Sue Minix is a member of Sisters in Crime, and when she isn't writing, you can find her reading, watching old movies, or hiking the New Mexico desert with her furry best friend.

A
Murderous
Plot

SUE MINIX

avon.

Published by AVON
A division of HarperCollins*Publishers*
1 London Bridge Street
London SE1 9GF

www.harpercollins.co.uk

HarperCollins*Publishers*
Macken House
39/40 Mayor Street Upper
Dublin 1
D01 C9W8
Ireland

A Paperback Original 2024
24 25 26 27 28 LBC 7 6 5 4 3
First published in Great Britain by HarperCollins*Publishers* 2024

Typeset in Sabon LT Std by HarperCollins*Publishers* India

Printed and bound in the United States

*To Julie and Jeannine, without whom
this series might never have been possible.*

CHAPTER ONE

Waking up in the morning was like trying to pull myself out of quicksand. Every time I gained an inch, my cocoon yanked me back two, enveloping me in its warmth and sense of security. A cozy cave where reality was forbidden and the outside world not only didn't exist but *never* existed. Kind of like the fictional world I'd created in my mystery series, which never existed, but felt as real as the comforter that covered my head.

And I wouldn't mind spending the rest of the day wrapped in my comfy sheath, except today was Saturday, and I had to get ready for my meeting with the Riddleton Runners at eight. Once a week, I met four of my friends at the park for a few laps around the mile-long track. Well, the real runners in the group managed a few laps. I'd yet to achieve two without doubling over with my hands on my knees, panting as if I'd just run five miles with Bigfoot chasing me.

I dragged the cover off, peeled open an eyelid, and searched for the clock on the nightstand, shielding my exposed eye from the sunlight streaming through the blinds with one hand. Nothing destroyed my cocoon-based fantasy faster than a blast of bright yellow light in

1

the eyes. Seven o'clock already. Time to get up. A word flew from my lips that, luckily, nobody else could hear.

Wrestling my arm from under the blanket, I felt around the other side of the bed. No boyfriend. No dog. Eric must've already gotten up and taken my German shepherd, Savannah, with him. Although, I should've realized Savannah was gone because she didn't throw her eighty-five pounds across my chest the instant I moved.

Perfect. I could snooze for a while longer. I snuggled into the pillow and drew the covers back over my head. My cocoon sucked me in like I was the caterpillar that built it. Too bad I'd never be a butterfly.

"Jen!" Eric's tenor voice filtered through the blanket.

A groan slipped out, and I burrowed deeper as if, like an infant, he'd think I'd disappeared if he couldn't see me.

Peekaboo.

"Jen, I know you hear me."

"Go away!"

"Come on. Get up. We need to leave soon."

Nope. Sleep weighed down my eyelids. "No, I don't. I have an hour."

"An hour to actually be there." Eric chuckled. "There's coffee, and I made breakfast. You should eat before we go."

"I'm not hungry." An audible stomach gurgle called out my fib. I'd bet he couldn't hear it, though. And I'd probably lose as usual. Nothing I did got past him.

"Liar."

"Am not!"

"You're always hungry."

"No, I'm always eating. That's not the same thing."

He snagged the blanket, but I swatted his hand away. "Okay. Have it your way." He whistled for the dog.

Uh-oh. I curled into the fetal position and protected my head with my arms. Savannah charged onto the bed, clawed the blanket off, and stuck her snout in my eye. I flailed my arms, blinking back the tears. She grabbed a corner of the comforter and leaped to the floor, dragging it into the living room like a goliath superhero's cape. I really needed to remember to tuck that thing under the mattress when I made the bed. Except I rarely made the bed.

Eric posed on the edge of the mattress and grinned. "Good morning, sweetheart."

I bit back the two-word expression my mother had washed my mouth out with soap for saying in the third grade. Instead, I stuffed my head under the pillow. "Whether or not it's a good morning is a matter of opinion."

"Any morning I wake up with you is a good morning." He smacked my leg. "Now, get up. Your breakfast is getting cold."

He really could be sweet when he wanted to be. Actually, he was always sweet. I was the one with disposition problems. Up and down, affable and grumpy. Poor guy never knew what he'd be facing from one minute to the next. And yet he stayed. I'd never figure that one out.

I came by my issues honestly, though. Between my stepfather, who blamed me for everything that'd ever gone wrong in his life, and my mother, who always made me feel like I was chasing butterflies through a minefield, I never stood a chance. If it weren't for my best friend and her family, I wouldn't have met a stable human being until I went to college. And college kids weren't known for being stable.

No wonder I was so messed up. Eric deserved better, and I resolved to give it to him. Starting tomorrow. Maybe the day after.

Throwing the pillow at him, I extracted myself from the tangled sheet and sent him a faux glare. "You know, you're lucky I love you."

"I know." He stood and sidestepped toward the door. "I'll meet you in the kitchen in five minutes, coffee in hand."

Eric O'Malley stood a head taller than I did, but we probably wore the same size jeans. Not that we'd ever swapped, but it might be fun to try it one day. For me, anyway. A rookie detective with the Riddleton Police Department, Eric's buzz-cut hair was the color of an orange and a tomato that'd spent five minutes together in a blender. Add a swath of freckles across his pallid cheeks, and he resembled Opie Taylor in a grown-up suit. But he was a keeper, as my mother liked to remind me daily.

I slowly lowered my feet to the floor as if testing the surface of an ice-covered lake. I stood there for a minute, making sure it would hold my weight. Unfortunately, it did. I needed to eat a few more chocolate chip muffins. That might do it.

Out of excuses, I headed for the bathroom while the aroma of freshly brewed coffee and bacon wafting down the hall tantalized my nose, and my stomach encouraged me to hurry. Eric had the right idea about me eating before our run. I required little fuel for the smidgeon of energy I used pacing around the track barely faster than a walk, but a rumbling stomach would be a distraction, and I had enough trouble focusing already.

4

When I flipped on the light, the mirror above the sink reflected the sleep-induced creases in my face and around my light-blue eyes, along with a severe case of bedhead. My short, black hair had evolved into a mass of spikes and cowlicks, creating a modern art masterpiece Picasso would envy.

After completing my ablutions, I stuck my head under the running faucet and drowned my hair, the only way sure to tame it, then ran a comb through the soggy mass and made my way to the kitchen, looking like the star of a 1960s Brylcreem commercial. A little dab'll do ya, and the wet head lived happily ever after in my house. Especially first thing in the morning.

I chased the coffee-and-bacon lure to the kitchen and arrived with thirty seconds to spare. Eric smiled and handed me my "Creativity Begins With Coffee" mug, the contents already fixed with two sugars and cream, just the way I liked it. I breathed in the robust aroma and sipped, swirling the flavors around my tongue as if the store-brand brew had come out of a 1982 Chateau Lafite Rothschild bottle.

After a hug and a kiss for the chef, I claimed my seat, and Eric set a plate of eggs over medium, bacon, and toast in front of me. I smiled at him with a mouthful of chewy, salty meat when he took the chair beside me. Savannah poked my knee to remind me she was available for cleanup, and my heart filled with contentment. I could get used to this.

Eric swallowed the bite of toast he'd dipped in egg yolk and asked, "Are you getting excited yet?"

I lowered my eyebrows and cocked my head in confusion. "Excited about what?"

"Your new release. It's in two weeks, right?"

The second book of my Davenport Twins Mystery series, *Twin Terror*, was about to come out and, to be honest, I felt more nervous than excited. The first book, *Double Trouble*, had been a smash hit. I couldn't imagine the second would do nearly as well. I slid my remaining egg from one side of the plate to the other. "Yup. Fifteen days, to be exact, but who's counting?"

"Sounds like you are." He laid his fork down and took my hand. "You don't seem very enthusiastic about the book coming out. What's wrong?"

How much time you got? "Just worried, I guess. Just because the first book sold a lot of copies doesn't mean people actually liked what they read. If the second one doesn't sell, the publishing team might change their minds about the rest of the series. And even if they don't, people might not read the third because they didn't like the second."

"I think you're worrying too much. You're a great writer and they're lucky to have you. Don't forget that." He squeezed my hand. "Have they come up with a name for number three yet?"

"I haven't heard anything about it. I guess they were so far behind on book two they didn't consider it a priority. Why, you have a suggestion?"

"Uh-uh." He poked a hole in his second egg to free the yolk from captivity. "You're the writer. I'm just a lowly rookie detective in a small-town police department."

I wiped my greasy fingers on the napkin in my lap. "Lowly detective my foot. You'd be surprised at how much creativity you use to solve crimes. You just don't see it that way."

He dunked another triangle of toast into yolk and

met my gaze. "Maybe. But I prefer to think I use logic and deduction. And lots of legwork."

"If you insist. I still say it takes at least some creativity. After all, what's deduction if not taking the facts and molding them into a conclusion?"

"Okay. You could be right. Especially with the tough cases." He set his plate down for Savannah to prewash. "I'm going to get dressed."

By the time I'd wiped up the last of the yolk with the last of my toast, he'd returned wearing his Christmas colors: forest-green running shorts and a red Riddleton High Track tank top. One day, I'd have to take him shopping for more running clothes so we could celebrate a different holiday once in a while. Halloween was next week. Black and orange might be an excellent place to start, as long as the orange didn't clash too much with his hair. We could always make both shorts and shirt orange and pass him off as a tall, skinny pumpkin.

I gave Savannah my plate, swallowed the last of my coffee, and headed for the bedroom to change into my Gamecocks sweats. If I thought about it, though, I was no better than he because I always wore the same thing, too. Perhaps we both needed to expand our wardrobes.

Eric and I strolled hand in hand down Park Street, enjoying the light, brisk breeze and mid-autumn sunshine falling from the azure sky. Savannah alternately trotted and pranced on my left, anticipating our run, which was the highlight of her week. As much as she loved being in my company most of the time, Saturday morning in the park offered the strenuous exercise a dog her size needed. She looked forward to the trip almost as much as I dreaded it.

7

Exercise for the sake of exercise had never been part of my routine, but, during my struggles with writer's block, Eric had convinced me to try running with his group once a week. He swore it would help, and, though I hated to admit it, he turned out to be right. I could never be sure if the fresh air, the camaraderie, the influx of oxygen, or some combination of all three did the trick, but it worked. My words began to flow again, so here I was, way too early in the morning, ready to suffer for my art.

The 1940s-era A-frame houses lining the street slept along with their occupants. If anyone inside was awake, they hadn't yet made it out into the world. Too bad for them. They were missing the beginning of a glorious day. The irony of the thought wasn't lost on me, however, since Eric'd had to force me out of bed this morning.

In the name of community engagement, Riddleton's town council hosted holiday decoration contests where residents and business owners competed for a plastic trophy and the right to puff out their chests like a tabby who'd brought home a mouse for lunch. Participation in the Halloween contest averaged second only to Christmas in the annual calendar of events, and this year was shaping up to be no exception.

While the homeowners snoozed or sipped their first coffee of the day, decomposing hands waved to us from makeshift graves, witches stirred their otherworldly concoctions in cardboard cauldrons, and ghosts of all shapes and sizes haunted our path. Eric and I took turns pointing out the attractions we found most entertaining. Savannah glanced over her shoulder and trotted as close to the curb as possible without slipping off into the street to ensure no supernatural being could reach her.

As we approached the wrought-iron gates of Riddleton Park, I spotted a small figure perched on the stone bench beside the entrance. It had to be Lacey Stanley, my bookstore business partner, and a mid-thirties, married mother of three. She wore her long brown hair in a convenient ponytail most of the time, and her runner's body showed only a slight bump where, a few months ago, a seven-pound, ten-ounce baby had been.

The other two members of our group wouldn't be here today, which left the three of us to fend for ourselves. No problem, however. Lacey had just built herself back up to light jogging, which matched my running speed, and Eric could run circles around us as if we were a mobile maypole. I also might convince him to take Savannah for a sprint around the track as a treat for them both. Pretty sure it wouldn't take much persuasion for him to agree.

Savannah leaped and lunged, almost yanking my shoulder out of its socket, when she saw Aunt Lacey. I let her go since nobody else was around, despite the clearly posted rule stating all dogs must be leashed. Besides, she had a leash on. The sign didn't say I had to be holding the other end.

Lacey braced herself in self-defense, putting her hand out in a "stop" gesture as the slightly overweight German shepherd barreled toward her. Savannah dropped to her haunches and wiggled her entire body as if I'd just inserted fresh batteries into the Energizer Bunny.

"Good girl!" Lacey said and leaned down in her black leggings and royal-blue tank top to scratch the dog's chest.

Eric chuckled. "I thought she was going to plow you under for a minute."

"No way. Jen's put a lot of work into training her. And me." She grinned in my direction. "It's amazing how effective something as simple as putting your hand out can be."

I nodded. "No kidding. The rest of her training was a bit more challenging, though."

Lacey gestured toward the gate. "We ready to stretch?"

Not a chance. Stretching for me was as much fun as riding a mechanical bull with no handholds. My muscles and I played tug-of-war every time I tried it, and I firmly believed some people weren't meant to be limber. Asking me to stretch was like expecting a power pole to bend with the wind. No way that would ever happen. Still, Lacey and Eric insisted on loosening up before running, so I went along to get along.

We worked through the routine, and I closed my ears to the screams from my extremities, focusing on the way the sunlight danced in the branches instead. Drops lingering after last night's rain glittered like diamonds on the pine needles while the tree trunks remained hidden in shadow, surrounded by wisps of fog. A peaceful yet ethereal scene. Like the opening of a horror movie. Goose bumps popped up on my forearms.

As I bent to stretch my hamstrings and calves, a flicker of movement in the shadows caught my eye. Not really movement, though, more like a momentary hitch in the atmosphere. I stopped in mid-stretch, focused on the area by the nearest tree, but saw nothing. Only the occasional falling diamond interrupted the gloom surrounding it. Must've been my imagination.

I dropped back down to touch my toes. Or try to touch my toes, anyway. Once in a while, I succeeded, but today wasn't one of those days. My shrieking hamstrings won the battle this time. As I mimicked Lacey's upper arm stretch, Eric pointed toward the tree I'd been watching and said, "Hey, who's that?"

Lacey and I turned in that direction. Emerging from the shadows, a man staggered zombie-like toward us, a dark stain soaked into the front of his light-colored shirt.

CHAPTER TWO

The man's pale skin, black pants, and white shirt jumped out at me when he approached. Not to mention the stain that looked suspiciously like blood. If I didn't know better, I'd think he'd escaped from the county morgue or the haunted house attraction going on at the community center. *A preview of his Halloween costume?* My pulse quickened as dread crept into my chest. Nope, not a costume. A real-life victim who needed our help.

From his uneven gait and obvious disorientation, he might be injured. We all exchanged glances, then ran to intercept him, dead pine needles sliding under our feet. Whatever the reason for his behavior, we couldn't leave him wandering around the park where anything might happen. Anything more than what already did, that is.

I slowed to a walk as features came into focus on his ashen face. Disheveled dark hair clung to his forehead above wide, darting, mud-brown eyes, seemingly unable to focus on anything. His trembling hands were smeared in what appeared to be the same brownish substance that coated the front of his shirt.

Lacey gasped and froze, hands covering her mouth, saucer-like eyes peering over them. Unlike me, she had little experience with situations like this. I wish I could say the same. Some people believed I sought out these circumstances. I'd happily live forever without ever finding another dead body or, in this case, an injured person, but somehow, they always found me.

I followed Eric, who slowly approached the man. "Sir, are you all right?" Eric asked, stopping in his path.

The man's gaze swung in all directions. He drunkenly lurched toward us, hair matted with blood plastered to his scalp.

Eric took the man by the arm, halting his forward progression. "Sir, what happened to you? Do you need help? What's your name?"

The man's mouth opened and closed soundlessly. His eyes ceased their aimless searching and came to rest on Eric's face, but no recognition glimmered in them. Nothing at all, in fact. As if he'd never seen another human before. I shuddered.

Eric looked back. "Lacey, call 911. Tell them we need police and an ambulance." He turned back to the man. "Sir, are you injured? What's your name?"

The man studied the toes of the dusty black oxfords poking out from under the hem of his expensive black slacks. When he looked up again, his face wore a mask of confusion. "I . . . I don't know."

I stepped to Eric's side and touched the sleeve of the stranger's white long-sleeve shirt, crisp under my fingertips, to draw his attention to me. Savannah sniffed his leg. "What about ID? Do you have a wallet? A phone, maybe?"

He reached a bloody hand toward his pants pocket. Eric reflexively grabbed his arm. "Do you mind if I do that for you?"

13

The man shook his head, winced, and raised his arms as if Eric was holding him at gunpoint.

Eric patted him down, looking for a way to identify the guy and, if I knew him, weapons. He found nothing. No wallet, no phone, and no weapons.

"What do you think?" I asked him when he met my gaze and shrugged.

The stranger cut off Eric's attempt at a reply. "My head hurts really bad. Is that why I can't remember anything?"

"I don't know, but I promise we'll do everything we can to find the answers to all your questions. First, we need to get you to the hospital."

Eric guided the agitated man to the stone bench outside the park gate, but he refused to sit, choosing instead to pace furiously up and down the length of it, muttering to himself. His blood-covered, tailored white shirt clung to his torso as he alternated between crossing his arms and waving them. The unmatted part of his dark brown hair riffled in the slight breeze, but the front and back remained stuck fast by blood and sweat.

I watched him stride back and forth, head down, only occasionally offering me a glimpse of his face. His eyes were filled with uncertainty and fear. And anger. I kept my distance as he waved his arms around, yelling indecipherable words.

Eric stepped into his path and raised his hands palm out to calm him down. "I understand you're frustrated."

The man stomped forward and bumped his chest against Eric's, pushing him back a step. "What do you think you understand? You don't understand anything. Leave me alone!"

"Just take it easy. We'll get this all sorted out. I promise."

Oh boy. Eric had broken the cardinal rule of police work: make no promises. Although he only said it would get sorted. He didn't promise a particular outcome. But would the man remember it that way? His volatility, bordering on dangerous, could be a result of the blow to his head. Still, I hoped Eric could keep him calm long enough for the doctors to help him regain his memory.

After disconnecting her call to emergency services, Lacey turned. "The police and an ambulance are on their way. I hope they get here soon."

The understatement of the year. "Me too. He's getting a little too agitated for my comfort. I don't want Eric to get hurt."

"I suspect he's had to deal with worse during his career." She laid a reassuring hand on my arm. "Have you ever seen that guy before?"

I dug deep into my memory, finding nothing helpful. He didn't even seem familiar. "No, never. You?"

She shook her head. "Not that I remember, but if he came into the bookstore on a busy day I wouldn't recognize him."

"I know what you mean. I pay more attention to the books than the people carrying them. Unless I think they might be interesting characters I can use in my novel."

Lacey chided me. "Our customers are all interesting characters. They keep us open, which is fascinating enough for me. You should try being more sociable once in a while. Give them a reason to come back."

Being sociable went against my introverted nature. I'd spent most of my childhood alone in my room, reading or writing, with few opportunities to develop adequate social skills and few people in my life with whom to practice. With the help of my friends, like Lacey, I'd improved significantly in the last couple of years, though.

Head down, I peered up at her from under my eyebrows. "Yes, ma'am. I'll try to do better in the future."

Lacey grinned. "Be sure you do."

I snapped off a mock salute, and we strolled over to where Eric had finally convinced the stranger to stand still. I reached for his arm to encourage him to sit, and Eric grabbed my hand in midair. "That shirt is evidence. You'll contaminate it."

He should've thought of that before I touched it the first time. At least he could be my witness when they found my fingerprints and DNA on it. "Evidence of what? It's obvious what happened. Either he fell and hit his head, losing his wallet and phone in the process, or somebody struck and robbed him." I immediately recognized the contradiction in my two statements.

Eric pointed it out for me anyway. "If somebody hit him, there might be something on that shirt we can use to catch the offender." He placed a hand on each of my shoulders and focused his emerald eyes on my blue ones. "Besides, things aren't always as they appear. We can't assume all that blood is his. What if he's the one who attacked someone and was injured when the victim fought back? He might be the perpetrator."

"And stole his wallet and phone? I'd think a victim would just run away, not rob his attacker first."

"I'm just trying to keep an open mind. That's my job."

The guy jerked his head up and grimaced from the

pain. "What are you saying? I hurt someone? Wouldn't I remember that? I *know* I couldn't forget something like that!"

Eric put his hands up again. "I'm not saying that at all. We have no idea what happened to you, and, until we do, we can't make any assumptions. It's as much for your protection as anything. The important thing right now is we get you the help you need."

"It doesn't feel like it." The man's knees buckled, forcing him to sit on the bench. "It feels like you're trying to pin something on me."

I sat beside him, careful not to touch anything. "You need to relax. You've lost a lot of blood, and getting upset will only make things worse. Nobody's saying you did anything wrong. We don't know what happened to you, and you can't tell us."

He covered his face with his hands, revealing a deep cut in the webbing between his right thumb and forefinger. "Why can't I remember?"

I leaned over and peered at the back of his head. The hair was matted with drying blood, and I couldn't see through to the scalp. The smell of blood and hair products flooded my nostrils. "That head wound probably has something to do with it, but at least it isn't bleeding anymore. It's not unusual for people to have memory problems after a trauma. I'm sure the doctor will be able to tell you more, though. After they do some tests."

He nodded and picked at the dried blood on his manicured fingernails.

His blood from the cut on his hand or remnants from another victim?

Between his shirt, his hands, and his head, there

seemed to be a significant amount of it on him. Could Eric be right? Did this guy get hurt while injuring someone else?

I looked up at Eric and, over his shoulder, glimpsed his partner, Detective Francine Havermayer, sprinting across the parking lot. I touched Eric's arm and jutted my chin in her direction. "I didn't know she could run. Don't they give you guys vehicles anymore?"

Pointing to the last house on the left before the park, he said, "She lives right over there. Moved last month. Guess she figured it made more sense to walk. Well, run."

"Since when does she do anything that makes sense?" Detective Havermayer and I had issues with each other that began the first time we met. Actually, our difficulties started *before* we met on her part, since she'd been hostile toward me at our first encounter.

I still had no idea what her problem was. Even Eric had no success prying it out of her during the six months of his detective training. Maybe someday she'd let it slip. Until then, we tolerated each other. Barely.

Havermayer pulled up beside us, lungs working overtime to make up for the shortage of oxygen created by her race across the parking lot. She wiped the perspiration off her forehead with the sleeve of her unzipped gray hoodie, which covered a navy blue Riddleton Police Department T-shirt tucked into her jeans. A pair of scuffed brown Doc Martens topped off her unusual-for-her ensemble.

I lifted my eyebrows, it being the first time I'd ever seen her wearing anything other than a starched and pressed black suit over a crisp white blouse. The first time she didn't look as though she'd just stepped off the cover of *Vogue*. "You feeling all right, Detective?"

18

She flashed her shamrock eyes at me. "Fine. Why?"

Strange. "No reason. Just wondering."

Her shoulder-length sandy-blond hair bounced in place when she shook her head in disgust, turning to Eric. "What's going on, and why is *she* here?"

Eric gave her the *Reader's Digest* condensed version of what we knew so far, which was basically nothing. Havermayer listened without comment, then approached the injured man and identified herself. "My partner tells me you say you can't remember what happened to your head and how you got that blood all over your shirt. Is that correct?"

The man nodded, made brief eye contact, then looked away. "I have no idea what happened to me."

Havermayer studied his profile as if deciding whether to believe him. "What's the last thing you *do* remember?"

He scrunched up his face in concentration. "Waking up under a tree with a splitting headache, covered in blood."

"Nothing before that? What were you doing in the park?"

"I don't know. I don't know. I don't know!" He balled his fists at his sides. "I can't remember anything!"

Havermayer put her hands up. "Okay. Calm down. I'm trying to help you."

"I don't see how asking me questions you know I can't answer is helping. I've already told you I don't remember."

"You're right. I'm sorry," she said in a soothing voice.

I'm sorry? I never dreamed Havermayer even had those two words in her vocabulary. I certainly hadn't heard them before. Even when she'd been proven wrong about me being a murderer more than once, she never apologized. Only acted as if I'd gotten away with something once again. I examined her profile. It seemed normal, but it couldn't be.

Who are you, and what've you done with Detective Havermayer?

An ambulance, followed by a van load of crime scene techs, interrupted my musings. The search for the real Havermayer would have to wait. She had to be in there somewhere, though, unless she was actually changing. Nah. Personal growth only happened to people who accepted that they needed it. She'd never admit being wrong about anything. At least she hadn't so far.

I eased Savannah back out of the way as two blue-clad paramedics approached with a stretcher. They loaded the man onto it and did a quick assessment before wheeling him back to the truck. Havermayer walked alongside, telling Eric she'd ride with the man to the hospital. He nodded and agreed to take charge of the scene.

A tech strung yellow crime scene tape, which augmented the seasonal decorations planted around the park. Lacey tugged on my sleeve. "I'm going to head out. I need to open the store soon. Now that Kirby's opened a section of his resort, we actually have people waiting for us to unlock the door on weekends these days."

Simeon Kirby was the developer from Spartanburg who'd rolled into town and decided Riddleton needed to be a tourist hot spot. His resort on the shore of Lake Dester would almost ensure it happened no matter how the residents felt about it. I, for one, was dead set against filling our quaint, cozy hometown with a mass of visiting humanity six months out of the year. It might be good for business, but definitely lousy for our way of life.

Of course, Kirby didn't care what I thought. He made it clear he believed the influx of money would make any inconvenience worthwhile. His vision for Riddleton entailed creating a miniature Myrtle Beach, only on the lake rather than the ocean. He'd met my suggestion that he get his eyes checked with a sneer. No surprise.

I sealed my lips against a nasty retort. Lacey was thrilled with the uptick in the bookstore business. I was, too—just not with what we'd eventually have to sacrifice to maintain it. The increased traffic, loss of privacy, and potential rise in crime would have a huge impact on our day-to-day living. However, I *did* enjoy not having to worry about how we'd pay every bill as it came in. Nothing in life came free, as my mother loved to remind me. Once again, she was right.

Squeezing her shoulder, I said, "All right. I'm going to hang here for a little bit, then I'll meet you up there."

Lacey waved to Eric, who was absorbed in instructing the crime scene techs and didn't see it, and waited for the ambulance to pass before heading to her car.

CHAPTER THREE

When the techs fanned out into the trees to search for evidence, Eric waved me over. "I'm going to be stuck here a while. You might as well go on home."

In your dreams. "I'd rather stay. I have a vested interest in how this turns out."

He chuckled. "Really? How so?"

"I was here, right? That makes me interested."

He cocked an eyebrow.

My cheeks heated. "I don't know. It sounded good, though, didn't it?"

"It did." He threw an arm around my shoulder and drew me to him. "It was complete nonsense, but it did sound good."

I kissed him, and my lips tingled. "Not nonsense. I want to know who that man is as much as you do."

"I know you do. But it's a police matter now. No place for amateurs."

"Oh, really!" I playfully pushed him away. "Since when am I an amateur?"

"Since you're not in law enforcement. You've always been an amateur."

"I might not be a cop, but I've solved as many cases as you have."

He tugged me back and brushed the hair off my forehead, leaving it tingling where his fingertips touched. "True, but I have work to do. This whole park has to be searched, and, as you can see, we don't have a lot of people to do it."

Perfect! "So let me help."

"I can't, Jen," he said, regret tingeing his voice. "I know how much you want to jump in, but I just can't let you."

"All right, I'll keep you company then. I won't touch, only make sure you don't miss anything. Four eyes are better than two, right? And besides . . ." I patted Savannah's head. "I've got the Bionic Nose here to sniff out clues."

"Jen, this isn't an episode of *Scooby-Doo, Where Are You!*" His solemn gaze met my mischievous one. "You're not going to let this go, are you?"

"Nope."

Eric's shoulders sagged in surrender. "Fine." He glanced at the tiny section of the crime scene covered so far. "You can come with me, but no going off on your own and no interfering. And you'll have to wear gloves like the rest of us. All right?"

"Deal." I stuck out my hand for him to shake. He kissed me instead, sandwiching my proffered hand between us. Even better.

Eric handed me a pair of disposable nitrile gloves and held up the yellow tape for me to duck under. Savannah stopped on the other side with her nose in the air as if she knew it was her job to find something important. He led me to the opposite side of the park from where the techs were working their way around witches and goblins and orange lights strung through the tree branches. "We'll start on this side and meet the others in the middle."

"Sounds good. Lead the way, Columbo."

He rolled his eyes and escorted us past plastic tombstones crookedly aligned in a makeshift cemetery to the far-right corner of the park by the ball fields. We followed the baseball field fence, searching the ground for anything that seemed out of place. Anything not installed by the decorating committee last week.

Savannah sniffed along with us, squatting to mark a few places for future reference—hers, not ours. The park served as a doggie Western Union where messages were left and answered daily. My German shepherd diligently responded to every communication she found.

When we reached the perimeter track after finding nothing other than candy wrappers and cigarette butts, we turned around and came back down. Perhaps I should've heeded Eric's advice about going home. It didn't seem I'd accomplish much here, and my unfinished manuscript waited patiently for me on my laptop. I'd never be able to focus on it, though. Not with an investigation going on here.

About the time my neck began to cramp on the third round trip with nothing to show for it, Savannah lifted her nose again and pulled toward a pine tree about ten yards away. I nudged Eric. "I think she's got something."

He squinted in that direction, checking out the area around the tree visible from where we stood. "It's probably nothing, but let's follow her anyway, just in case."

I let her have her head, and she lurched forward, taking me with her, except my feet didn't move as

24

nimbly as hers did. I stumbled, pitching headfirst toward the ground. Eric grabbed the back of my sweatshirt, stopping me from doing a face-plant. Savannah waited impatiently, tugging on her leash.

More irritated than curious at this point, I followed until she stopped. Her find turned out to be anything *but* nothing. At the base of the tree she led us to, we spotted a pool of dark liquid the size of an eight-by-ten envelope.

Blood? So much of it had seeped into the ground that I couldn't tell for certain, but, if I had to guess, I'd say yes. Along the outer edge of the puddle, a small semiautomatic pistol flattened the grass, and half-inch-wide holes, about an inch deep, littered the ground as if the palmetto bugs had been searching for buried treasure.

I hauled Savannah back a few feet so she wouldn't contaminate the evidence and exchanged a glance with Eric. Had we found the location of the stranger's attack? If so, why would the attacker have left the gun behind? And what made those tiny holes? Always questions, never answers. Not yet, anyway.

Eric squatted for a closer look. "I think we've found a crime scene."

He called over one of the crime scene techs to take pictures of what Savannah had sniffed out and collect the evidence. "Looks like the Bionic Nose came through for us," he said with a grin, kneeling to peer at the gun. "It's a thirty-two caliber. And it has what looks like blood and hair on the grip and some blood around the hammer."

Peeking over his shoulder at the gruesome sight, I held Savannah behind my back and my breakfast in my belly.

I'd seen blood and dead bodies before, but somehow the combination of blood and hair on the butt of the gun seemed more real. More visceral. Especially since I might've seen where it came from firsthand. The leash slipped through my sweaty palm, and I grabbed it with both hands to keep my German shepherd from getting too close. "You think that's what someone used to hit the amnesia guy?"

"Possibly. We'll have a better idea after the lab geeks analyze it." He squinted at the deep-red pool just beyond the toes of his running shoes. "It's an awful lot of blood for that small head wound, even if they bleed a lot. I wonder if the guy was injured somewhere else, too, and we didn't notice."

The distinctive metallic scent wafted up to my nose, and my stomach lurched. I covered my nostrils with my hand as a barricade. "I don't know, babe. Unless the stain on his shirt came from an abdominal wound, but he didn't seem to be in pain anywhere except his head. However, he had to get walloped pretty hard to forget everything he ever knew. I suspect that injury might turn out to be worse than it appeared."

Eric stood and joined me to make room for the tech to do his work. "You're assuming he *has* amnesia. I'm not so sure about that. I mean, think about it. What better way to get away with assaulting someone than pretending you're the victim?"

Interesting concept. "I hadn't considered that possibility. You really think he's faking? What did he do, though, slam his head against a tree to set up an alibi? He couldn't have hit himself with the gun hard enough to cause the damage we saw. Not in that location, for sure. He'd have to be a contortionist."

"Maybe, but we'll know more when the results come back on that blood and hair. If it's not his . . ." Eric shrugged.

The tech photographed the evidence, then bagged the gun and took swabs of the blood for testing. He peered up at us. "Scalp wounds bleed a lot, but I'm not sure your guy would've been walking and talking if he'd lost this much from a single blow. If it's not all his, we might have a second victim somewhere."

Eric ran a hand over his reddish-orange buzz cut, considering the prospect of another casualty. "Go ahead and get those swabs back to the lab, so we'll know what we're dealing with here."

"Yes, sir." The tech gathered his supplies and took off in a fast walk toward the van.

"What now?" I asked, scratching my best girl under the chin. I might have to make her my detective partner if she kept finding evidence for us. Although, I wouldn't mind a bit if she never discovered another scene like this one.

Stroking Savannah's head, Eric checked on the progress of the remaining techs, who were still only a third of the way across the park. "Now, unless you're too tired, we take the Nose here back to where we left off. We still have a lot of ground to cover."

Despite my aching neck and queasy stomach, I refused to quit. There might be something else useful out there. Something that could reveal whether our amnesiac friend was telling the truth. "We're good. Lead on."

We'd only managed another couple of unproductive rounds when Chief of Police Stan Olinski made his way through the trees to us, the sunlight reflecting off the stars adorning the collar of his freshly ironed navy-blue uniform shirt. A big change from the slept-in-his-clothes appearance of his detective days. And an even bigger change from the football-player-grunge look he wore so proudly when we dated in high school. Either his fiancée—otherwise known as my best friend—was rubbing off on him, or she was ironing his uniforms for him. I placed my bet on the latter.

Olinski had asked me to marry him after graduation, and took ten years to forgive me for turning him down. Becoming Little Jenny Homemaker had no place in my plans. I wanted to write the Great American Novel. To be the next Hemingway or Twain or Faulkner. Not that *that* ever happened, either, but I could live with writing a successful—so far—mystery series.

No matter how my writing career turned out, I had no regrets about not jumping into a lifelong commitment with my high school boyfriend. Especially since he'd recently proposed to my best friend, and—unlike me—she'd been thrilled to accept. A win for everyone.

Olinski dropped a hand onto Eric's shoulder. "Have a good run this morning?"

Eric snickered. "Not hardly. Didn't even make it through the pre-run stretch."

"So I heard. What've you found?"

I opened my mouth to respond, and Olinski glared and pointed at me. "Not you. Him. You're not involved in this."

Ha! I was right smack in the middle of it, as far as I could tell. Of course, he *was* the chief of police. That still didn't give him the last word, in my opinion. "But—"

"No. Not a word. You need to leave this alone, Jen. It's a police matter, and, unless there's been some change in your status I'm unaware of, you're not police."

Fuming inside, I recognized the warning expression on his face. Now wouldn't be the time to remind him the latest unofficial poll ranked me as the best amateur detective in Riddleton. I doubted a proper time for that existed, in his opinion. Still, I claimed the title with pride. I'd earned it the hard way.

Eric filled him in on our encounter with the amnesiac man and the blood pool and gun Savannah had discovered by the tree. "Now we have to establish whether the guy was the victim or the perpetrator or maybe both. And whether there's someone else out there we need to be looking for."

Olinski gestured toward the crime scene techs still scouring every blade of grass in their section of the park. "All right. I'll see what they've uncovered, and we'll decide where to go from there." He gave me a pointed glance. "And that 'we' doesn't include you. Understood?"

I sighed out my frustration, clenching my unencumbered fist by my side. "Understood."

Eric scowled at Olinski's back as he strode away. "I'm sorry he came down on you like that. It was uncalled for."

Funny, Eric didn't act like it bothered him when it was happening. "That's how he usually reacts when something like this occurs. Not that it matters. I always end up involved anyway. Why didn't you say anything to him?"

A red background highlighted the freckles on his cheeks. "He's my boss, and I just got promoted. I'd like to keep it that way. Besides, he's right about you not interfering. It's too dangerous for you. What could I say that wouldn't get us both in trouble?"

"Exactly what I just said. I don't interfere. I help. You

don't mind when you get the credit for my work," I said, though I didn't really mean it. Eric was supportive even when he might get in hot water for it.

He responded before I could take it back. "I never take credit for your work. That's how he knows when you involve yourself in our investigations. I always tell him where I got my information from." Eric took my hands in his. "I don't want to fight with you."

Pulling my hands back, I wrapped my arms around him and rested my cheek on his chest. "I don't want to fight either. I'm sorry about what I said. He makes me grumpy." I angled my head back to look him in the eye. "But you have to admit he *was* being a butt."

He kissed me. "I agree. He was being a total butt. And next time he acts like that, I'll take him out to the woodshed and tan his hide with a switch. Good enough?"

"Perfect. At least he didn't tell me I had to leave. Letting Savannah help you look for clues isn't interfering, right?"

"Well, since she just found what looks like our primary crime scene, I'm willing to take my chances."

Savannah nudged my leg, and we resumed our search. Every so often, she'd stop to sniff the air, but she didn't lead me in any particular direction. After another half hour of strolling back and forth across the park like we were enjoying the first warm day of spring, we caught up with the crime scene techs. We'd found nothing else of interest in this case.

I had, however, learned how messy Riddleton residents could be when watching baseball games. I'd have to suggest trash cans on all the benches in the stands at the next town council meeting. Not that it would make a difference. The junk would still find its way to the ground.

As soon as they noticed his arrival, Eric was immediately surrounded by techs with evidence bags. Apparently, they'd had more success than we did. A blind person would probably have had more success than we did.

I tapped him on the shoulder. "I'm taking off. It looks like you're going to be busy for a while sorting through all this stuff."

Turning, he said, "Yeah. Hopefully, some of this stuff—as you so delicately put it—will tell us who our amnesiac friend is. It doesn't look too promising, though."

"You never know. Sometimes, the clue that cracks the case appears completely innocuous at first. This might be one of those times."

He held up crossed fingers and kissed me goodbye. "I'll stop by the store when I'm done here. With something relevant to report, I hope."

"Me too." I led Savannah toward home, and she showed her disappointment at missing her run by turning back toward the park every few steps with longing in her soft brown eyes. She knew just how to make me feel like a three-year-old caught with cookie crumbs on my face in church. Never dreamed I'd be living with a nun one day.

"I'm sorry, little girl. We can't run today. We can try again tomorrow by ourselves." The words jumped out before I thought about them. I didn't love running in the first place, but doing it by myself was torturous, every stride a result of sheer willpower. And my will didn't last very long. My German shepherd needed the exercise, though. I sighed and shook my head. The sacrifices I made for my dog.

Savannah gave up trying to take me back about halfway home, and I walked her around the block as a consolation prize. We ran into my best friend, Brittany Dunlop, on the sidewalk in front of our building, coming home from work at the library. She was wearing a knee-length plaid skirt and white silk blouse.

Brittany and I had been inseparable since we'd decorated each other with fingerpaints in kindergarten. Tweedledum and Tweedledummer, my stepfather used to call us. We didn't care, though. We had each other. Over the years, she'd been the only person in my life I could count on, no matter what. Until I met Eric.

Now, the two shared the responsibility of saving me from myself. A monumental task given how much trouble I seemed to get into.

CHAPTER FOUR

Savannah's disappointment at not being allowed to run flew out of her head the instant she saw her favorite aunt. Brittany defended herself against the bounding dog until she sat at her feet. A few ear and chest scratches satisfied the neglected beast, and she turned her attention to the oak tree while we talked.

Brittany tucked back a lock of her honey-blond hair that always looked as if she'd stuck her finger in an electrical socket. It immediately fell down again. "You're late today. A long run or just slower than usual?"

"No run at all, actually." I told her about the amnesiac stranger and the subsequent search for clues to his identity. "My girl here is so disappointed I'm thinking of taking her out tomorrow to make up for it. Care to join us?"

She flashed her caesious-blue eyes at me over the frames of her tiger-striped glasses as if I'd used my outside voice in the library reading room.

I guess not. "Okay, never mind. Just thought I'd ask."

"What did you expect? You know I don't run. Besides, I'm having breakfast with Olinski tomorrow." Her cheeks flushed under sparkling eyes.

"Oh, so you'd rather have breakfast with your fiancé than run with your best friend. I know where I stand now," I teased.

"Yup. You got it," she replied with a smile quickly replaced by a furrowed brow. "So, what's the deal with that guy who can't remember his name? Did you find anything that might tell you who he is or what happened to him?"

We mounted the steps to our apartments located across the hall from each other on the second floor, Savannah leading the way. "We're hoping the blood on the ground or the gun will help with that. At least tell us whether he's the victim or the perpetrator. Although they might not have anything to do with him at all. For all we know, he could be an innocent bystander who saw something he shouldn't have."

Brittany unlocked her door. "Well, good luck. I'll try to pump Olinski for info if I can. I figure you're dying to jump into the investigation."

She knew me well. "As usual, you're correct, but both Olinski and Eric have already warned me off. Not that I'd ever let that stop me."

"Not in a million years. I know."

I laughed. "Talk to you later?"

"Of course. I'll let you know if I find out anything."

"Me too." I opened the door, and Savannah ran for her water dish. Apparently, clue-hunting made her thirstier than running. We hunted a lot longer than we usually ran, though. Perhaps that had something to do with it.

After a quick shower and a change of clothes, Savannah and I strolled down Main Street to the bookstore. At a little after eleven, a few puffy clouds had joined the sun in the otherwise clear sky, and the temperature climbed closer to seventy. The epitome of a gorgeous fall day and a welcome prelude to the gray chill and icy rains we'd endure come winter.

The Dollar General and Goodwill had their share of Saturday morning shoppers, and the Dandy Diner was busy as well. However, the town hall, which was closed, and the police station were quiet. I suspected the cops had plenty to keep them busy inside, though, given the day's developments. At the very least, they had a guy with no idea who he was to deal with.

I considered stopping in to see how the identity search was progressing but vetoed the idea since nobody would be happy to see me, and Eric would tell me when they learned something if he could. One of the many benefits of being in a romantic relationship with a police detective. I got the inside scoop firsthand when they let him share it, which was never often enough to suit me. If they wouldn't let me investigate for myself, the least they could do was tell me what they knew. For some reason, they didn't see it that way.

Go figure.

When I opened the door, Ravenous Readers buzzed with its share of customers as well. The partially open resort had fulfilled its promise and brought more visitors to Riddleton. So far, my expected unmanageable traffic and increase in crime had yet to appear, but it was too soon to tell what the future would bring. It would be one time I'd be happy to admit to being wrong, though. However, my gut told me to give it until the resort was completed and fully occupied before Googling recipes for crow.

In a search for Lacey, her second-favorite aunt, Savannah expertly negotiated the browsers camped out by the hand-hewn cherry bookcases along the wall. Carved wooden plaques identified the genres in alphabetical order from Art to Writing, and several people rifled through our newly added Used Book section. To my German shepherd's chagrin, none of them was her personal treat dispenser, otherwise known as my business partner.

When Savannah's ears went back and her tail spun into propeller mode, I knew she'd found her target standing at the cash register. Time to collect her "I'm here, now show me how much you love me" treat. Lacey obliged with a smile and fished the bag of bacon snacks from under the counter. My dog had her wrapped around her not-so-little paw. And all it took was espresso eyes and a wagging tail.

When Lacey held out her hands in an "all gone" gesture, Savannah wandered out onto the sales floor to introduce herself to all her prospective new friends. Most responded with smiles and pets, a few ignored her, and one man I didn't recognize glared at me from across the room.

I poked Lacey and jutted my chin in his direction. "You know that guy?" Peering closely at his chestnut hair and the caterpillars perched on his Neanderthal-like brow ridges, I said, "I don't think I've ever seen him in here before."

"Me either, but he looks familiar somehow. Maybe he's related to someone in town."

"Perhaps, but he doesn't like Savannah, so he's free to leave as far as I'm concerned."

Lacey laughed. "We can't throw everyone out who doesn't like your dog, Jen. Some people don't like dogs."

"And I don't trust anyone who doesn't like dogs. Who doesn't like unconditional love?"

"Agreed. We'll make that the store motto: never trust anyone who doesn't like dogs. Then the dog-haters might self-select, and we won't have to throw them out."

I put my hand up for a high five, and she slapped my palm.

"Before I forget, can you cover for me on Monday? Brielle has a doctor's appointment."

"Sure, no problem." I studied her expression. "Anything I need to worry about?"

She smiled. "Nope. Just a three-month checkup. Hopefully, she'll hit all her milestones."

"I'm sure she will. She takes after you," I said with a smile. Lacey hadn't been late for work once since we took over the store. "How are the kids handling the new addition? Are they feeling neglected yet?"

"Brianna's not thrilled at having competition in the family. She loves being Daddy's little girl. But Benny adores being a big brother."

"Brianna will come around—don't worry."

"I hope so. There's a ten-year age gap between them, so I'm not sure they'll ever be close. That's a lot to overcome."

Having had no siblings of my own, I knew of nothing to allay her fears. "Give it some time. She'll love her baby sister. I'm sure of it."

Lacey stared at a spot in the distance. "I hope so. Ben's been paying her as much extra attention as he can since we brought the baby home. Maybe she'll figure out he still loves her even with another girl in the house. It's hard for him, though, because he wants to bond with the baby, too."

"He's a good man. He'll figure out how to do both. I have no doubt."

She smiled. "I know he'll try his best to do right by all our kids. With luck, that'll be enough for Brianna."

After ten minutes of ardent argument, Lacey finally let me take over the register so she could get off her feet for a while. Working all day then caring for a new baby all night took its toll on her. I could see the fatigue in her eyes and the sluggish way she moved. Sluggish for Lacey, that is. Normally, she zipped around the store like a jackrabbit being chased by a fox. Exhaustion had her moving at *my* pace.

I tried to help in any way I could but, to her, accepting that help was a form of surrender. She finally agreed to take a break, then headed for the stockroom to grab more books for the shelves. Not exactly what I had in mind, but it didn't surprise me at all.

The problem was I had no authority over her anymore since we became equal partners earlier this year when the store needed an influx of cash to stay open. Even if our relationship hadn't changed, I couldn't have stopped her, anyway. Her mulish streak exploded out for at least a mile in all directions. Nothing could make her change her mind once she'd decided on a course of action. Not even overwhelming fatigue.

Adjusting to the new dynamic created a challenge for all of us, but we'd worked it out and, honestly, nothing had changed. Lacey had always run the store the way she wanted. The only difference now was I no longer had the final say in disputes, which proved beneficial since, in my ignorance, I usually landed on the wrong side of things.

Working her maternity leave had given me a much greater understanding of how much she did around here. I muddled through the necessities, but it was the little things she understood that made the most significant difference. Things like merchandising and upselling. My English degree prepared me for none of that. Or anything else outside of academia or publishing. Lucky for me, my writing career had succeeded so far. Too bad writing success didn't translate into wads of cash coming in. Enough to support myself, but not much more.

After checking out a couple of golden-age women collecting mysteries, I took advantage of a lull to wander over to the coffee bar. Charlie Nichols, also known as our barista-in-chief and, for the moment, the Lone Ranger, leaned on the counter, waiting for a mid-thirties blonde to choose her morning snack.

If nothing else, Charlie kept us entertained with his unique clothing line. Today's outfit included powder blue pants with a matching pullover shirt, a red kerchief around his neck, a black mask over his eyes, a Stetson on his head, and, of course, his gun belt and cowboy boots. God only knew what he'd come in wearing tomorrow.

Computer geek Charlie lived in my building, and, when he offered to help out at the bookstore, we made a deal. He'd give up his delusions of a potential romantic relationship with me, and I'd let him wear whatever he wanted to work.

No question I got the better end of the arrangement. He'd contributed much more to the store than khaki pants and a red Ravenous Readers polo shirt ever could have. To my surprise, he'd turned out to be a reliable and dedicated addition to the bookstore staff. The customers loved him, as did Lacey and I.

I retrieved my "Writer in Residence" mug from under the counter near the pastry case stocked with fresh cookies, muffins, and croissants—courtesy of Bob's Bakery across the street—and filled it with coffee from the urn. The hearty aroma wafted from the cup to my nose, and contentment washed over me. This was my place, and I loved it. I belonged somewhere for the first time in my life. Something I never thought I'd feel when I first took over, and I had Lacey and Charlie to thank for it.

The ceramic warmed my palm as I stirred in cream and sugar. My neck muscles loosened, letting me momentarily forget the morning's challenges. I relaxed into it, and my mind drifted as I watched Charlie whirl around the space in the store he'd made his own.

He prepared an espresso for the blonde to go along with the oatmeal raisin cookies she'd selected and doffed his hat when she dropped her change in his tip jar. He not only dressed in character but acted the part as well. The blonde carried her goodies to a table, smiling and shaking her head.

Our customers responded well to him. Some because they saw him as a kindred spirit who showed an ability to be himself no matter what people thought. Others came in because they thought him weird and wanted to see what he would be up to next. Every day was an adventure. *Who's Charlie going to be today?*

I didn't care which category—kindred spirit or weirdo—our regulars fell into as long as they continued to show up. It didn't matter as much what the tourists thought. We'd probably never see them again anyway, no matter how well or poorly we treated them. Or how entertaining we turned out to be.

A few children wandered around the kids' section behind us, filled with child-sized tables and activity zones, along with hundreds of titles selected to satisfy each level of reader. All nestled under the protective eyes of a pair of life-sized giraffes, which bookended the heading "Ravenous Kids" painted on the wall in rainbow colors.

Lacey had remodeled the area earlier this year, adding new bookcases and rearranging and increasing the available stock. The positive response from parents and kids made the section the focal point of the store. Exactly what we planned. *Score one for Lacey.*

Smiling as I looked around at a half-dozen people flipping through books, I realized the bookstore might actually make it. The financial struggles we'd fought through lay in the past, never to return unless something extraordinary happened. I could relax and enjoy my coffee without that burning in the pit of my stomach every time I remembered the stack of unpaid bills on my desk. The bills still existed, but they remained unpaid only because I'd been too preoccupied to pay them, not because the money wasn't there.

A middle-aged couple I'd never seen before, in shorts and polo shirts, made their way toward the register. Lacey was still in the stockroom, so I set my mug behind the pastry case and headed that way. Ringing up customers was one of my favorite things to do. I must've been a cashier in a former life. Or I'd totally missed my calling in this one.

The woman smiled as she set two biographies and a do-it-yourself book on plumbing repair on the counter. I hoped they had some hands-on experience to go with that guide. If not, I should probably snag them a copy of *Swimming for Dummies* as well.

I smiled back and scanned the biography of Paul Newman I didn't even know we had in stock. "Did you find everything you needed today?"

"We did, thank you," the woman replied, straightening the collar of her white polo shirt. "Plenty to keep us busy for the rest of our visit to the resort."

Were they staying in one of the unfinished rooms? Perhaps they received a discount for doing their own plumbing work. "How are you enjoying your trip?"

"Lake Dester is beautiful this time of year. The leaves are turning, and the sun reflects off the water like it's littered with jewels. It's wonderful."

The man grunted. "Yeah, wonderful if you like having nothing to do all day."

She squeezed his arm, a fake smile on her face. "That's why they call it a vacation, dear." To me, she said, "Don't mind him. He's just grumpy because the exercise facilities aren't finished yet. He can't go a day without pedaling that stationary bike until his legs fall off while listening to the stock market reports."

No response seemed my best play if I wanted to get out of the conversation unscathed, so I bagged their books while he tapped his credit card on the machine. "Thanks for stopping by. I hope you enjoy the rest of your vacation."

"We will." She herded her husband out the door.

CHAPTER FIVE

I retrieved my coffee about the time Lacey came out of the stockroom pushing a cartload of books and carrying the old life-size cardboard cutout of me under one arm. I stepped in front of her. "Where do you think you're going with that thing?"

It'd taken me months to convince her that our customers had no interest in being assaulted by an overgrown picture of me and a table full of my books every time they walked in the door. I found it disturbing, and I couldn't imagine they felt any differently. And blatant self-promotion was undignified, in my opinion. My publisher vehemently disagreed, and I couldn't fault them for that. If I didn't promote my books, who would? There had to be a better way, though. Something that didn't involve freaking people out.

"I'm putting your display back up. You have a new book coming in a couple of weeks, remember? People need a reminder to catch up on the series before then. Most authors would love having their books displayed at the front of the store."

She was right, of course, but I still hadn't figured out how to *be* an author. "Okay, but how about something that doesn't scare the bejesus out of them? Like a table in the corner by the restroom or something. Or a polite reminder by the register. People might buy the book on impulse that way. Like a candy bar by the grocery store checkout."

She pushed past me while Savannah led the way, prancing. "Nonsense. You're the only one who has a problem with it."

"Well, yeah! How would you like to have to stare at a ginormous picture of yourself all day? It's creepy."

"You're a bestselling author. Deal with it," she said with a grin. As we passed the coffee bar, Lacey called over her shoulder, "Charlie, would you grab the table from the back for me?"

Tipping his hat, he replied, "I'd be proud to, ma'am." He climbed on his imaginary horse with his arm in the air. "Hi-Yo, Silver! Away!"

Lacey and I burst out laughing. When I caught my breath, I said, "I wonder how he's going to carry it back on horseback."

"Very carefully, I'd think. I just hope he doesn't come back with an imaginary table on his imaginary horse." She propped the cutout in position between the front door and the right-side window, poised for a frontal attack.

"I wouldn't put it past him." I peered at my smiling face and grimaced. "You know, I swear this thing follows me with its eyes like the painting in *The Picture of Dorian Gray*."

"I'll bet it does." She straightened the books on the cart, placing copies of *Double Trouble* in three stacks of five. "It probably wants to make sure you don't do anything to embarrass it."

Fat chance. "I couldn't possibly embarrass *it* more than it embarrasses me."

"You'll get over it. Besides, don't you want to sell your books? You get paid both ways. Profits from the store and royalties from your publisher. What's wrong with that?"

Arrgh! Logic I couldn't argue with. Lacey must've been taking advice from Brittany.

Charlie showed up, sans horse, with table, sparing me the necessity of responding to her comment. Good thing since I didn't have a reasonable reply. Of course I wanted to sell my books, just not in such an ostentatious way. If I wanted to be the center of attention, I'd have become an actor or a circus clown, not a writer.

However, deep down, I knew deferring to Lacey's expertise was the best way to go. A way of giving the customers what they didn't even know they wanted. But I didn't have to like it. Especially when it came to me and my books.

After setting up the folding table and helping Lacey spread the cloth over it, Charlie glanced at the Used Book section, which had about half the books it could hold. "Do you want me to bring up some more used books?"

"If you don't mind," Lacey replied. "There's one more box back there."

When he left to retrieve them, she arranged the copies of *Double Trouble* on the table. I had to admit she had a flair for merchandising. Definitely not my forte.

"We have to make a decision about the used books," I said.

"I can't believe we went through all the ones we got from Gil in only nine months."

When the used bookstore threatening to steal a chunk of our business closed before it opened because the owner died, we picked up their inventory and the new bookcases for the kids' section for next to nothing. Now we had to decide whether to continue selling used books or return to our previous policy of new books only. The numbers would give us the answer to that question, though. Numbers dictated everything we did.

Something else I had no talent for.

Lacey put the finishing touches on the new display. Like it or not, I had to admit it looked pretty good.

"The used books definitely went fast," she continued. "And there was no significant dip in our new-book sales. Mostly, they seemed to be add-ons."

Losing new-book sales had been my greatest fear when we decided to sell the used ones. It seemed I was wrong. Again. "Okay, so what do you want to do? Should we buy more and make the section permanent or quit while we're ahead?"

"Before we decide, I think we should check into wholesalers and see what our profit margin will be. We basically got this crop for free since the bookcases would've cost a lot more by themselves than what we paid for all of it."

Charlie returned with the box of paperbacks and began restocking the shelves, which were each dedicated to a specific genre. Once on the shelf, they were then arranged alphabetically by the author's last name. The customers seemed to appreciate the layout because they could as easily hunt for specific books as browse for something to read. How would they feel if we stopped selling them altogether?

I gave him a hand, sliding paperbacks into the correct

spaces. "When we're done here, would you go online and look for used book wholesalers and get us an idea what we'd have to pay for stock if we keep this section open?"

He smiled at me with a book in each hand. "Sure thing, Boss. Do you have a specific amount in mind?"

"Not really. We've been selling them for half the cover price. Anything that lets us turn a profit at that amount would work. So sayeth the numbers."

He shelved his books and considered me thoughtfully. "We could always use them as a loss leader."

A loss leader? New one on me. "What's that?"

"Something you sell below cost to get people in the door, hoping they'll also buy something else you make money on. Grocery stores do it all the time."

"You mean like selling canned peas at two for a dollar, hoping someone'll buy a ribeye to go with them?"

"Exactly."

"We'd have to advertise them at that price to bring people in, though. I'll ask Lacey about it, but I don't think we need to go that far. Ravenous Readers is still primarily a new-book bookstore. I'm not sure we want to push the used books to the point that people are only coming in to buy *them*. I'd much rather they come in for a new book and find a used one they want, too."

He nodded. "Gotcha. I'll see what I can find."

"Thanks." I retrieved the last three books from the box and tucked them into the mystery shelf, which still looked a little bare. Maybe we should take trade-ins, too. Nah, that would make us too much like a used bookstore and would definitely affect new-book sales. Although, I'd been wrong on that subject before.

Charlie took the empty carton back to the stockroom.

The bells over the front door jingled, and I looked up in time to see Eric do a double-take and step away from Lacey's display. Exactly what I'd been complaining about.

He looked at me, then back to the cardboard cutout picture of me. "Jeez, Jen, getting a little full of yourself?"

I pointed to Lacey. "Don't look at me. It's all *her* doing."

Lacey dropped her hands on her hips. "Well, I think it looks wonderful. Wait and see. We'll sell all those books by the end of next week. When I add the new one to the extra copies of these I have coming in around the same time, they'll all fly out of here. I guarantee it."

"Now, who's getting full of herself?" I teased. "I think you're overestimating the power of my smile."

She picked up one copy and held it under her chin. "More like you're underestimating your talent. *Double Trouble* was a smash hit, remember? *Twin Terror* will be, too. I guarantee it."

My cheeks burned. Even after all this time, I still hadn't adjusted to knowing people enjoyed my writing. "I wish I shared your certainty. It would make my life a lot less stressful right now. I'm worried about how the second book will be received."

Eric took my hand. "Relax. You're gonna do great. I have faith in you."

I looked into his eyes. They sparkled, but fatigue had etched lines on his face around them. "Thank you, but you're only saying that because you love me."

Eager to change the subject, I led him to the coffee bar and poured him a cup—black, no sugar, the way he liked it. He said he'd grown accustomed to drinking his coffee that way because the police station break

48

room always ran out of cream and sugar. "How's the investigation going? Have you learned anything new about our forgetful friend?"

He blew away the steam and sipped. "No, not really. Havermayer couldn't get anything out of him, and neither did the psychiatrist who interviewed him at the hospital. The doctor thinks his amnesia is real. Caused by the blow to the back of his head. I still have my doubts, though. He might be faking to get out of trouble."

"Possibly, but I'm not sure I agree. He seemed legit to me."

"Either way, we have to go with the doctor's diagnosis for the time being. No way to prove he's faking unless we catch him letting a memory slip. And he's not talking, so no possibility of that."

"Not much help. Where is he now?"

"Havermayer brought him back to the station after the doctor released him. We still have to address the issue of the blood and the gun. The blood and hair on the pistol match his, but the pool we found by the tree doesn't, which means we have another victim."

I sat across from him at an empty table. "That complicates things. You think he hurt someone, then got clobbered by somebody else?"

"I don't know what to think. We didn't find his fingerprints on the gun, so it's possible he didn't use it. However, the blood by the tree matches the blood on his shirt. We have no idea how this all fits together, though. He might've tried to help the other victim and wiped his hands on his shirt. Then, the real killer knocked him out. In other words, it doesn't feel like we know much more than we did this morning."

My coffee had cooled, but I didn't want to interrupt the conversation to add more to heat it. "What're you going to do with him?"

"We'll hold him for investigation for now. Work to find out who he is, at least. We're checking missing persons reports now."

"Did the techs find anything else interesting?"

He barked a laugh. "Yeah, absolutely. Seventeen candy wrappers, a used condom, an empty Bob's Bakery bag, a poker chip, and twelve cigarette butts. All of which have to be processed. Talk about a waste of time and resources."

"Maybe not. You never know. That empty bag might break the case."

He drained the last of his coffee. "Nah, if anything, it'll be the condom or maybe the poker chip."

"Seriously? A poker chip?"

"Believe it or not, underground gambling has become a bit of a problem in Riddleton."

I laughed. "You're kidding. Now you're cracking down on Friday night poker games?"

The front door opened, and Eric stood. Officer Zach Vick, son of the former police chief, who'd died last summer, waved Eric over with one hand and massaged the back of his neck with the other.

"I'll be right back," Eric said, setting his empty cup on the table.

I refilled it for him and topped off my own while waiting for his return. My heart swelled with pride as I watched him work. He took his job seriously and was determined to be the best detective possible. I could see him replacing Olinski as chief of police one day if he wanted, although he'd never expressed an interest in that. His goal was to be as good as Havermayer. I believed he could do better.

Eric listened as Zach delivered his message, then bolted out the door. He made his way back to our table. One look at the freckles standing out on his ashen face like chocolate sprinkles on vanilla ice cream told me something important had happened. And it wasn't good.

"What's going on?" I asked, concern heavy in my voice.

He took a large swallow of his fresh coffee and dropped into his seat with a sigh. "Simeon Kirby's body's been found in the back of Havermayer's car. He was shot three times—two in the chest and one in the gut—and they found his wallet and Rolex under the driver's seat. Havermayer's been detained for questioning in the murder."

CHAPTER SIX

Eric kissed me and sprinted out of the store. I sat, stunned, unsure what to do or how to feel. On one hand, Havermayer being accused of murder based on circumstantial evidence was like a dream come true. She'd done it to me often enough. This was payback to the nth degree, and yet I experienced no joy in her predicament. Two wrongs definitely didn't make a right, as my kindergarten teacher loved to say. Took me long enough to listen. Maybe I was finally growing up.

My stomach churned coffee and acid back up into my esophagus. Simeon Kirby, my nemesis second only to Havermayer, had died, and contradictory feelings muddled my brain. I wanted him to go home to Spartanburg, not die, but either way he was out of my life for good. Knowing that if Havermayer herself wasn't a suspect she'd be pointing a finger at me didn't help any either. Everyone knew how I felt about him, which made me the perfect prime suspect. Should I be grateful the body was found in her car? I shuddered at the prospect.

But I knew there was no way Havermayer had murdered Simeon Kirby or anyone else. That level of flexibility didn't exist in her makeup. Flexibility required seeing the big picture. Not something she was known for. In her way of looking at things, the forest was always hidden by the trees. Pretty sure the rule book had her name on the copyright page, and she'd ignore no statute written in it. Certainly not one as big as murder.

Putting all that to the side, what motive did she have? As far as I knew, she'd never conversed with the man. Even if she did, those discussions included nothing volatile enough to make her want to kill him. Not without me having heard about it. The gossip train would've stopped at every station in town within minutes had Havermayer argued with Kirby. Given how many people the detective had alienated over the years, it might be only seconds before everyone knew what had happened. Nope, no way she killed him.

Charlie parked himself in Eric's vacated seat across the table from me, concern and confusion oozing from his eyes. "What's going on? Why'd Eric run out like that?" He gave me a side-eye. "Did you dump him or something stupid like that?"

"What? No! Why would you ask that?"

"He took off like Jack the Ripper was chasing him. You must've said something that upset him. You're good at that, you know."

"Gee, thanks for the reminder." I shook my head, mildly irritated that he could think so little of me. "Not me this time. Zach."

He pinched his eyebrows. "When was Zach here? I didn't see him come in."

Typical Charlie. Oblivious to everything going on around him when he had a research project to do. A positive thing in, my opinion, since he usually did his research for me. "When you had your nose buried in your computer, apparently. Simeon Kirby is dead. Somebody shot him."

His brows shot up to his hairline. "You're kidding. And Havermayer thinks you did it, right? That's what usually happens."

I gave him a half-smile. "Probably, but for once she's got bigger problems right now. They found Kirby's body in the back of her car, along with his wallet and expensive watch. She's being detained for questioning."

His eyes widened to the point he resembled a pug. "Holy cow! I can't believe she finally has to walk in your shoes. It's about time she tried them on. What're you gonna do?"

Conflicting options ran through my head, as always. My first instinct was the same as any time someone I knew had been falsely accused. Jump in and find exculpatory evidence. But this time, Detective Havermayer occupied the hot seat. The detective who constantly put me in the position of having to defend myself against her accusations. That made it a tougher decision.

Even if I wanted to help, and I wasn't sure I did, she would never accept it. She couldn't ask me to check into her situation after all the times she'd cautioned me to stay out of police investigations. Unless she wanted to win the election for Riddleton's biggest hypocrite, and that, too, went against her nature. Right up there with murdering someone.

I met Charlie's gaze. "Me? I doubt I'll do anything. Havermayer can take care of herself. She always does. And she has the whole police department to help her. She doesn't need or want any interference from me. Even when I sailed in the same boat, she objected to me working to clear my name. I don't see her attitude changing anytime soon, even if I did try to help her."

"Come on," he said, leaning back in his chair. "If it were anyone else you knew, you'd jump on the first horse you saw and ride to the rescue. That's who you are."

"Maybe, but anyone else would need rescuing from *her* false accusations. I haven't heard of her making any against anyone else in this case. I suspect she's a little busy trying to get back on the right side of the interrogation table."

Charlie crossed his arms. "So, you're really not gonna help? What happened to your mystery writer's curiosity? Are you gonna let this challenge go unaccepted? That doesn't sound like the Jen I know."

Irritation crept into my voice. "No, I'm not going to help. If I risk getting myself in trouble, it'll be for someone who can't help themselves. Someone who needs me to fight for them because there *is* nobody else. Havermayer has all the resources she needs and the benefit of the doubt to boot, which is more than she ever gives anyone else. She doesn't need my help."

"True. She does have the benefit of the doubt. No way any of the people she works with believe she killed Kirby, no matter what the evidence says. They'll work overtime if they have to. Whatever it takes to clear her. Which doesn't mean she can't use your help, by the way. Just sayin'." He stood and retrieved his computer from the coffee bar. "You want to see what I found for the wholesalers?"

Embracing the subject change, I leaned toward him and said, "Sure. Whatcha got? Will we be able to find books we can afford?"

He shifted to a seat beside me so we could both see the screen, and we huddled over it while he flipped through and explained our options. He'd found several distributors that could accommodate bulk orders within our price range if we chose our inventory carefully. It seemed like a workable plan.

I waved Lacey over to show her what Charlie had discovered. We went through all the options again and crunched the numbers. "I think we can do it," I told her. "Actually, I think we *should* do it."

Lacey concurred. From the look of it, we would stay in the used book business for the foreseeable future. The add-on sales contributed enough to our bottom line to make the trouble worth our while. "Do you have any idea where the genre plaques over the bookcases came from?" I asked her. "We need to get one for the Used Book section since we've decided to keep it. That cardboard sign we've been using looks a little tacky."

"A little?" She laughed. "I don't know, but I'm sure there's some paperwork in that office somewhere. I'll take a look when I get a chance."

"May the Force be with you," Charlie said with a grin. "I wouldn't want to have to find anything in there."

She cocked an eyebrow at him. "And what, exactly, does the Lone Ranger know about the Force?"

His grin turned sheepish. "Sorry, I slipped into the wrong character there for a minute." He puffed his chest out with his fists on his hips, looking more like Superman in a Halloween costume than the Lone Ranger. "It won't happen again, Kemosabe."

"Wait a minute," I said. "Isn't that what we're supposed to call you?"

He jiggled his eyebrows. "Since neither one of you seem interested in playing Tonto, I have to improvise."

Lacey and I gave a gold-medal performance of the synchronized eye roll.

We had a steady stream of customers for the rest of the afternoon. Lacey handled the floor and the cash register while Charlie controlled the coffee and pastry distribution. I jumped in wherever needed, although those two operated with expert efficiency most of the time. I did my best to be useful, even if it only meant fetching water for the coffee pot. At least I didn't have to pump it out of a well.

At five forty-five, Charlie and I broke down the coffee bar, carrying empty trays and utensils to the wash sink. While cleaning the espresso machine, he said, "I almost forgot. Lacey mentioned you found a man who can't remember who he is this morning. Whatever happened with him?"

I sprayed glass cleaner on the pastry case. "He still doesn't remember anything. Eric said they're checking missing persons reports. If that doesn't turn up anything, I think they'll have to post his picture around town and hope somebody recognizes him. Or Veronica could send out a town-wide email with his photo attached."

"Huh. Is he from around here, you think?"

"I don't know. I didn't recognize him, and neither did anyone else who saw him this morning at the park. He might be new to the area, though."

He snapped the nozzle back in and replaced the now-clean drip tray. "I wonder if he's one of the workers from the resort. I wouldn't think we'd recognize too many of them. They don't make it to town very often."

A stubborn smudge on the glass required another

squirt. Probably the remnants of some kid's cookie fingers. "Could be, but I don't think so. He wore expensive dress clothes, and his hands were impeccably manicured under all the blood. Definitely not a construction worker."

"What about a supervisor? I don't think walking around with a clipboard all day would hurt his manicure too much."

"It's possible, but what was he doing in the park dressed like he'd just come back from a casual meeting with the governor?"

"Good question. Guess you'll figure it out when you find out who he is."

"What's this *you* stuff? I told you I'm not getting involved."

He lifted one eyebrow. "Whatever you say."

I walked away, shaking my head. If he thought I'd get involved in this mess, he was nuts. Well, even more nuts than usual.

I vacuumed the carpet with Savannah's snarling assistance while Charlie washed the dishes. Lacey checked out our last two customers and locked the door behind them when they left. She closed out the register, and I put the vacuum cleaner back in the stockroom.

Charlie came out of the utility room, wiping his hands on a towel. "How'd we do today? It seemed pretty busy to me."

Lacey collected the reports spitting out of the printer and peered at the one with the sales totals. "Congratulations, everyone! We just had our best non-holiday-season Saturday. If this keeps up, we'll be in the black in no time."

"Yay!" Charlie clapped his hands. "Looks like the

resort is helping our business just like Kirby said it would. Without any of the negative stuff we've been worried about. I feel bad he died, now."

I'd never admit it out loud, and if anyone asked I'd deny I ever thought it, but he was correct about the increased business. Though, I still had concerns about what would happen when the project was completed and the resort fully occupied. However, since Kirby had died, whether that would ever happen now remained a question. Would his family or business partners take over? I had no idea.

He'd been in town for almost a year, and I still knew virtually nothing about him. Most of my interactions with the man had been hostile, so I couldn't blame myself for not wanting to learn more. I wasn't interested in knowing my enemy or keeping him close, only getting rid of him before he irreparably damaged the atmosphere in my hometown.

I texted Eric to see if he might have time for dinner. No surprise, he didn't. Not with a murder and identifying our amnesiac stranger on his plate with no help from his partner, who currently occupied a holding cell. A picture of Havermayer in an orange jumpsuit, huddling in a corner while a crowd of convicts she'd sent to jail closed in on her, popped into my head. I shook it away, not wanting to be that person. *But it was fun while it lasted.*

Besides, Havermayer would never make it to the Sutton County Jail if the Riddleton Police Department had anything to say about it, so no orange jumpsuit. And even if, for some strange reason, she *did* end up over there, they'd keep her in protective custody for just that possibility. She'd never have to face an angry mob howling for revenge. Nor did she deserve to. I still found it impossible to believe she had anything to do with Simeon Kirby's death.

Making the safe assumption that Olinski would be just as occupied with the day's events as Eric, I called Brittany.

She answered on the second ring. "Hey, how are you? Heard they still don't know who the guy you found in the park is."

"From the rumor mill or Olinski?"

"A little of both, but mostly Olinski."

Must be nice dating the chief of police. Maybe someday Eric would hold that position, and he could tell me whatever he wanted with nobody to slap his wrist for it. "Funny how he's so forthcoming with you, but when I ask a simple question I'm interfering in his investigation."

Her guffaw had me pulling the phone away from my ear. "That's because you usually are trying to interfere. And you never ask simple questions."

I stuck out my lower lip. "It wasn't that funny. And I don't interfere; I help." Someday, somebody would believe me when I said that.

She sobered. "I'm sorry. How about we have a girls' night since the boys are both busy with the case? Then I can make it up to you."

"All right, but it's going to take lots of wine to soothe my injured feelings." Not true, but I enjoyed tugging on her proverbial pigtails sometimes.

"I'll bet. Don't worry, I have plenty. You want to swing by the diner on your way home? I've been craving some of Angus's fried chicken."

My eyebrows shot up. "*Craving* craving? Or I haven't had it in a while craving?"

Brittany sighed into my ear. "No, I'm not expecting, Jen. Ever since Lacey got pregnant, that's the first place your mind goes. If I didn't know better, I'd wonder if *you* weren't the one with baby fever."

Not in this lifetime. "But, you *do* know better, don't you. I'll see you in a little bit."

Brittany disconnected without a reply.

CHAPTER SEVEN

Proprietor Angus Halliburton and Jacob, the grill cook, were manning the almost empty diner when I walked in. Not unusual for a Saturday night, when most people traveled to restaurants in Blackburn or Sutton for *real* dates. There was always Bannister's Bar and Grill on Second Street if they wanted to watch a ball game while they ate or didn't want to travel.

"Hi, Jen," Angus said, wiping down the counter, black combover flopping in rhythm. "Heard you had a busy morning at the park. Sorry I missed it."

Angus was a regular member of the Riddleton Runners and my usual Saturday running partner, but couldn't participate this morning because his assistant manager, Marcus Jones, was out of town. I would've missed trotting alongside him if we'd had the opportunity to run. Amnesia man picked the perfect day to show up.

"*You* may have missed it, but clearly the rumormongers didn't."

As the engineer of the town gossip train, Angus often knew things before anyone else did. He loved to regale me with stories while we ran, which took my mind off my aching legs and wheezing lungs. Not that

I was particularly interested in the intimate details of my neighbors' lives, but my nodding and laughing in all the proper places made him happy. And that made me happy.

Angus leaned on the counter. "Of course not! Everything that happens around here runs through me. You should know that by now." He wiped his hands on the apron concealing his ample midsection, even though it was already covered in ketchup, mustard, and who knew what else.

I *did* know that, and Angus's information had come in handy more than once during my investigations, I had to admit. "When is Marcus coming back?"

"They're supposed to be back tomorrow night, but I heard a couple of cops talking over lunch about how they might call Ingrid back early to do Kirby's autopsy."

Ingrid Kensington was our town doctor, who doubled as a part-time pathologist and was also Marcus's girlfriend. She'd moved to Riddleton from London after the state offered to pay her way through medical school in exchange for five years as a small-town doctor. I could listen to her talk all day, even if I couldn't always understand her. Her words looked like English and sounded like English, but they were often Greek to me.

I scooted onto a stool at the counter, and Savannah nestled at my feet with her chin on the footrest. "I hate that they have to call her in. She and Marcus deserve some time away."

Angus shook his head and poured me a Mountain Dew. "I know, but there's no telling what she might find. Maybe he had a heart attack before the gunshots killed him."

"Anything's possible, but I doubt that's what happened.

I know they have to retrieve the bullets for examination. I just think it stinks, that's all."

He handed me my drink. "Did you want something to eat? You haven't had your daily bacon cheeseburger yet."

"Not tonight. Can I get two fried chicken dinners to go, please? Actually, make that three. Eric probably hasn't eaten since breakfast." I peeled the wrapper off my straw, feeling like I'd forgotten something. I'd figure it out eventually. "I'm hanging with Brittany tonight since the boys are working, and she's craving your fried chicken. Guess she hasn't had it in a while."

He perked up. "Craving? Is she—"

"No, she's not pregnant," I said with a laugh. "Apparently, Lacey's put that idea in all our heads. I said the same thing when she told me."

"Oh, too bad."

I sucked on my straw, savoring the fizzy sweetness of my drink. "If you ask me, little Brielle's all the baby we need around here for the time being."

His eyes took on a faraway look. "No, you can never have too many babies."

There had to be a story behind that look. "Do you have any kids, Angus?"

Strangely, the gossipmonger was great about passing on information about everyone but himself. All I knew about him was he used to be a bank loan officer in New Hampshire.

"No, my wife and I never had any. We always thought we'd have plenty of time later to start a family. Stupid assumption."

I swallowed the lump that had suddenly formed in my throat. "What happened?"

"Brain cancer. It happened so fast that I never had time to wrap my head around it. One minute, she was fine; the next, she was gone. She was only thirty-three."

No wonder he never talked about his past. It was too painful. The lump settled in my chest. "I'm so sorry, Angus. I had no idea."

"It's okay. I moved here so I could get away from the constant reminders of what we had and what could've been." He smiled and looked around the diner. "So, here I am. Brand-new diner, brand-new life."

I reached across the counter and grasped his hand. "Well, I hate the reason you had to come here, but I'm grateful you did."

"I'll bet. You'd have starved to death years ago if it weren't for me."

Our laughter broke the tension, but his story still haunted me.

Jacob loaded our meals into Styrofoam containers and brought them up to the register. Angus packed three large and one small box into a plastic bag for me. Then he poured the rest of my drink into a to-go cup.

"Hey, what's in the smaller one?" I asked, confused since I'd only ordered the three fried chicken dinners.

He opened it and showed me a plain hamburger patty. "You forgot to get something for my favorite customer."

Oops. Angus might've just saved my life. Savannah would never have forgiven me. If *never* lasted only about five seconds. "Thank you. I know she would've been heartbroken if she didn't get her own personal hamburger."

"Well, we certainly can't have that, can we?"

"No, definitely not." I plucked two crumpled twenties

out of my pocket, handed them to him, and grabbed the food bag. "Thanks, Angus. You have a good night."

"You, too. See you tomorrow?"

I smiled and opened the door. "You can count on it."

When we invited ourselves into her apartment after leaving Eric's dinner with the duty sergeant, Brittany was balanced on a step stool, draping fake cobwebs across the ceiling to go with the life-size cardboard witch propped in the corner. Maybe I could swap the witch for the one of me Lacey had up in the store. It would attract more attention and be less frightening.

Savannah charged, and I dropped the food on the coffee table to catch her before she knocked my best friend on her keister. The stool was only two feet high, but a fall could still do some damage. My plans for the evening didn't include a trip to the emergency room. Although, at least we'd be going there for somebody besides me for a change.

I grabbed the dog's collar and dragged her back while Brittany descended the two steps to floor level. "If I'd known you needed cobwebs, I'd have brought you some of mine," I said.

Brittany squatted to scratch Savannah's neck and peered up at me. "No, thanks. Yours come with the spiders that created them."

"See? Two for the price of one. It's a bargain at any price, but for you, no charge."

"You sound like an electronics store commercial at three in the morning." She pulled a chilled bottle of wine out of the fridge while I retrieved our dinner. "Besides, my mother always taught me, 'You get what you pay for.'"

66

"Your mother's a wise woman."

"Don't tell *her* that. It'll go straight to her head."

I picked up the plastic bag and adjusted the decoration I'd nudged out of line when I dropped the food. Brittany had alternated black and orange votive candles across the coffee table, separated by goblins of varying shapes and sizes.

"When did you become such a Halloween buff? I don't remember you ever decorating your apartment before." I carried the bag to the kitchen.

Brittany doled the food onto plates, although I'd have been content eating out of the container. "I was feeling creative, and I had some stuff left over from doing the library, so I brought it home."

"Creative, huh? In that case, I'm glad your wedding's not scheduled until June, so you can't get 'creative' with that. I'd hate to see how I look in an orange maid of honor dress."

"How do you know it wouldn't be black?"

"I assumed your wedding dress would be black, and we'd have to wear orange for contrast. I think Olinski would look terrific in an orange tux, don't you?"

She handed me my plate and a wineglass half filled with white Moscato. "Oh, definitely. It would bring out the brown in his eyes."

I plopped down on the love seat. Savannah positioned herself at my feet. "Maybe, but black would hide the wrinkles in his suit better."

"Uh-uh. No wrinkles at my wedding, thank you."

"Oh, so he's coming naked. Your mother'll *love* that."

"Very funny." She forked up some mashed potatoes. "I think he's been looking very sharp lately."

No argument from me about that. His uniform had

knife-edge creases these days, as opposed to the "I've been wearing this suit for three days" crinkles of his detective years. "I noticed. I figured you've been ironing his uniforms for him."

"Not all of them. I do a couple for demonstration, and he does the rest."

More proof those two were much better suited for each other than he and I were. Pretty sure I wouldn't have had the patience to demonstrate, and he would've expected me to iron them all. Maybe he'd changed. Maybe we'd both changed. "Good for you. You've found a way to tame the tiger. Impressive, I must say. You should write a book called '*How to Train a Man.*'"

"I'll leave the writing to you." She chuckled. "Besides, he's not a tiger. He's a pussycat."

Seriously? That sounded nothing like the linebacker I'd dated. I shook my head and bit into a juicy chicken leg, letting Angus's perfect mix of seasonings entertain my taste buds.

Brittany swallowed her mouthful. "Hey, you want to see some of the wedding stuff while we eat?" Without waiting for a reply, she jumped up and retrieved a bridal magazine at least an inch thick from a foot-high stack of them on her dining room table.

If I said "no," would it make a difference? Probably not. I *was* the maid of honor, though, so my job description included looking at wedding stuff. Especially since it was for Brittany. "Sure, why not? It'll be fun." Like driving a thousand miles with no bathroom stops.

She sat and patted the couch beside her. "Come sit over here with me so you can see what I've been looking at."

I wrenched my feet out from under the two-ton dog

68

and moved to the other side of the coffee table. Savannah followed and squeezed between me and the arm of the couch. The magazine was open to a dog-eared page depicting a wedding dress that looked like it had come from an 1860s dressmaker—crinoline, lace, and all. The lace veil puddled on the floor, and the waist had been cinched so tight the model resembled a dinner bell.

"Is this the dress you want?" I asked, mentally begging her to decline. If her dress looked like that, would mine be from the Civil War era, too? I'd be Little Bo Peep without the staff.

"Oh, no," she chuckled. "I want something much simpler. I just like to look at this one. It's gorgeous, don't you think?"

On Scarlett O'Hara, maybe. "Absolutely. Is there a picture of something more suited to *you* in there?"

She flipped forward a few pages to a simple V-neck dress with cap sleeves. "This one is more my style *and* my price range."

Breathing a silent sigh of relief, I said, "I think you'll be beautiful in it."

Although, if this bridal gown had to make the bride the center of attention, our bridesmaid dresses would probably be potato sacks. Fine with me. I might wear it again someday. Perhaps for the sack race at next year's Founder's Day picnic, coincidentally scheduled for two weeks after the wedding. Perfect timing.

Brittany turned to a dog-eared page with wedding cakes on it. "How are you doing with your list?"

My list? Oh yeah, my to-do list for the wedding. If I ever got married, I'd definitely elope. No way I was going through all this again. Of course, it would be a great way to get revenge on Brittany for making me do it. The to-do list would have *her* name on it. "So far, Bob's agreed to make the cake, and Angus will cater. He needs a head count, and you need to stop by and go over the menu with him."

"Okay. What about the music?"

"Have you decided if you want a band or a DJ yet?"

"I'm not sure. I keep going back and forth. I'll discuss it with Olinski and get back to you on that one."

Her phone rang, and she picked it up to check the screen. "Speak of the devil."

Saved by the bell. I could safely table the discussion of flowers and invitations and centerpieces for another day.

I took Savannah for a walk. Not that we had any secrets from each other, and Brittany'd never ask me to leave the room, but she needed privacy sometimes, too. I'd been selfish where Brittany was concerned for most of our friendship. I wanted to do better. To not only be okay with sharing her but to be supportive as well. It wasn't easy, though. I was dying to pepper Olinski with questions while she had him on the phone.

The sun hadn't quite set yet as the clocks didn't fall back for another couple of weeks, but the dark-gray sky zipped toward black, and the air had chilled. I shivered in my sweatshirt, which was all I'd needed to be comfortable this afternoon. Autumn often brought wide temperature swings each day as the warmth from the sun rapidly dissipated when it went down in the evening. Welcome to South Carolina, where, if you didn't like the temperature, you only had to wait a little while. It would change.

CHAPTER EIGHT

When we returned from our stroll around the block, Brittany was paging through her magazine, her phone lying beside her on the couch.

"Where'd you go?" she asked.

I unleashed the dog. "Savannah hadn't been out in a while, so it seemed like a good time to take her for a walk. And I figured you needed some private mushy time with your fiancé."

She laughed. "Yeah, right. With half the police force for an audience. Olinski has enough trouble telling me he loves me when we're alone. No chance he'd say anything mushy with all the guys around."

"Huh. I guess he hasn't changed as much as I thought. I was sure he'd have gotten over his embarrassment by now."

"Nope. Some things will probably never change. He still puts on his macho persona with his uniform every morning."

"Persona being the word of the day." After refilling our wineglasses, I stretched out on the love seat. "Did he have anything interesting to report? Any news on amnesia guy?"

"Now, you know he told me not to tell you anything."

"When has that ever stopped you?"

She shrugged. "We're almost married. I'm not allowed to tell anyone what he tells me."

I crossed my arms. "Nice try. First of all, you're not married yet, and, secondly, that only means you can't be compelled to testify against him at trial. It has nothing to do with sharing information with your best friend."

"I know. Actually, he didn't even tell me not to say anything to you. I made that up. There's nothing interesting to share."

I punched her lightly in the arm as payback. "There's no news at all about the guy from the park this morning?"

Brittany sipped her wine. "Nothing, other than they're calling him Dan now."

"Why Dan?"

She shrugged. "Why not? They have to call him something."

"I suppose. Is Havermayer still being detained for Kirby's murder? Did she have an alibi?"

"He didn't say if they were still holding her, but he told me this afternoon she said she was home alone that night. Kirby's family showed up to claim the body, though."

I sat up, and Savannah immediately climbed into the empty space. "Ingrid hasn't done the autopsy yet, has she?"

"I don't think so. Olinski wanted to question them first, anyway. Get their alibis and all that. Just because Kirby was shot here doesn't mean it was someone from here who shot him."

"Who all showed up?"

"The wife and two of his kids. The eldest son and

his daughter. He has another son nobody's been able to reach, which, from what they said about it, is unusual for him."

Strange that Kirby's son disappeared around the same time Kirby was murdered. Could he be the killer?

Or better yet, could he be our amnesiac friend Dan? The family lived in Spartanburg, though, which made it unlikely that one of Simeon Kirby's sons would be found wandering around Riddleton Park with a head wound. Why would he be here in the first place?

"Does Olinski have any thoughts about who the killer might be?" I asked Brittany.

"If he does, he didn't say. It's probably too soon to speculate unless there's only one person with a motive, and I doubt that's the case. Although, what Havermayer's motive might be, I can't fathom, but I'm betting she's still in custody."

"Being accused based on circumstantial evidence. Sound familiar? You can call it karma as far as I'm concerned." I flashed her a grin. "However, I'm betting on the wife. Being married to Kirby couldn't have been easy. The guy was a jerk who only cared about making money. He didn't strike me as much of a family man."

Brittany drained her glass. "That's how he seemed to you, but you only met Kirby the businessman. He could've been a loving, devoted husband for all you know."

I raised my eyebrows, and we both started laughing.

When Brittany could breathe again, she said, "Yeah, you're probably right. The guy was a jerk." She leaned forward to set her empty glass on the table. "But you know it's possible his wife liked him that way. She might've only been in it for the money to begin with."

"Could be. Or maybe one of the kids offed him to get their inheritance sooner. His reward for devoting his life to making money."

Times like this, I appreciated that I grew up without money. My life was difficult but simple. Rich people have more luxuries but a lot more complications to go along with them. I hated my stepfather growing up, but at least he never had to worry about me bumping him off for my inheritance. There was only so much beer I could drink, and that's likely all he would leave me. It was all he ever had.

Brittany frowned. "My father worked hard to take care of us, and I'd never murder him for his money."

"True, but he loved you, and you knew it. He always made time for his family. Since Simeon Kirby's been in Riddleton for almost a year now, I doubt anyone could say the same about him."

She nodded her agreement and refilled her glass. "So, who do you think killed him?"

"Without any evidence, I'd have to speculate."

"When's that ever stopped you before?"

I balled up a napkin and threw it at her. "Usually, when I speculate, I at least have something to go on. I have nothing at all at the moment."

She gave me her "I've got a secret" smile. "Not nothing. Olinski told me the blood on Dan's shirt matches Simeon Kirby."

There could only be one reason Kirby's blood was on Dan's shirt: he was there when Kirby was murdered. Could he be the killer? It didn't seem likely, given his condition when we found him. Maybe he was a witness to the shooting, and the killer tried to stop him from talking. The head wound was supposed to kill him.

74

It didn't work, but the amnesia solved the problem, anyway. Dan couldn't tell the cops anything. Not even his name.

My eyebrows shot up. "That does change things. But Dan had a head wound that knocked him out and gave him amnesia. If he killed Kirby, who hit *him*?"

"What if Kirby hit him, then Dan got the gun away from him and shot him in self-defense before he passed out?"

From Brittany's point of view, the idea seemed reasonable since she hadn't seen Dan in the park this morning. I could see no possible way he maintained consciousness long enough to take the gun away from Kirby and shoot him.

But I'd been wrong before.

I awoke Sunday morning to the smell of bacon frying and coffee brewing. Unless Savannah had grown thumbs overnight, Eric must've come in late last night, because he wasn't here when I went to bed. Strange. He usually went home when he had to work late. Stranger still, I didn't hear him come in. Apparently, the stress of my long day yesterday tired me out more than I'd realized.

I swung my legs over the side of the bed, unhindered by my German shepherd, who was probably begging for bacon. After a pit stop in the bathroom, I found them in the kitchen—Eric frying eggs, the dog dripping saliva on the floor.

"Good morning! What time did you get in last night?" I asked Eric.

He turned to me and smiled, but his fatigue cast a shadow over his attempt to show happiness at my arrival. He wore it like a mantle of rocks bowing his shoulders and lining his face. "More like early this morning. It was after two. I hope you don't mind. I didn't feel like driving back to my place."

"Not at all." I wrapped my arms around him and nuzzled against his back, breathing in his clean man scent. A mixture of soap, aftershave, and just plain Eric. "I love having you here in the morning."

"You mean you love having breakfast ready for you when you get up." He turned around, leaned down, and kissed me, his shower-wet hair dampening my cheek.

"That too." I filled my mug with coffee, added cream and sugar, and warmed my hands with the heated ceramic. "Did you get a chance to eat your dinner last night?"

"I did. Thanks for thinking of me."

"I'm always thinking of you."

He kissed me again. "You're sweet."

Embarrassment heated my cheeks. "Shut up and finish fixing my breakfast. I'm hungry."

He pulled the pan off the stove and made like he'd dump my eggs in the trash.

I shot him my best "You wouldn't dare!" look.

He laughed.

My toast popped and I slathered it with butter. "Did you make any progress in the case?"

"Which one?"

"Either. Both. I missed you last night. I'd like to know it wasn't for nothing."

Eric slid the eggs onto a plate, added bacon and toast, and handed it to me. The smells triggered a fountain in my mouth. Funny how the aroma of bacon could do that, whether I was hungry or not. Today, though, I was starving.

I thanked him and claimed my place at the table, waiting for him to join me. Savannah abandoned the kitchen long enough to check my path for leavings, then returned to sit at Eric's feet. A twinge of jealousy popped up until I remembered it was the food she wanted more than me, not my boyfriend. A minor difference but an important one to my fragile ego.

While he flipped his eggs, I asked, "Did you learn anything new about Dan? Like his real name? And why are you calling him Dan, anyway?"

He chuckled and shook his head. "One of the guys found a lost dog a few weeks ago and called him Dan until he could find the owner. We figured our guy was just another stray, so we're calling him Dan, too. Maybe it'll bring us luck finding his owner."

Interesting way to think about a lost, injured human, but it made me all warm and fuzzy inside knowing Eric felt comfortable sharing it with me. Gallows humor kept cops and medical professionals from losing their minds. "From the sound of things, you might need to work on his memory more than finding his so-called owner. Brittany told me Olinski mentioned the blood on Dan's shirt matches Simeon Kirby's. Is Dan now a suspect in the murder, or are you sticking with Havermayer?"

"Brittany shouldn't be running her mouth. Then again, neither should Olinski. I guess if he thought it was okay to tell her, it's okay for her to tell you." Eric claimed the seat at the end of the table. "We're looking at them both, although we're having trouble finding a motive for Havermayer to kill him. She didn't like him much, but that's no reason for murder."

"Obviously, or she'd have killed me years ago." It wasn't like she hadn't tried through legal channels every time she falsely accused me of murder. If she'd made any of those accusations stick, I might've faced the death penalty. "What makes you think she doesn't like him? I didn't realize she'd even interacted with him that much."

He dunked his toast into an egg yolk with one hand and propped up his chin with the other. "I imagine her problem with him was much the same as yours. She doesn't like change."

"What do you mean? I have nothing against change unless it's going to make things worse. In this case, Kirby's plans were going to hurt the town. That's why I didn't like the idea of the resort. It would turn Riddleton into a tourist trap instead of the quaint little hamlet I've grown to love."

"I'm not sure if that was her reason or not, but she definitely didn't like the resort."

"You think she murdered him to put an end to the project?"

He bit off a piece of bacon and stared at a spot over my left shoulder while he chewed. After swallowing, he said, "I don't see how that would work. Kirby will leave the resort to his beneficiaries, whoever they may be, and they'll finish or sell it to another developer. It might be delayed while the will is in probate, but the resort is here to stay, I suspect."

I ate in silence while waiting for the disappointment to dissipate. "You're probably right. Who found the body?"

"Havermayer's neighbor spotted it when she stopped to chat with Havermayer while she picked up her car after dropping Dan off at the station."

"Wish I'd been around to see the look on her face. Just to see *her* off balance for a change. Did she freak?"

He tried to hide a smirk. "No way. Sorry to disappoint you, but she's a trained detective. She preserved the scene and called it in." He picked up another slice of toast. "It's a little weird knowing my partner's being investigated, though."

"I'll bet. On some level, it must feel like you're being investigated, too." I lifted my lip in a half-smirk. "Although it hasn't seemed to affect your appetite any."

"I'm a growing boy." He chuckled and wiped up a smear of yolk with his toast. "It does feel a little like I'm being looked at, too. Although nobody's said anything about me being involved. The other team is working on it. I have to figure out who Dan is. I wouldn't mind some help, but we're not exactly equipped to handle two major investigations at the same time."

Riddleton was a small town with a small-town police department. One of the other reasons I'd been so against Kirby's development plans. We'd already had more than our share of murders since I'd been back. The last thing we needed was an increase in crime overall. I had no factual basis for that assumption, only that it seemed reasonable that more people around would mean more crime.

It took all my willpower to keep from offering to help Eric with his investigation. Number one, he'd probably turn me down flat. He wanted me safely tucked away at home or in the bookstore, minding my own business. Number two, Olinski would never allow it. And number three, Havermayer had been after me since the day we met, and she had the entire police force behind her. She wouldn't need or want my help. Still, I didn't want to be the person who wouldn't help because I didn't like her. I'd stick with the first two reasons for now.

I stabbed a forkful of egg. "Brittany thinks Dan might've killed Kirby. I don't see how since he was knocked out by that whack on the head. Do you still think he might be faking the amnesia?"

"I don't know. The doctor at the hospital didn't think so. I'm in no position to say he's wrong, but my gut tells me there's more to this story than we know yet."

Good old cop gut. "My writer's gut says the same thing. There's always a story behind the story. We just have to figure out what it is."

"We? You know how Olinski feels about you interfering in our investigations."

"I didn't mean 'we' as in you and me. I have no intention of sticking my nose into this one. It's all yours."

"Good, if it's true. There's obviously some connection between these two cases. Between the three of us detectives, we'll get to the bottom of it."

I wiped my plate clean with my last bite of toast. "Well, let me ask you this. If Brittany's right, and Dan is involved in Kirby's murder, how did he get the body into Havermayer's car?"

"That's one of the reasons I never said Brittany was right. There's no way Dan stayed conscious long enough to kill Kirby and transport his body across the street to put it in the car. And Havermayer's car was locked. How did *anybody* get the body in there?"

"Are you sure she locked it?"

"She said she always locked it. And the doors were secure when we got there."

"She could've locked them while she waited for you."

Eric set his plate on the floor for Savannah to prewash. "Come on, Jen. She's a detective. She'd never tamper with a crime scene."

"She would if she was the perpetrator. It wouldn't be the first time a cop's ever committed a crime, would it?"

"No, but now we're back to motive. And you're starting to sound like her when she's talking about you. Why on Earth would she want to kill Kirby?"

I gave him a pass on accusing me of sounding like Havermayer. He was tired and frustrated and didn't know what he was saying. I couldn't possibly be anything like his partner. "Great question, but so far we have no idea why anyone wanted to kill Kirby. Other than the obvious. He was obnoxious, and he had money. A deadly combination if you ask me."

He stood and stretched his arms over his head. "You okay with cleaning up? I have to get to work."

"Of course." I glanced at the clock. Seven thirty. "You sure they're expecting you in so early? You didn't get home until after two."

He slipped on his navy blue suit jacket and kissed me. "The sooner I clear Havermayer, the sooner I can help with the rest of the investigation."

I wished him luck. Clearing Havermayer of Kirby's murder would be a more difficult task than usual. Because she was a member of the police force, the proof of her innocence would have to be clear and indisputable to avoid any appearance of impropriety. He'd almost have to find the real killer to eliminate her as a suspect. A challenging task for a rookie detective working without his partner. Even if he did have help from another team of detectives, he had the greater incentive to get Havermayer out of jail. And I knew him well enough to know he believed clearing her was his responsibility alone.

My laptop screen stared back at me as I sat, fingers poised over the keyboard, waiting for inspiration to strike. Straight-laced, analytic Dana and social butterfly Daniel Davenport, the twin stars of my Davenport Twins Mystery series, were struggling to solve their fourth murder in two years. High school juniors when this all began, they were currently wading through the second semester of their freshman year in college. Luckily for most of us, our late-teen years weren't nearly as eventful as what I'd put those poor kids through.

In their story, the head cheerleader was murdered right after the midterms, and Dana's roommate became the prime suspect because she hadn't made the team after the victim convinced the coach she wasn't good enough. Dana and Daniel jumped into action to help her clear her name. They'd gathered all the clues and interviewed all the suspects. Now, it was time for me to pull it all together. To bring all of the storylines full circle and reveal the killer.

Yup, that's all I had to do.

The book was due on the last day of December, which left me one more month to write and a month to rewrite. Normally, I got stuck at the beginning and the middle, but this time I'd created such a tangled web of red herrings that I'd confused myself. How could I expect the reader to make sense of it? Perhaps I could turn it into one of those "choose your own ending" books kids loved so much. But my books were written for older teens and adults. I suspected that option might not be well received by my readers. Or my publisher for that matter.

Amid the debate on where to send the twins next, my phone rang. My mother, right on time with her Sunday morning call. She was never a minute late for anything. Unfortunately, I'd inherited my punctuality from my father's side of the family.

CHAPTER NINE

I swiped the screen, my finger running across my mother's smiling face in my college graduation photo. "Hi, Mom!"

A few breaths bounced off my eardrums before she replied in a voice low and hesitant. "Hi, honey, how are you?"

"I'm fine. What's going on?"

"Nothing. Why do you ask?"

Great, it's one of those days. My mother loved to make sure I knew something was wrong but made me pull it out of her like a splinter. For some reason, she believed it made her look strong. Like she refused to burden others with her problems unless they insisted. The Queen of Self-Delusion, crown, scepter, and robe all included for one low price.

"Because you sound like the world's coming to an end. So, unless it's your turn to be Chicken Little in the school play, something's wrong. What is it?"

"Nothing that won't keep, dear. Tell me about the man you met in the park yesterday."

Argh! I clenched my free hand, but asking again would be a waste of time. She'd tell me when she was ready. I filled her in on our encounter with Dan. "How did you find out?"

"Oh, you know, I talk to people. I heard the developer fellow who's building the resort on the lake was killed, too. What do you know about that?"

I laughed. "What makes you think I know anything about that?"

"You always know when somebody's dead. It's your special gift."

Yeah, the one I'd love to return to the store the next day. "I wouldn't exactly call it a gift. People tell me things, too. One of the advantages of having a cop for a boyfriend."

"Boyfriend? You need to marry that man before he changes his mind. He's a keeper, you know. Don't let him get away."

Her demeanor brightened like someone had flipped a light switch. A conversation with my mother was like hauling TNT over a mountain pass after a landslide. Everything would be fine for a while, and then you blew up.

We were halfway through that pass.

"Yes, Mother, I know." I sighed. "You remind me of that every time we talk."

"So, what's the problem?"

I clenched my fist again. "I'm not ready to get married, and neither is he. We're taking things slow."

"Slow my foot. You're scared."

Duh. "You bet I'm scared. With my track record, I need to be extra careful not to mess things up this time."

I'd had two serious relationships with men in my life. One I walked out on, and the other walked out on me. No matter who left whom, though, it was my fault both times. I refused to make the same mistakes with Eric. I loved him in a way I'd loved no one else before.

"Just don't be so careful he gets tired of waiting. There are plenty of other fish in the sea. Make sure he doesn't go looking for his fishing pole."

I sent her a mental eye roll. "Yes, Mother. I'll be careful. Can we talk about something else now? Like, what's bothering you?"

"I told you, everything's fine. Who does Eric think killed that man?"

Nifty subject change. "The police have two suspects: Detective Havermayer and the guy from the park."

"They think a detective murdered a man she hardly knows just because they found his body in her car? Are you going to help her like you helped all those other people?"

My mother certainly keeps informed. "She doesn't need my help. She has all the cops helping her."

"Obviously not, or she wouldn't be in jail. You need to do something. Find out who really murdered that man. She needs you."

Since when did my mother want me to get involved with murder investigations? What happened to her fearing for my safety?

"I think she'd rather face the death penalty than accept help from me."

"You might be wrong there. I think she'd welcome any assistance she can get right now. At least, that's what I've heard. You should talk to her."

"Seriously, Mom, where are you getting all this stuff from?"

"I told you. I talk to people."

Must be nice. "Okay, so how about talking to me?

Why were you upset? Is Gary all right? Are *you* all right?"

No reply. The sniffles floating over the airwaves told me she was crying. We'd hit a boulder, and the bomb had gone off. Now, I had to clean up the mess.

My stepfather Gary was diagnosed with colon cancer last year. After surgery and chemotherapy, he went into remission. The only thing I could think of that would have my mother this upset and unwilling to discuss it was the cancer had returned.

"Mom? Please talk to me. I want to help."

She blew her nose, then said, "There's nothing you can do. The cancer came back, and it's spread to his liver."

I hated my stepfather growing up, but we made our peace when he got sick. We'd never be best friends, but I no longer wanted him to die. And more important, my mother didn't want him to die. Anxiety bubbled into my chest. I wiped sweaty palms on my pants legs one at a time.

"I'm so sorry. What does the doctor say?"

"Not much. They're going to run some scans next week to see if it's spread anywhere else. If it's only his liver, they'll treat it the same way they did the first time. If they find it anywhere else, though . . ."

I already knew the end of that sentence. She didn't have to finish it. If the cancer had spread throughout his body, there would be nothing they could do for him. The boulder dropped into my belly.

Forget Havermayer. I had to go see my mother. Luckily, it's only a twenty-minute drive.

* * *

After an interminable evening with my stoic mother and uncommunicative stepfather, followed by a restless night's sleep, Charlie, Savannah, and I arrived at Ravenous Readers at the same time Monday morning: nine forty-five. I'd almost forgotten I had to cover for Lacey today so she could make her baby daughter's doctor's appointment. I was happily writing away when I remembered mid-sentence at nine thirty and had to rush, throwing on my khaki-and-red uniform and Nikes and racing the dog out the door.

Charlie had ditched his uniform as usual. This time for a Luke Skywalker impersonation—white pants and a matching tunic with brown leggings and a broad black utility belt sporting an oversized silver buckle with a blue lightsaber carried in his right hand. Guess he decided we needed a little help from the Force running the bookstore in Lacey's absence.

Savannah trotted through the store, searching everywhere for Aunt Lacey, disappointment clear on her face when she finally gave up and followed me around instead. I opened the register for business and handed her a bacon treat from the bag Lacey kept under the counter. She accepted it from me, but I could tell it just wasn't the same.

I set up the kids' section for Story Time while Charlie slash Luke started the coffee and fetched the pastries from Bob's Bakery. Bob Underwood had learned to bake from his grandmother and launched his business right after high school graduation almost forty years ago. His croissant sandwiches and overfilled donuts were an instant success, but, as most businesses in small towns did, he struggled at times.

When Ravenous Readers opened, he agreed to

provide the baked goods for the store to sell, hoping to increase his customer base. After two and a half years, I still had no idea if it worked or not, but he had a carton of goodies ready for us to pick up every morning. I could only assume he got something out of the arrangement other than the minimal amount he billed us once a month.

By the time I finished loading the child-sized chairs with crayons and paper crowns for the kids to color, Charlie returned with a box of croissants, muffins, and cookies. I turned the closed sign to open, then helped load the display trays and slide them into place in the pastry case. Opening chores complete, I stood in the store and looked around to make sure we'd missed nothing important.

No customers wandered around, and we'd finished setting up, so I grabbed the feather duster and went to work on the bookcases. Charlie emptied coffee into the urn and started a new pot.

"What're you reading for Story Time today?" he asked when I got close enough to hear.

"Lacey left copies of *Simon's New Bed* on the table next to her throne, so I'm guessing that's what I'm supposed to read."

He emptied prepackaged grounds into the filter. "I don't suppose you'd consider letting me do it this time."

Our barista had taken over for Lacey before and done a splendid job. The children loved him. Or, to be more precise, who he pretended to be. "Why wouldn't I?"

"I don't know." He pressed the button to start the water flowing. "Lacey usually does it, and you're working for her. I thought you might want to do the reading."

I reached under the counter for my mug. "Nah, I've seen the movie. You can read the book to the kids if you want."

He showed me all of his five thousand dollars' worth of dental work. "Thanks."

"When you're through with the kids, would you mind seeing what you can find out about the Kirby clan?"

"I thought you were staying out of this one."

"I am. Just satisfying my writer's curiosity."

Charlie twisted his lips into a half-smile. "Sure you are."

I crossed my arms and scowled. "I am! I told Eric I'd stay out of it and I will."

"Okay. I'll take your word for it. Although, I was looking forward to diving into this one. It's an interesting case." He cocked his head. "Didn't I check Kirby out for you when he first came here in January?"

"Yeah, but now he's dead, and we need to know what's going on with the rest of the family. Especially his wife. If it weren't for Havermayer and Dan, she'd be the prime suspect right now. She still is in my book."

The spouse was almost always the first one the police looked at when someone was murdered. They were usually the ones with the most to gain. Or at least the most motive. People killed their partners for money or jealousy or, sometimes, just plain hate. Nobody could hate somebody as much as the person who once loved them, a phenomenon I understood well when my boyfriend unexpectedly left me to take a job in Paris. I killed him many times in my mind. Human nature at its worst.

"But we're not investigating, right?"

"Right."

Charlie wiped his hands on a towel. "Who's Dan?"

"That's what the cops are calling the guy with amnesia." I told him what Eric had said about the coworker who'd found the lost dog despite how ridiculous the story sounded.

"I guess that makes sense. To somebody." He laughed. "So, does this mean you're going to try to help Havermayer? You know she hates you, right?"

Was hate too strong a word? Maybe. Or maybe, given her behavior, it fit perfectly. Either way, as my mother reminded me last night at dinner, I wasn't Havermayer. "For the moment, I'm only indulging my curiosity. I love a good mystery, and this might turn out to be one. If I find something useful to the investigation, I'll tell Eric and let him decide what to do with it. Havermayer doesn't even come into it."

"If you say so." He suppressed a smile. "Personally, I think you're trying to score brownie points with her."

"I couldn't score points with her if I were the only player in the game. She hates me, remember?"

The front door bells jingled, and I turned to see Veronica Winslow, Riddleton's mayor, enter, holding the hands of her twin four-year-olds, Peter and Parker. When the boys saw Charlie, they wrenched their hands free and ran to the coffee bar, yelling, "Luke Skywalker! Luke Skywalker! Can I play with your lightsaber?"

Veronica chuckled and rolled her eyes. "They saw *Star Wars* for the first time the other night, and that's all they talk about anymore. Charlie being dressed that way is the bonus they've been craving."

"I guess Charlie picked the right day to try out his new outfit."

"That he did."

Charlie collected the twins, and I placed two chocolate chip cookies each on plates for them. Savannah twirled around my legs as I delivered the goodies, then sank between their feet to collect crumbs. I grinned at Veronica as I returned to the coffee bar. "Well, we've got three happy campers, anyway. You want some coffee?"

"Sure. What do you mean three?"

"Peter, Parker, and Savannah. The kids love *Star Wars* and cookies, and the dog loves cookie crumbs. A match made in heaven."

Two women and one man came in with six children between them. Pretty good turnout for a Monday. I loaded cookies on plates for the new arrivals and helped Charlie get them all settled.

"What time should I start reading?" he asked.

I glanced at the clock. Ten thirty-two. "Give it a few more minutes in case we have stragglers. If they're not here by ten thirty-five, go ahead and start."

"You got it, Boss."

I shook my head on the way back to the coffee bar. He really shouldn't still call me that since I wasn't the boss anymore. Good thing Lacey didn't mind. I guess we both realized he considered it a term of respect, and he never disrespected Lacey, so no reason for either of us to object. Regardless, she could've made an issue of it and didn't, and I respected her for that, among many other things.

After topping off my cup, I took a seat across from Veronica at a table by the Mystery section. "Have you heard about all the excitement this weekend?"

"Of course. I know everything that goes on around here. Courtesy of Angus, if nothing else. He tells me whatever he hears. And some of it even turns out to be true," she said with a smile. "Most of it, actually."

"Yeah, he's good about that. And correct a surprising percentage of the time."

"Well, in this case, I got my information from the police department in my daily briefing from Chief Olinski this morning."

Olinski briefed the mayor every morning? I had no idea. No wonder she was always on top of things. "Have they learned anything new?"

"I'm not sure. He told me everything that happened this weekend, but I don't know what you would call new."

I recounted what I knew about Dan and also Simeon Kirby's murder. She listened without comment, nodding in places until I finished. "And that story about how they started calling him Dan sounds dumber every time I tell it. I hope they figure out who he really is soon."

"Guess I do have some fresh information for you. Dan, as you call him, is actually Elliott Kirby, Simeon's youngest son. His older brother, Simeon Junior, recognized him at the station."

Holy cow! That fleeting thought I'd had and dismissed turned out to be right. But that still didn't explain how he could've killed him. "Well, that certainly makes things more interesting since Simeon's blood was on Elliott's shirt. Do they think he killed his father?"

"According to Olinski, he's a person of interest, just as he has been all along. They released him into the custody of his family, though. Unlike Havermayer. They're hoping it'll jog his memory to be around people who know him. And they're not allowed to leave town with him, so they're staying at the resort for the time being."

Surprising they didn't release the detective when they learned Elliott's identity. The half of me that believed in her innocence felt sorry for her, but the other half, the one that believed in karma, still struggled with being happy she was getting what she deserved. The war between my sides seemed never-ending.

Elliott likely had more motive and opportunity than Havermayer did. But that still left the question of how he got the body into her car. For that matter, how did *anyone* get Kirby's body in her vehicle?

Story Time let out, and the Winslow twins ran up to their mother, yammering about the new bed Simon got and demanding a copy of the book to take home. Veronica smiled and nodded as they described the story to her, then gave me a questioning glance over their heads.

"I'll get you a copy," I said over the din. On my way back to the kids' section to collect the book, I waved goodbye to the other parents and their excited youngsters. A mixture of pride and gratitude swirled through my chest. We'd accomplished our goal of encouraging young people to read and making a difference in the lives of these children.

Charlie returned the tiny chairs to their homes under the tables while Savannah vacuumed the carpet. I patted his shoulder as I passed. "Great job, Charlie. The kids loved it."

His cheeks pinked. "Thanks, Boss. It was fun."

I snagged Veronica's book from the table and carried it to the register, where she waited with the boys, who were having an imaginary sword fight behind her.

"Let me guess," I said. "Lightsabers?"

She sighed. "Lightsabers. I'm guessing they'll be next on the list of things they want."

"Sorry. I guess we'll have to be more careful how we dress Charlie from now on."

"No, it was only a matter of time. They were already hinting about it. I'm sure it'll be on the top of their list for Santa this year." She smiled as Peter pretended to die after being stabbed with Parker's saber. "I'm enjoying them now while I can. They'll be teenagers soon enough."

Veronica handed the book to the boys, and they argued over who'd get to carry it. "You sure you don't want one of your own?" she asked with a grin.

"Positive. See you later."

I rested an elbow on the counter with my chin in my hand. Eric and I hadn't yet discussed the subject of children. It seemed so far down the road, why bother at this point? But if he wanted them and I didn't—which at the moment seemed quite likely—it made our future together untenable. Our relationship would be doomed to fail. Even if he could live without having kids, would he be happy? Maybe, but not as happy as he'd be when he had an orange-haired brood with freckles running around the house. And he'd be nothing like my stepfather.

Eric was a good guy. He deserved happiness. We needed to have the children conversation as soon as possible. Then, if we weren't in the same place, we could go our separate ways. Get out before we got in too deep. Yup, that's what we needed to do. Tonight. Better to be unhappy for a little while than for the rest of my life.

"Jen?"

I blinked and found Charlie staring at me like I had two noses. "Hey. What's up?"

"Nothing. You were gone there for a minute. Are you okay?"

I'll let you know tomorrow. "I'm fine. Just thinking. I know you're not used to it, but I do exercise my brain every once in a while."

He chuckled. "Okay, just don't give yourself a headache."

"I won't. I'm going to give you one instead. Veronica just told me Dan has been identified as Elliott Kirby, one of Simeon's sons."

"Whoa! I didn't expect that."

"Me either. I know I asked you to check into the whole family, but can you start with him instead of the wife? Him having amnesia and being covered in his father's blood is skating dangerously close to coincidence territory for me."

"And we all know how you feel about coincidences." He drew his lightsaber and pointed it toward the ceiling. "They must die!"

My guffaw turned a few heads in the Romance section, and Savannah came running to see what was going on. Maybe I didn't want to have kids because they might turn out as crazy as Charlie.

Or worse.

They might turn out as crazy as me.

CHAPTER TEN

The rest of the morning passed uneventfully, with a few customers in and out purchasing nothing. Average for a Monday. Charlie played on his computer, researching the Kirbys, and I juggled characters in my head, trying to decide who'd murdered the head cheerleader. It was the first time I'd ever started writing a mystery without knowing the identity of the killer.

I hoped it would also be the last.

I'd narrowed the choices down to two by the time Eric came in with burgers and fries for all of us, including Charlie.

What a sweetheart.

I gave him a hug and a kiss. "I missed you this morning."

"Me or my cooking?" He unloaded the bags from the Dandy Diner. "I ran out of clean clothes at your place, so I had to go home last night."

"Guess we'll have to clear out a little more space in the closet for you." I waved Charlie over so his food wouldn't get cold.

"Or we could get a bigger place." Eric peeked at me out of the corner of his eye. "Together."

Panic zoomed through my chest, and my heart galloped like a thoroughbred in the Kentucky Derby. My lungs trapped the air in them. I couldn't move. The word "together" played on a loop in my head. He wanted us to move in together. In the same place.

Calm down, Jen.

Deep breath in, slow breath out.

Oh, crap!

I bit into my bacon cheeseburger, and the mix of flavors bathed my taste buds, overshadowing my anxiety. Nothing like the perfect burger to make the world seem right again. For the moment. Eric had made a passing comment about us moving in together, and, as usual, I'd freaked out. My typical overreaction to anything that even hinted at commitment. I loved him. Why did the idea of moving our relationship to the next level paralyze me?

Eric and Charlie were discussing Simeon Kirby's family, and I tuned back in to the conversation in time to hear Eric say, "And his wife was almost hysterical."

"Hysterical about what?" I asked.

"Welcome back," he replied. "Where'd you go?"

No place he would appreciate. A conversation best had in private. Or better yet, not at all. "No place important. I was only thinking. We can talk about it later."

Charlie shrank into his seat and played with his French fries as if he'd rather be anywhere else. He'd never been one for drama, preferring to live in the worlds he created for himself.

Eric studied me with sadness in his eyes as if he knew what I'd been thinking about. "I can't wait," he said in a tone heavy with sarcasm.

98

Ignore it. It'll be okay. "What were you saying about Kirby's wife?"

He dunked a fry in ketchup. "Virginia was distraught. Basically nonfunctional. Her son, Simeon Junior, had to answer all our questions."

"I heard he's the one who recognized our amnesia guy as his brother Elliott."

"That's right." He gave me a questioning glance. "How did you know?"

"I have my sources," I replied with a coy smile. "Who else from the family showed up?"

"Only the daughter, Marion. She's a real piece of work."

"How so?" Charlie asked.

Eric sighed. "Let's just say she wasn't overwhelmed with sadness at her father's death unless she covered her grief with anger. If I had to guess, I'd say she hated her father but is smart enough not to show her joy at his demise."

My ears perked. "Hated him enough to kill him?"

"I don't know. We'll have to see what our investigation turns up. We haven't questioned them yet."

Strange. Usually, they questioned potential suspects right away before they could get their stories straight. "When are you going to do that?"

"This afternoon, probably. Once we get the autopsy results back. Ingrid's working on it now. It's a shame she was out of town all weekend. It would've been nice to have that information when the family came in."

I swallowed my mouthful of fries. "She and Marcus deserved some time away. How was she supposed to know Kirby would be murdered while she was gone?"

Blond eyebrows lowered, Eric replied, "I didn't say

she shouldn't have gone, only that we could've used the information sooner. Unfortunately, we couldn't reach her in time."

Touchy. Time to change the subject. "How's Havermayer holding up? Have you released her yet?"

"Olinski will likely let her go this afternoon. It looks like she was set up. We haven't found anything close to a motive yet. She didn't even know the guy."

"Uh, not necessarily," Charlie muttered.

Eric jerked his head around. "What do you mean?"

"I'm sorry. Did I say that out loud? I didn't mean to."

"Well, you did, so come on, spill it. What do you know?"

Charlie's face turned the color of the ketchup dripping off the end of his fry. "I don't *know* anything. I've heard a few things, though. But it's all rumor and innuendo. You can't take it seriously."

"All right. I won't assume it's true, but I might look into it, if it seems plausible enough. Please tell me what you've heard."

"Angus told me that someone told him that Kirby and Havermayer were seen together outside a motel in Sutton."

My brows shot up, eyes wide. "You think Havermayer and Kirby were having an affair?"

Charlie put his hands up. "I don't think anything. I'm only telling you what I heard."

I exchanged a glance with Eric. "Any possibility it's true? Would Havermayer do something like that?"

He shrugged. "I have no idea. She never discusses her personal life. To tell the truth, I was starting to wonder if she was gay and just not ready to share that with me."

"Why would she keep it a secret? This is the twenty-first century, not the 1950s. Even here in Riddleton."

"How should I know? Some people are private, I guess." Eric handed the last bite of his burger to Savannah. "Of course, an affair with a married man *is* something most people would keep secret."

"Sure, but Kirby? I was under the impression she didn't like him much. I know she didn't like his plans for Riddleton."

Gathering his trash, Eric stood. "I guess I'll put it on the list of things that need looking into." He leaned over and kissed me. "I have to get back to work."

"Thanks for lunch," Charlie said.

"Yes, that was very sweet of you." I walked him to the door, the cardboard cutout of me watching us like a chaperone. *Creepy.* "Call me later?"

"You bet." He threw me a wink, the bells jingled, and he left.

I turned back to Charlie and rubbed my hands together. "All right. What did you find out about the Kirby family?"

He cleared the table and retrieved his notebook from behind the coffee bar. "Where would you like me to start?"

"At the beginning. It appears to me a lot is going on in that family that could make one of them a killer."

He flipped back to the first page and read from his notes. According to Charlie's research, Virginia Madison had married Simeon Kirby thirty-five years ago in Spartanburg, where the family still lived. She came from a wealthy family, and her father bankrolled Kirby's construction company. They had three children: Simeon Junior, Marion Kirby Jenkins, and Elliott. All three worked with their father in some capacity and most likely expected to inherit equal shares of the company along with their mother.

I stopped him. "Basically, what you're saying is all four of them had a financial motive to kill him. Not only the wife."

"Based on what I found, yes. Of course, I only put this together from bits and pieces I ran across in their social media accounts and interviews. I don't know how accurate it is."

"I get that. Keep going."

"I didn't have time to dig up much more. So far, I have Junior as his father's right-hand man in the company. Marion is the finance person. She handles the books. And Elliott is the on-site supervisor. Elliott is the only one who's actually been working here in Riddleton with his father. The other two pass through once in a while."

I tapped my fingers on the table. "In that case, Elliott seems to be our prime suspect. He's the one with the access, and he had his father's blood on his shirt and hands." Except we still had the problem of how he killed his father after he got knocked out. Or who knocked him out after he killed his father. My writer's gut had questions. Many questions.

"Could be. But I wouldn't rule anyone else out just yet if I were you. He might've interrupted the murder or been intended to be the next victim."

"Of course not. Everybody's still on the suspect table. Why don't you get back on your computer and see what else you can find out? We need to know more about the family dynamic to narrow it down. And the business. There may be some skeletons in that construction trailer they have out there."

"You got it, Boss. I'm on the case."

The rest of the afternoon passed quickly. A steady flow of customers kept us busy, and I used the little bit of free time remaining to clear the stack of bills on my desk. Amazingly, we still had money left in the account when I finished.

My happiness was interrupted by the thought that Kirby's death might put an end to our success. What would happen to us if the resort was never completed and people stopped coming? After all, how many folks would want to stay in a resort with no facilities? No exercise room or swimming pool. At least it had a restaurant, although the menu was limited. Sure, there were always people who wanted a nice, quiet vacation on the lake. But what else did Riddleton have to offer? In truth, not much.

I couldn't deny my pleasure at the idea that Kirby's plans for Riddleton might never be realized. But, as much as I hated to admit it, the tourists staying in the unfinished resort had put our business in the black. Just as Kirby had predicted. Perhaps the family would finish the place and leave the rest of the town alone. Assuming they weren't all in jail for killing him.

We closed the store at six, and I headed for the diner to grab dinner on the way home. The Monday evening crowd filled a quarter of the tables, and, being mostly locals, Angus made it clear Savannah could stay. I spotted Ingrid and Marcus at a booth on the back wall, and we joined them.

"Hey, guys, mind if we interrupt your dinner break?"

Marcus moved to sit next to Ingrid, and I loaded my German shepherd onto the bench near the wall. "How was your trip?" Ingrid and Marcus had taken his daughters to Six Flags Over Georgia for a weekend break.

They smiled at each other, and Ingrid replied, "Brilliant! We had a lovely time. The girls rode every ride they were tall enough for."

Marcus took her hand. "Too bad we came back to such a mess, though."

Marcus Jones was a former felon I'd met a couple of years ago who'd turned his life around after getting out of prison. Angus hired him as a cook and recently promoted him to assistant manager. He'd worked hard to make a better life for his children than he'd had growing up and seeing him and Ingrid together made me believe that anything was possible. Now, if I could only translate that to my own life, I'd be in great shape.

"No kidding. Simeon Kirby picked a terrible weekend to die," I replied.

Ingrid cocked an eyebrow and shook out her short loose curls. "Is there a good weekend to die?"

Heat rushed into my face. "No, of course not. I only meant it was inconvenient that you were out of town and awful that you had to come back to this."

She showed me her slightly crooked smile. "I know, luv. I was only having you on."

For once, I didn't need a translator to tell me she was only teasing me. I'd had enough conversations with her to have finally picked up on some of the odd expressions she used. Odd to Americans, that is. I figured they were perfectly normal in London.

Angus's new server, Gretchen, came over to take my order. "What can I get for you tonight?" she asked, holding the pen top against her lower lip.

Her acne-dotted baby face made her seem barely

old enough for high school, let alone holding down a full-time job. I had to assume Angus had done the requisite checks, though, and she was at least sixteen. Either way, it was great to have a server who didn't already know what I wanted to eat. It let me pretend I'd actually considered the entire menu before ordering. Like a normal person.

I asked for fish and chips since I'd already had my bacon cheeseburger for today and a Mountain Dew to drink. Gretchen dutifully recorded my request and returned with my soda a minute later.

While I stripped the paper off my straw, I asked Ingrid, "How'd the autopsy go this morning? Anything exciting or unusual?"

She sipped her tea and shook her head. "No, not at all. Pretty standard for a death by gunshot wound. One shot to the chest, one to the abdomen, and one to the heart, which killed him instantly. The poor chap didn't stand a chance, I'm afraid. I did find a hair on his chest that didn't belong to him, though. I sent it in for testing. Hopefully, they'll eventually have a suspect to match it to."

They might already have one. We found him wandering around the park, covered in the victim's blood. "Were you able to establish what kind of gun they used?"

"That's the strange thing. Two different weapons were involved. I retrieved nine-millimeter bullets from the chest and the heart, but a thirty-two-caliber round made the wound in the abdomen."

"Interesting. We found a thirty-two at the crime scene but no other weapons."

"Didn't you find a guy out there, too? And the

guy didn't remember nothing that happened to him?" Marcus asked.

The gossip train was barreling down the tracks. *Toot! Toot!* "We did, and his blood and hair were on the gun as if someone hit him with it. He turned out to be the victim's son."

Marcus sat back in his seat. "Sounds like they found the killer then. No long, drawn-out investigation needed this time."

"Not necessarily. He might've shot Kirby, but then who knocked *him* out? He'd been struck in the head with the pistol. That's how his blood and hair got on it. And where did his wallet, his phone, and the other gun go? Somebody else had to be there."

Ingrid studied me over the top of the glass she held with both hands. "Somebody with a different gun. What are you going to do?"

Why did everyone keep asking me that? This case had nothing to do with me. Any interest I had in it was only professional curiosity. As a mystery writer, I was bound to be curious, right? Plus, I might get ideas for my book. "The police are handling this case. I'm going to stay out of it like I'm supposed to."

They glanced at each other and laughed.

I scowled at them. "What's so funny?"

Ingrid sobered up first. "You always say that, luv. And then you jump in anyway."

"Not this time. Unless somebody's accused me, and I haven't heard about that happening just yet. And Havermayer's a suspect herself, so I doubt anyone's looking at me."

"Havermayer's a suspect? How did that happen?" Ingrid asked, her eyes wide.

"They didn't tell you? The body was found in her car, and Kirby's wallet and phone were under the driver's seat."

"No, they never mentioned it. Of course, if the scene isn't relevant to my autopsy, they sometimes don't." She met my gaze. "So, you're really going to tell me you have an opportunity to be a hero for your nemesis, and you're going to let it pass?"

I'd never had any interest in being a hero for anyone, let alone Detective Havermayer. I had nothing to prove to her, and nothing I ever did would make a difference in how she felt about me. Not that it mattered. I didn't need her approval. I only wished she didn't take out her animosity toward me on Eric.

"First of all, she'd never accept any kind of help from me, even if she was dying from some rare disease and I had the only cure. Second, they don't really think she did it. They're only holding her because they have to until she's cleared as a suspect. And the whole department is focused on clearing her."

"Okay, if you say so." Ingrid smiled. "Although I do have to wonder why you've been asking all these questions then. You certainly sound interested in the case."

"It's an interesting case. Why shouldn't I ask questions?"

Her smile evolved into a smirk. "No reason." She glanced over at the front counter. "I wonder what's going on up there."

Marcus and I turned to find Angus having an animated discussion with Zach Vick.

"Zach's ordering food, I imagine. What else would they be talking about?" I said.

"I don't know," Marcus replied. "Angus seems pretty excited."

I chuckled. "There's no such thing as mundane chit-chat to Angus. He makes every conversation seem like he's learning the secrets of the Kennedy assassination."

"That's because he usually *is* getting the scoop on something important."

Zach left the diner empty-handed, and Angus marched straight toward our table.

"Looks like we're about to find out," Ingrid said, grinning.

When Angus arrived, red-faced and puffing, I scooted over and hauled Savannah into my lap to make room for him to sit. We waited for him to catch his breath.

After a minute, he looked around the table and said, "You'll never guess what Zach just told me."

"They're outlawing gossip in Riddleton?" I quipped.

He rolled his eyes at me. "No. Try again."

"Why don't you just tell us, Angus?" Ingrid said.

"Fine. You know that guy with amnesia in the park Saturday?"

He was all excited because Zach told Angus his name, and he assumed we didn't know. *Typical.* "Sorry to burst your bubble, Angus, but we already know he's been identified. His name is Elliott Kirby."

Angus waved a hand at me. "Yeah, yeah. Very nice. But did you also know when they searched Havermayer's house, they found Elliott's wallet and phone in a desk drawer?"

No, I definitely didn't know that.

CHAPTER ELEVEN

I tossed and turned all night leading into Tuesday morning, often reaching for comfort from Eric, only to find Savannah in his place. He must've gone home after work. Or perhaps he worked all night. No telling with him, although he could've mentioned not being able to make it home when he called earlier. However, when he had a case like this one, he couldn't focus on anything else until he solved it. And he'd never had a case in which his partner was a suspect before.

Angus's words at the diner last night whirled through my brain, manifesting in my dreams as Havermayer chasing me with a knife or shooting at me from behind a tree. My subconscious was desperately trying to tell me something I was sure I didn't want to hear. Although Havermayer was always after me for some reason or other, why should this situation be any different? She'd have to get me in my dreams, though, because this time she was the one who'd been falsely accused and arrested.

As convinced as I was of her innocence, the amount of evidence stacking up against her concerned me. The real murderer framed her. But how? How did they get

Kirby's body, wallet, and phone into Havermayer's car? If her vehicle matched Eric's, she had a key fob to lock and unlock it. The fob was programmed to only work on her car. The fob for Eric's department Suburban didn't work on hers and vice versa. He accidentally tried it one day and couldn't get in.

Forgetting the car for the moment, how did they plant Elliott's wallet and phone in a desk drawer in her house? Even if a key fob malfunction enabled them to place the body in her car, it wouldn't work on her front door. The only way to access her home would be with a key to one of the doors. Unless she left her doors unlocked when she came to the park. Because the crime rate in town remained low, many people in Riddleton did. But Havermayer was a cop. She would know better.

Maybe Eric would have some ideas. He'd been so busy we hadn't spoken since lunch yesterday, other than a "yes, I'm still alive, but no time to talk" call last night. As much as I tried to deny my reactions because they made me feel dependent and vulnerable, I missed him. And I needed to verify what Angus told us last night. Even though he seemed to get the information from Zach, as a patrol officer Zach wouldn't be directly involved in the heart of the investigation. His information might be second-hand as well.

Eric's name was at the top of my frequent contacts list, and I tapped the photo of the two of us smiling into each other's eyes taken last Valentine's Day. The day I'd finally broken down and given him the key to my apartment. A decision I'd yet to regret. We'd grown closer since then, and our relationship had deepened. I suspected the hot breakfast he served me almost every morning didn't hurt anything, either.

110

He answered on the fourth ring right before his voicemail picked up. "Hey, babe, I'm super busy, so I only have a few minutes. What's up?"

"I have some questions, but mostly I wanted to hear your voice. I feel like I haven't seen you in a year."

"I feel the same way, but it's only been since lunch yesterday, remember?"

"I know. I guess I've gotten spoiled having you around so much."

He chuckled. "In that case, it's good for you to miss me once in a while. It'll remind you of how much you love me."

I shifted the phone to my other ear. "Maybe I'll just stop missing you altogether. You're getting a little full of yourself."

"Yeah, right. Like that's gonna happen. Hold on a sec." He moved the phone away and spoke to someone in the background, then came back on the line. "I have to go in a minute. What did you want to ask me?"

Disappointment flitted through my chest, but I couldn't take it personally. He had to work. Havermayer's future depended on it. "Angus said you found Elliott Kirby's wallet and phone in Havermayer's house. Is that true, or did the gossip train jump off the rails?"

Eric sighed into my ear. "Unfortunately, it's true. The techs found them in the bottom drawer of her desk under some papers."

"Does that mean she's the prime suspect now?"

He hesitated, then said, "It's leaning that way. Especially since the autopsy showed two different weapons were used. A nine mil and a thirty-two. Havermayer happens to own one of each. Her duty weapon is a nine millimeter, and her backup gun is a thirty-two caliber. And her backup gun is missing, but the serial number doesn't match the one we found in the park. Still, it doesn't look good for her right now."

"What about ballistics? Do either of the guns match the bullets?"

"The results haven't come in yet. The ballistics lab in Sutton is way behind right now."

"Too bad we can't have one here in Riddleton."

"I wouldn't want to have enough shootings here to justify it. Would you?"

"No, of course not. I didn't think about it that way."

I needed to let him go, but my mind searched for another question instead. Finally, one came. "How's Havermayer holding up through all this?"

"Oh, you know how she is. She's mad as hell. But underneath, I think she's a little depressed. She hasn't had a single visitor since she's been locked up."

Her personality probably had something to do with that. She'd alienated half the town over the years. "That's too bad."

He breathed into the phone, and I could hear the hamster wheel turning in his head. "You wouldn't consider visiting her, would you? It would help keep her spirits up while we sort everything out."

Me visit Havermayer in jail? He must've lost his mind. "I'm pretty sure I'd be the last person she wanted to see."

"I don't know about that. You know what it's like to sit in jail even though you've done nothing wrong. You can commiserate with her, and it might be a way to change her opinion of you." He stopped for a breath, then continued, "If nothing else, she'd have to wonder about all the times she's falsely accused you. Maybe

112

she'll think twice next time. If there is a next time. Who knows? You might even become friends by the time it's all over."

Friends? With Detective Havermayer? I sealed my lips to keep from laughing out loud. I didn't want to hurt his feelings. "I don't know, Eric. Let me think about it, okay?"

"Please do. Look, they're calling me. I'll talk to you later if I can."

"I love you."

"Love you too. Bye."

I swiped the red button to disconnect the call and sat with the phone in my hand, watching Savannah's rib cage rise and fall as she slept. "You hear that, little girl? Eric wants me to visit Havermayer in jail. Isn't that ridiculous?"

She cracked her eyelids open and thumped her tail, then went back to sleep.

I nuked a fresh cup of coffee and sat cross-legged on the couch next to the dog, who grumbled and scooted over a half inch or so. Her version of making room. Good thing for her I wasn't a Great Dane with the same mindset. She'd be on the floor.

I sipped my drink, the warmth filling the hollow in my chest, and mulled over my boyfriend's suggestion that I visit my archenemy in jail. He, of all people, understood how much his partner hated me. And how much I returned the feeling.

Why wasn't it enough for him that I believed in her innocence? That's more benefit than she would've given me. If our positions were reversed, she'd have me standing before a judge already. A situation I'd already experienced once before at her hands. She had me locked up and never once showed any concern about my well-being. No way I could visit her just because nobody else would.

Eric asked too much of me.

Warming my hands with the cup, I stared into the murky beige liquid while my conscience tugged at me. Did I want to be like Detective Havermayer? Of course not. She came off as cold and unfeeling. Narrow-minded and judgmental. Not who I wanted to be. Not who I believed I was, but some people said the same things about me. Were they correct? I didn't think so, and Havermayer probably didn't agree with those characterizations about herself either. Finally, something we had in common. Not enough to base a friendship on, though.

Tired of arguing with myself, I replaced my house-only sweats with jeans and a sweatshirt, woke Savannah, and headed for the bookstore. No way I could focus on writing, and Charlie and Lacey would provide enough distraction that I could put Havermayer out of my mind for a little while. Maybe Charlie had learned something interesting about the Kirby family. Proving the detective innocent would be better than a fifteen-minute visit, right? Right.

Savannah and I checked on the progress of the Halloween decorations as we strolled down Main Street. I had to scope out the competition, although, unless Lacey worked on them earlier this morning, we hadn't begun to decorate yet. Not that we had any chance of winning the contest. We'd only won one, and that was only because the true winner bowed out at the last minute. Still, I maintained hope we'd win in our own right one day, which required knowing what we were up against.

The Dollar General, next door to our apartment complex, had strung orange and black bunting across the façade below the sign and had an animatronic witch stirring the contents of a cauldron and cackling in one window. Definitely an outside decoration. I wouldn't want anything inside loud enough to be heard through window glass. The other window hadn't been touched yet. I'd have to check back later and see what they came up with.

We crossed Oak Street and passed the Goodwill, which had nothing in the windows that could be called a contest entry. They relied on donations, though, and often waited until the last minute to see what leftovers people might offer. As a result, their decorations usually seemed a mishmash of concepts, but I suspected winning the contest was never their goal.

Angus had begun a sketch on one window of the Dandy Diner, but it was too soon to tell what it was supposed to be. Whatever he came up with, he'd make it excellent without a doubt. Angus had a knack for designing the perfect scenes for the occasion and painting them well. The former banker in New Hampshire turned diner owner in South Carolina had missed his calling twice. He should've been an artist.

On the other side of Oak Street, the town hall and the police department remained unadorned. The police had been too busy. Not sure what the town's excuse might be. If I knew Veronica, she wanted everything to be perfect, and that took time. I suspected something spectacular would magically appear on the building before the end of the week.

Lacey hadn't yet begun work on Ravenous Readers' windows either. She probably had a notebook full of sketches inside to show me, though. I didn't know why she insisted on getting my approval every time. She had all the talent. I had the artistic ability of a rotten tree stump. And that was a generous assessment.

I opened the front door in time to make way for the Story Time crowd to exit. Restraining Savannah with one hand, I held the door open with the other, smiling and nodding. When the threshold finally cleared, we found Lacey and Charlie cleaning up the kids' section. One long-haired thirty-something woman perused the Romance section.

She looked up and smiled as I approached. "I love this store. You have a great selection for such a small place."

"Thank you." Filled with a mix of embarrassment and pride, I eased Savannah away from sniffing her new-found friend.

The woman squatted to scratch the dog's neck. "I think it's terrific that you have a dog in here sometimes. I love them, but I can't have one at home. My landlord won't allow it."

"That's too bad. She's my first, and I never dreamed I'd have a dog, but now I can't imagine life without her." I glanced at my German shepherd, who arched her neck and pushed into the woman's hand. "Feel free to enjoy her as long as you like. She doesn't seem to mind. And if I can help you find anything, please let me know."

"I will, thanks."

Disco Charlie—decked out in his tight black leather pants, satin purple paisley shirt, and sparkly purple platform shoes—danced back to the coffee bar. I joined him there and fished my mug from under the counter near the pastry case. He rearranged the goodies to fill

116

the empty spaces on the trays while I filled my cup from the urn.

"Busy morning?" I asked. "The turnout for Story Time looked pretty good."

He waved the tongs. "Eight kids. Not bad for a Tuesday."

"They must've all come out at once. It seemed like more, but I can live with eight. Much better than the one or two we used to get."

"Definitely. It's a lot more fun now."

"Speaking of fun, have you had any luck learning anything interesting about the Kirbys?"

"A little." He moved the last croissant into place and closed the case. "It seems Simeon and his wife, Virginia, had some marital trouble. She filed for divorce at one point, then changed her mind."

Now we're getting somewhere. "That makes her a pretty good candidate for prime suspect, don't you think?"

"Could be, but they've also been in marriage counseling ever since."

"Maybe it wasn't going well. After all, Kirby's been here in Riddleton for months. That can't be good for a rocky marriage." I helped myself to a chocolate chip muffin. "Anything else? What about Elliott?"

"I couldn't find much on him. He's not big on social media, but his sister Marion is. From what I could find, she hated her father. Blamed him for pushing her into a loveless marriage just because the guy invested in Kirby's company."

Suspect number two? "That tracks with what Eric told me. You think she hated him enough to kill him?"

Charlie shrugged. "No telling. People have been

murdered for less. Plus, there's the inheritance. Maybe she wants that money to get out of her marriage."

"It's possible, I guess. We'll have to keep an eye on that one."

"That's all I've got so far. I'll keep digging, though. That's the fun part, anyway."

"Thanks, Charlie."

Lacey, finished with the kids' section, waved me over to the front counter. She had her notebook in hand. Time to see what she'd come up with for the window decorations. Something brilliant, I'd bet.

"Whatcha got?" I asked, propping my elbows on the display case beside the register.

She handed me the book, open to the first design. "One of my better efforts, if I do say so myself. What do *you* think?"

I studied the drawing of the ghost of Mark Twain sitting in a wingback chair, reading to a group of goblin children sitting cross-legged on the floor before him. Above the ghostly Twain, the spirits of Tom Sawyer and Huckleberry Finn read along over his shoulder. "Cute! I like this one. Very fitting."

Lacey grinned. "I know, right? Turn the page."

The door drawing depicted a witch on her broom carrying a load of Halloween-themed books to the window on the other side. I flipped to the next page. The other window had mummies and zombies struggling to reach more Halloween-themed books floating above their heads. Lacey had outdone herself this time.

I tapped the drawing. "I love this. I had no idea there were so many books with Halloween as a backdrop. Do we have any in stock?"

"Some. I'm going to display them around the store as soon as we get the decorations up."

"I can help with that."

"Terrific. Let's knock that out before I get started on the windows."

We headed back to the stockroom to gather up the black and orange garland and cardboard ghosts, witches, and ghouls for the walls. Lacey carried the boxes, and I brought the ladder and the staple gun. We started at the corner by the window where I'd once spent so much time trying to write my second book. I shook away the memories of the writer's block that still tormented and paralyzed me.

I climbed the ladder, and Lacey handed me the garland, which I stapled to the wall above the bookcases. My short arms had me getting down and moving the ladder every few feet. We were in for a tedious morning. Maybe some chit-chat would help pass the time.

"How was Brielle's appointment yesterday?"

Lacey's smile stretched from ear to ear. "Great! She's right where she should be. A happy, healthy baby."

"I'm glad. She's a sweetheart."

"I agree. All things considered, she's given us very little trouble. She's not sleeping through the night yet, but she goes right back to sleep after I change and feed her."

"Lucky you."

"Definitely. How's your investigation going?"

It isn't yet. "I had an interesting conversation with Eric this morning. He thinks Havermayer is getting depressed, and he wants me to visit her in jail since nobody else has. I told him I'd consider it, but really, I think he's fifty cats away from crazy."

Lacey handed up another few feet of garland and a cardboard witch. "Why?"

"She hates me. I'm the last person she'd want to see. Especially with her on the wrong side of the barrier."

"I don't know, Jen. Jail is a lonely place to be. You, of all people, should understand that. I expect she'd be happy to see a friendly face. You *can* put on a friendly face, right?"

I barked a laugh. "For Havermayer? I'd win an Academy Award if I pulled it off."

"It would look great on your mantel."

"I don't have a mantel."

"You should get one." Her expression turned serious. "Please consider visiting her. It would make me happy. Eric, too."

As usual, I had no argument for that. Something this important to my business partner and friend should be important to me too, right? I felt her chocolate brown eyes boring into the back of my head as I stapled the witch, flying her broom toward the window, into place.

Guess I'll be visiting Havermayer this afternoon.

120

CHAPTER TWELVE

People scurried around the Riddleton Police Department like squirrels gathering nuts for an arctic winter. Standing inside the doorway, I saw the uniformed and plain-clothed officers juggling the investigation that involved one of their own, along with their regular duties. Although, who worked on which, I couldn't tell. To say the scene was pure chaos would be like saying the Hindenburg disaster was a campfire in the sky.

I ventured down the hall between the faded gray walls full of photographs of uniformed officers from Riddleton's past, none of them in memoriam. As far as I knew, Riddleton had never lost an officer in the line of duty. One benefit of being a small-town cop. Most never even drew their weapons during their entire careers. And I'd never heard a single one of them complain about it.

The yellowed tile squeaked under my Nikes as I approached the duty sergeant's desk, which blocked the hallway between an alcove on one side and the break room on the other. The alcove held the doorway to the steps leading to the basement housing the property and locker rooms. I'd spent some time down there a while back while trying to get Eric cleared of a crime he didn't commit. It seemed I'd spent a big chunk of my time since I moved back to Riddleton defending people who'd been falsely accused. Myself included.

The sergeant looked up from the file he was engrossed in. *Helping find Kirby's killer or only killing time?* "Can I help you?" he asked when I neared his station.

It took me a minute to force the words "I want to visit Detective Havermayer" out of my mouth. I still couldn't believe I would actually see someone in jail I knew hated me. Eric had better have big plans for showing his appreciation. A surf-and-turf dinner might do it. Maybe even some jewelry, although that would be silly since I never wore any.

My sweaty palms slid down my jeans while the duty sergeant made a call to arrange my visit, and perspiration dripped down my forehead despite the chill in the air. How bad could it be? I'd sit in the hard plastic chair, chat for a minute, make sure she didn't need anything, then get the heck out of there. Easy-peasy, right?

Not too late to back out, Jen.

I shook my head. Eric would kill me. No way to avoid going through with it without creating more problems for myself. The sergeant hung up the black plastic receiver, and Zach Vick came to escort me to the visiting area. I pushed my reluctant feet forward to follow him through the bullpen, where the detectives worked, to the back of the station, adrenaline zinging through my muscles. Forget fight. The urge was all flight, and it took every bit of strength I had to keep from turning around and running back out the door.

In the visiting area—a chilly, unadorned white room designed to be uncomfortable—Zach pointed to the seat on my side of the plexiglass barrier with holes drilled into it so we could hear each other. I shivered when my bottom hit the cold plastic. My legs bounced, and my fingers tapped on the counter between me and the divider as I waited for Havermayer to appear.

I had no reason to be agitated. Havermayer couldn't hurt me. The idea that she might even be happy to see me popped into my head, only to be immediately evicted. She'd rather spend a month in solitary confinement than a minute locked in a tiny room alone with me. Still, I could leave any time I wanted to. All the guards stood on her side of the glass. She was stuck here until they let her out. For once, I held a slight advantage over her. She'd find some way to turn it against me, though.

Deep breath in, slow breath out.

When Zach escorted the handcuffed Havermayer to her side of the window, I almost didn't recognize her. Her sallow cheeks had hollowed as if someone had removed all her molars like a 1940s leading lady, and her sandy hair stuck out in places like she'd used her fingers for a comb. Dark circles supported her lower eyelids, and that, along with the lines around her eyes and mouth, made me wonder if she hadn't slept since her detention.

And worst of all—in her mind, I'm sure—she wore the same clothing she had on when taken into custody. A huge departure from her usual posing-for-a-magazine-cover veneer. No photographers would be clamoring to take her picture today unless she posed for a mug shot.

Zach removed the handcuffs, and she took her seat, glaring at me.

"Come to gloat?" A sneer emphasized her question.

A wave of pity washed away the retort forming in my throat. Taking advantage of our reversed positions was out of the question, no matter how much I might want to. I refused to be like her. "No. I came to check on you."

Confusion flitted across her face before anger moved back in. "Why?"

I shrugged, and my legs finally settled. "Why not?"

A surprised expression momentarily replaced the anger. "What do you want, Jen? Did you come to see me brought low?" She stretched her arms out to the sides. "Well, here I am. Happy now?"

Her words went through me like a knife. Had someone asked me last week how I'd feel seeing Havermayer sitting in jail, falsely accused as she'd done to me, I'd have said thrilled. But I wasn't. She didn't deserve to be in here any more than I did, and it bothered me. And she honestly believed me to be guilty when she arrested me. I had no doubt she couldn't have killed Simeon Kirby, so how could I be happy?

"Actually, no, I'm not. You didn't murder Kirby. That's the difference between us. You're willing to believe I'm capable of murder and act accordingly. I'm *not* willing to believe the same of you."

Havermayer lowered her brows and trained her shamrock eyes on me. "How can you be so sure? All the evidence says I did it."

Running a hand through my hair, I probably made mine stick up like hers. "Another difference between us. I recognize the evidence isn't always correct. Especially when there's so much of it. You have a lot of traits I don't particularly like, but stupidity isn't one of them. There's no way you'd leave so many clues pointing to yourself. If you murdered someone, nobody would ever find the body."

A smile briefly creased her solemn face. "You're right,

of course. I had nothing to do with it. Now I'm trapped by the same rules I always applied to you. How's that for irony?"

"It's the very definition of the word." My smile matched hers. "Do you need anything?"

"I wouldn't mind some clean clothes, but my house is still a crime scene."

"I'm sure they have an orange jumpsuit in your size somewhere. Although, I don't think orange is a great color for you. It would clash with your eyes." After a moment, I said, "I'll see what I can do. Maybe Eric will escort me into the house to bring you some clothing."

Her mouth opened and closed before she uttered a quiet "Thank you." Embarrassment reddened her cheeks.

My instinct urged me to offer to help her find a way out of her situation, but my obstinate side argued. I didn't owe her anything, and she wouldn't appreciate my efforts, anyway. She'd get nasty with me as she always did when I wanted to help with an investigation. Why put myself in a position to be treated badly again? *Why should I help her?*

My mother's voice insinuated itself into the silent discussion. I'd asked her once why it was my responsibility to help someone I didn't even know who'd been falsely accused. Her response was: "Because you can, dear. Because you can."

She was right then, and she'd be right now if she said the same thing. Just because the victim was Detective Havermayer didn't make her any less a victim.

I locked my gaze on hers to ensure she understood I meant what I was about to say. "Now, what are we going to do about your situation?"

"What do you mean 'we?' There's nothing you can do to help me."

"You said it yourself. The police can't release you because the rules bind them the same way they did you. All they can do is keep looking for another suspect. And every time they look, they find more evidence steering them back toward you. You need someone like me."

Her fists clenched in frustration. "Yes, but all of that evidence was planted. The real killer is framing me, and there's nothing I can do about it."

"I know you're being set up, and so does the department, but their hands are tied. Mine aren't. I'm willing to help if you'll let me. You think I'm a silly mystery writer who thinks solving a crime on paper is the same as solving one in real life. I know it isn't. But, the concepts and methods are the same. And, as much as you don't want to acknowledge it, I have a decent success rate for an amateur."

Havermayer broke away from our staring contest. "Yes, you do," she said to her uncharacteristically dirty fingernails.

My eyes widened in shock, but I covered it with a dispassionate mask before she noticed. It took tremendous strength for her to admit that. I wouldn't rub her nose in it, no matter how tempting it might be. It was the first time she'd ever said anything nice about me.

Not wanting to force the issue, I waited for her to speak again. I'd offered to help, but I wouldn't beg her to let me. I'd already swallowed enough pride to keep me full until lunch tomorrow. Whether to accept my offer was up to her.

She struggled with the decision long enough that I

considered leaving her to deal with her own problems. Fine with me if she didn't want my help. When she finally looked back at me, her face wore a guise of neutrality so effective she'd win the jackpot in the World Series of Poker. I had no idea what she'd decided to do until she spoke.

"All right. I need help, and you're the only one offering right now."

I bit back a nasty response to her backhanded acceptance. As difficult as I found it to make the offer, it was ten times more so for her to accept. For us to work together to prove her innocence, we'd have to shelve our animosity for the time being.

Who knows? Maybe we'd end up friends when the case was done. Keeping myself from laughing out loud at the thought was a challenge, but if I did I'd have to explain my outburst to Havermayer. On second thought, maybe I should. I dare say she could use a good laugh right about now, too.

While I could put my ill feelings aside for the sake of the case, it'd be a lot easier if I knew the source of the difficulty to begin with. Now I had a chance to find out. "Okay, I'll help you, but before we begin I'd like to understand why you hate me so much."

Her fingernails grabbed her attention again, and her voice dropped to slightly above a whisper. "I don't hate you."

She sure fooled me. "What is it then? You've had a negative attitude toward me since the day we met. Why?"

Pressing her lips into a line, she scowled at me. "What did you expect? You waltz into town after all those years and think you own it." She threw her hands out to the sides. "Look at me, everyone! I'm a famous author. And just because you write mysteries doesn't make you a detective. You have everyone fooled except me."

What the hell? "I'm not like that at all. If anything, I crawled back to this place when everything else in my life fell apart. What makes you think I have it so easy anyway? You're the one with the awesome job and fancy clothes."

"Awesome job? How about sitting around writing all day and owning a business you inherited just because you wallowed in your misery, drinking coffee, and chumming up with the owner."

"Screw you!"

"Well, screw you, too!"

I stood, knocking my chair over. "Forget your stupid clothes. It'll do you some good to get a taste of how the rest of us live."

Havermayer covered her face with her hands. "Jen, wait."

I froze in place but didn't sit.

"I'm sorry."

The second time in one week she'd apologized. The first time ever to me. Still, it'd take a lot more than that after what she'd said.

"Please!"

I'm sorry and please at the same time. What was I supposed to do with that? I sighed and dropped into the plastic chair with my arms crossed. "What?"

Tears hovered in her lower eyelids. "I'm sorry I said those things."

"You're only saying that because you need my help."

"I understand why you think that, but it's not true.

However, you're right—I do need your help, and you have no reason to give it. I know that."

I met her gaze, focusing on the desperation in her eyes.

"Please, I'm begging you. Do you know what it takes for me to say that?"

I did. "All right, I'll help you. But one more outburst, and I'll take you down myself. Got it?"

"Look around." Grinning, she held her hands out to the sides. "Somebody beat you to it!"

"Then I guess we'd better put our heads together and see what we have to do to get you out of here, don't you think?"

"Definitely. What do you need from me to start investigating?"

It surprised me they let us talk for as long as we wanted. The last time I visited someone here, Zach hovered over us and cut off the conversation after fifteen minutes. The detainee being a detective in the department must've made the difference. I suspected Eric might've had something to do with it as well. No way he'd ask me to come here then not ensure I had as much time as I needed.

Despite the reason, Havermayer and I talked for another hour, and she filled me in on everything she'd told Olinski when he questioned her. When I asked how she thought the killer might've entered her house to leave Elliott's wallet and phone in her desk drawer, she said the only thing that came to mind was maybe she'd left in such a hurry Saturday morning she forgot to lock the door behind her or left a window open. If that's what happened, it meant the killer was still in the area when we discovered Elliott. Were they watching the whole time?

Other than that tidbit, she imparted little I didn't know already, courtesy of Eric and Angus, except neither of them mentioned that she'd seen people she didn't recognize entering the park on Friday night. And they left a gold Mercedes and a Chevy Suburban the same as Havermayer's in the parking lot. Could that be the way they left Kirby's body in Havermayer's car? A malfunctioning key fob?

I understood almost nothing about locks and even less about vehicle key fobs. Earlier, I'd wondered if it might be possible someone else's fob opened her car door. That didn't seem likely at the time. Otherwise, auto theft incidents would've skyrocketed since their invention. However, I had to find out for certain.

And for that, I needed Charlie.

CHAPTER THIRTEEN

When I made it back to the bookstore around three, business had slowed down. Not unusual for a Tuesday afternoon. Most Riddleton residents worked in Blackburn or Sutton, and the few vacationers from the resort had been in town for several days. We mostly saw them over the weekend when they realized there was little else to do in the area besides sit on the lakeshore and read. A trip to the unfinished resort was a true relaxation vacation.

I had an hour to kill before Eric would be available to take me over to Havermayer's house for her fresh clothing. Perhaps he'd let me poke around a little, too, while we were there. The crime scene techs had missed well-hidden things occasionally in the past, and another set of eyes wouldn't hurt, even if the techs had located all the evidence. And I wouldn't mind getting more insight into the mind of Detective Havermayer. I doubted Eric would share my view of the situation; however, it was worth a try.

Charlie studied his laptop screen, elbows propped on the pastry case. No sign of Lacey or Savannah anywhere. Perhaps we'd run out of treats, and my neglected German shepherd had dragged her off to the Dollar General for more. I'd learned the hard way that the cardinal rule of dog ownership was: Never run out of treats. Especially when your dog weighed almost as much as you did, and she had two hundred and forty pounds of pressure per square inch trapped in her jaws waiting to be released.

Savannah wouldn't hurt anyone intentionally, though, unless provoked. Maybe not even then. She loved everyone she met, classifying her as the proverbial "gentle giant." So much for the protective watchdog I thought the woman in Georgia had given me. However, I wouldn't have it any other way. Anyone threatening me would take one look at her and run, unwilling to take the chance. And if they didn't, they had no reason to hurt her since she'd never come after them.

Good enough for me.

Charlie looked up when I grabbed my mug. "Hey, Boss. How'd it go? Any fireworks?"

Filling my cup, I replied, "Surprisingly well. I think Detective Havermayer and I might actually be friends someday." A bit of an exaggeration, perhaps, but why not? I'd escaped with no fisticuffs, and it had nothing to do with the barrier between us.

He narrowed his eyelids. "Really? That *is* a surprise. How'd you manage that?"

"We had our first conversation ever without one of us accusing the other of wrongdoing." I stirred cream and sugar into my coffee. "It started out a little shaky, but eventually we agreed to work together. I think it'll make a difference in the way we interact with each other in the future. I hope, anyway."

"Congratulations! I'm so proud of you." He turned

his laptop for me to view a photo of Elliott Kirby on the screen. "You want to guess what I've been working on?"

"Gathering information on the Kirbys?"

He twirled in a circle, raising his arm up and down with his forefinger pointed in a disco dance move. "Yup, and I've found some interesting stuff."

More interesting than that silly dance? "Such as?"

"Guess who owns a nine-millimeter semiautomatic pistol."

The guessing game wore on my nerves, but Charlie enjoyed it, so I ignored my irritation and replied, "Santa Claus?"

He rolled his eyes. "No. Simeon Kirby Jr." After another twirl, he continued, "He purchased it at a gun shop in Spartanburg three years ago."

All right. Suspect number three. "That's awesome, Charlie. Thank you. Can you do one more thing for me?"

"What's that?"

"Can you find out what kinds of cars the Kirbys drive? Havermayer saw a couple of vehicles in the park's parking lot Friday night. One of them might belong to our killer. Also, look into whether it's possible for the key fob for one vehicle to open another. I'm thinking that might be how the killer got Kirby's body in Havermayer's car."

"Ooh, interesting. I never thought about something like that." His fingers flew across the keyboard. "I'll start on it right now."

"Thanks. Where's Lacey?"

"She's in the office ordering used books for us," he replied without looking up.

I topped off my coffee and headed back there.

When I hit the doorway, Lacey was clicking away on the computer mouse, and Savannah slept in her bed on the floor beside her, paws twitching and tail thumping against the wall. Good thing I wasn't here to rob the place. Our security system had completely broken down.

"How's it going?" I asked Lacey, parking myself in a chair by the desk.

She jerked her head up, startled. "Oh, hey, I didn't hear you come in."

I jutted my chin toward the still-snoozing dog. "That's okay. Neither did she."

"Yeah, she's pooped. Charlie's been running her up and down the store all afternoon. She might need a new stuffed bone. I think she's about worn that one out."

"It's about time. She's had it since her puppy days. I'm surprised the razor blades that passed for puppy teeth never shredded it."

I crumpled up a piece of paper and threw it at the sleeping dog. She snorted, rolled over, and went back to sleep.

My hero.

I gave up trying to rouse her. "Any luck finding us some cheap books? That section's looking a little bare."

"Actually, I did. Charlie found several decent wholesalers to choose from. I ordered a couple hundred. That should hold us for a little while."

"It'll get us through Christmas, anyway. People might buy new books as gifts and used ones for themselves. Unless, of course, they decide to read the gifts before they wrap them." Clasping my hands behind my head, I leaned back in my chair. "When are you going to start decorating the windows?"

"Right now," she said, standing. "I wanted to order

134

the books so we'll have them before we run out. Next up, window dressing."

"Sounds great. Do you mind babysitting Savannah for a little while longer? I'm going to Havermayer's house with Eric to collect some clean clothes for her. It's the least I can do. Today was the first time I'd ever seen her wear the same thing two days in a row, let alone more than half a week."

"She must be going crazy by now." Lacey rubbed the back of her neck. "No problem watching Savannah. Looks like she's going to sleep the rest of the day, anyway. Not that she's any trouble when she's awake." She inched her way around the desk so as not to disturb the dog. "How did your visit go?"

"Fine. Actually, better than fine." I filled her in on what Havermayer said about the vehicles in the parking lot but left out the personal aspects of our conversation.

"From the sound of it, your visit was almost civilized. How did you manage that?"

"Well, not the whole visit. I asked her point-blank why she hated me so much, and she exploded. I fired right back at her, though."

"When did you become so brave?"

"I can take her." I flexed what passed for my biceps. "Actually, a plexiglass barrier stood between us, and I could run if I needed to."

"That's the Jen I know. How did she answer your question?"

"She didn't say anything worth repeating, and I don't want to give her a *real* reason to hate me by telling you. At least, not before we free her from jail. Then she can hate me all she wants. It'll be like old times."

Lacey laughed. "I suspect if you get her out of jail, you'll be bosom buddies for life."

"Possibly. Or she might only be pretending to agree to a truce so I'll help her. For all I know, she's still holding a grudge."

"I doubt it. I believe she'd rather die in prison than pretend to be your friend when she isn't. That's not her style."

"You're probably right."

I huddled on the stoop attached to Havermayer's Lilliputian-sized red-brick house on the corner of Park Street and Second across from the park, waiting for Eric to let me in. The mid-autumn sun had fallen behind the trees and taken the temperature with it. My sweatshirt had been fine for the sunny afternoon, but now I'd begun to shiver. I hoped Eric arrived before frostbite set in.

A black Chevy Suburban rolled to a stop at the curb. Eric must've heard me complaining. I stood to greet him, and he smiled at me over the top of the vehicle as he closed the driver's side door. The loving expression on his face warmed me in a way no jacket ever could have.

"You ready to go?" he asked as he came around the car. "I know Havermayer will appreciate this. Maybe she'll be nicer to you from now on. It's amazing what clean clothes can do for someone's disposition."

"Really? It's never helped her before." I hadn't told Eric I'd made peace with his partner yet. "Still, I know what you mean," I continued. "I think I threw away the clothes I was wearing when they took me to jail. I never wanted to see them again. I can't imagine how yucky I'd have felt if I'd had to spend more than one night wearing them in lockup." I kissed him. "I have you to thank for getting me out so quickly."

He put on his little Opie Taylor face. "Aw, shucks, ma'am. 'Tweren't nothin'."

"'Twas too!"

We laughed, and he put his arm around my waist as we climbed the steps to the front door, still fragrant from a recent royal-blue paint job. He fumbled with the keys, then inserted one in the lock and turned. The mechanism clicked. Clearing away the crime scene tape, he opened the door.

"After you, ma'am."

I sashayed past. "Well, thank you, kind sir."

He doffed an imaginary hat and followed me in. "The bedrooms are on that end." He pointed to the side of the house closest to the park. "Havermayer's is the larger one on the left."

"And how would you know that?" I teased.

He turned red from the collar of his white shirt to the tops of his ears.

Taking his hand, I led him in that direction. "I had an idea. What do you think about looking around a little while we're here? Just to make sure the techs didn't miss anything."

"They were very thorough, Jen. We're here to get clothing and nothing else."

"What would it hurt to take a look? Worst case, we don't find anything. Best case, we find a piece of evidence that exonerates Havermayer. What do we have to lose?"

He stopped with his hands on my upper arms. "You? Nothing, but I could lose my job if I let you roam around her house. Havermayer would go ballistic."

"You're with me. What harm could I possibly do?"

"You don't have to look for trouble. It always finds you."

I batted my eyelashes at him. "But this time, I have a big, strong man to take care of me."

His green eyes sparkled. "Nice try." He opened the door on the left, which turned out to be Havermayer's bedroom. "There you go. Don't take too long. I have to get back to work."

"Fine." I glanced around the sparsely furnished room, seeing nothing I might use to carry her belongings in. A door in the wall drew my attention, so I rooted through her closet, searching for a suitcase. Spotting a small overnight case in the corner of the shelf, I stood on my tiptoes and grabbed the handle. It slid forward an inch, then stuck. I lost my balance and fell on my butt, grunting. Good thing it was well padded with chocolate chip muffins.

The suitcase broke free and followed me down, bouncing off the hardwood floor beside me. I covered my head with my arms until it landed.

"Jen, are you okay?" Eric called from the room across the hall.

Three strides later, he squatted beside me. "What happened? Are you hurt?"

"I'm fine." I stood and dusted myself off. "Nothing injured but my pride, as usual. The suitcase fell off the shelf."

When I reached down to grab it, a floorboard shifted under my foot. The falling case had knocked it loose, and one corner overlapped the next slat. I knelt to slide it back into position and noticed a strip of light-green tinted paper wedged between the other end of the loose board and the one beside it.

I pointed it out to Eric. "Hey, what's that?"

He bent over and peered at it, frowning. "I don't know, but don't touch it."

Reaching in his pocket for the small knife he always carried, he dropped onto his knees. "Go in the kitchen and see if you can find a bag for me to put this in."

For once, I followed instructions without comment or complaint. Not sure why. Perhaps Eric's serious expression encouraged me to behave myself for a change.

The old-fashioned kitchen, loaded with drawers and cabinets women in newer houses only dreamed of, occupied the far side of the house. I looked around but, naturally, Havermayer left nothing on her spotless countertops. I'd have to search, starting with the most reasonable place—drawers and cabinets in the cooking area by the stove—and work my way out.

Twelve drawers full of every knickknack, doodad, and cooking utensil imaginable and four cabinets of foodstuffs later, I found a box of gallon-size freezer bags. Of course, Havermayer couldn't make it easy and bring her own sandwiches for lunch. Nope, that tiny scrap of paper would go into a bag large enough to hold a whole ream.

I brought the bag to Eric, who'd used the tip of his knife to slide the slip out of the crack and onto the floor. As he eased the knife blade under the paper for transport, I leaned over for a clearer view. It was a corner of a light-green page with dark lines surrounding lighter ones. Like a bookkeeping ledger. Nothing written on the section we had, though. "What do you think it is?" I asked him.

He shrugged. "Could be anything or nothing. I'll take it back to the lab anyway, just in case. Who knows? It could be the innocuous clue that breaks the case you're so fond of."

"Ha-ha. More likely, it's just something dropped unnoticed by the previous owner when they were packing up to leave."

"I like my version better," he said with a wink.

"Let's bring it back to the station and see who's right." I headed toward the door.

Eri cleared his throat behind me. "Uh, Jen? Aren't you forgetting something?"

I turned back. "What?"

"Havermayer's clothing?"

CHAPTER FOURTEEN

When Savannah and I entered the apartment after our walk Wednesday morning, we found retired Riddleton Police Detective Jeremy Conway sitting on the couch with his scuffed cowboy boots on the coffee table, drinking coffee out of my favorite mug. My coffee that I hadn't even had any of yet. And using my mug. My irritation at his inviting himself into my apartment again tripled.

Conway had cleaned himself up since our last adventure together earlier this year when we'd helped identify a skeleton and bagged its murderer. Now, he came across less like a hobo riding the rails in the 1930s and more like a retiree who'd escaped from the 1960s. He'd drawn his shoulder-length white hair into a ponytail, and waggled his bushy black-and-gray eyebrows in response to my surprised expression. The only thing missing was a paper flower pinned to his tie-dyed T-shirt.

My vicious attack dog ran to greet him, though she'd only met him twice before. I'd say she had a good memory, but she reacted the same way the last time he'd broken into my apartment, and she'd had no idea who he might be. And I wasn't even home at the time. The first time it happened, I chose to believe she reserved her protective instincts for me alone, but, clearly, that wasn't the case.

Perhaps I'd gone a little too heavy on socialization during her puppyhood. Or she'd learned all her social skills from Daniel Davenport. Either way, I saw a new alarm system in my future.

I hung up her leash and poured myself some coffee in a plain white cup that came with my dishes. "I thought we agreed you wouldn't do anything like this again," I said to Conway.

He responded with a gap-toothed grin peeking out of a two-day growth of beard.

"Seriously. Why did you break into my apartment again? If you wanted to talk to me, all you had to do was call. I know you have my phone number. You've called me before."

"This was a lot more fun," he replied in his raspy voice, cultivated over years of alcohol consumption. "Why didn't you put a deadbolt on the door like I told you to?"

Sitting beside him on the couch, I replied, "I didn't think I needed to. You're the only one who's broken in since I had my locks changed, and I thought we'd resolved that problem."

Another grin accompanied by another waggle. "Think again 'cause here I am." He swallowed a gulp of coffee. "Your coffee stinks, by the way. Almost as bad as that swill they had at the police station. You really should invest in the good stuff. It'll change your life."

"My life is fine the way it is. Why are you here?"

He set his boots on the floor and shifted to look me

in the eye. "I thought you might like to help me get my friend Detective Havermayer out of jail. But if you're not interested . . ."

"Havermayer's your friend? I always thought she didn't have any. You either."

"I was her training detective. Taught her everything she knows."

I grimaced. "That explains her disposition. She must've got it from you."

"Now, now. No need to get nasty. I thought we were friends."

"Think again," I said with a smirk. In truth, I'd actually begun to like him, After all, he'd saved my life, so I owed him. I'd never mention it, though. His already overinflated head might pop and fly away.

Conway put his cup down on the table and stood, hitching up his faded baggy jeans. "All right. I'm going out to the resort to talk to Kirby's family and need some backup, but I can see you don't want to come along, so I'll just take off now."

"Wait a minute." I grabbed the sleeve of his red plaid flannel shirt. "I didn't say I wasn't interested. I'm just grumpy because you invaded my space again. It makes me feel unsafe."

"You *are* unsafe. I'm telling you, get a deadbolt. A kindergartener can get in that door."

"All right, fine. I'll take care of it. Pour yourself another cup of coffee while I get dressed." My house-only sweats were fine for walking the dog, but nothing that involved being out with the general public.

"Pass on the coffee. We can pick up something drinkable on the way. I'll just play with your roommate here until you're ready." He snapped up Savannah's tug toy and dangled it in front of her snout. She snagged her end, set her feet, and pulled, growling.

At least he likes dogs. I had to give him that. "Suit yourself. I'll be right back."

I ducked into the bedroom and closed the door, not trusting him to not invite himself into my bedroom as well. My jeans and sweatshirt from yesterday were piled on the chair. After adding clean underwear, a T-shirt, and socks to the ensemble, I was ready to go within five minutes.

In the background, the battle for supremacy over the tug toy raged. My dog sounded like a wolf with a fresh kill while fighting for the toy. We'd have to translate that enthusiasm to uninvited strangers in the living room. The word "attack" might be a good one to add to her training repertoire.

After a quick trip to the bathroom mirror to brush my hair into something acceptable for the rest of the world, I returned to the living room in time to see Savannah yank the toy out of Conway's hand. "Looks like we know who the tough one is now, don't we?"

He waved a hand at me. "Nah, I let her win. I didn't want her to hurt herself."

Another macho man defending his masculinity. "Whatever you say." I grabbed my keys and a chew stick for Savannah. "I'm ready whenever you are. Unless you want to challenge her to a rematch."

"Nope, I'm good. Besides, she needs to rest up. I won't let her win again."

I tossed my girl her treat, and we trotted down the steps to the parking lot. Climbing into the passenger side of his black Ford Bronco, I pushed the floorboard clutter—mostly empty fast-food bags and cardboard

"What is it you'd like to know, Mr. Conway?" Virginia asked, twisting the sleeve of her white cotton blouse between the fingers of her other hand.

Conway conjured up a fake smile of his own. "We're hoping to get a clearer picture of what happened Friday night. If you could all recount your movements, it would help tremendously."

Stephanie was the first to speak up. "I was home with my husband all night. I believe the police have already verified that."

One spouse giving an alibi for the other. What could go wrong with that?

A nod from Conway in her direction prompted a response from Marion. "I was also home with my husband all night. Also verified by the police."

Two for two.

"I spent the evening with my husband as well," Virginia said. "But we had dinner with friends in Spartanburg."

"And afterward?" I asked.

"Simeon dropped me off at home and came here to meet with Simeon Jr. and Elliott. They'd had a meeting with one of the company's investors, and Simeon wanted to find out how it went."

"Why didn't he just call?" Conway asked.

"He preferred to meet face-to-face."

"Spartanburg is a hundred and fifteen miles from here, Mrs. Kirby. A two-hour drive. That seems a long way to go when a phone call would suffice."

Virginia glanced at Stephanie, then quickly away. "I don't know what to tell you. Obviously, he came here as he said he would." She dabbed a fingertip in the corner of her eye to keep a tear from ruining her mascara.

coffee cups—away from my feet. At least we had one thing in common. Before I totaled it after being pushed off the road, my car always looked like this, too. However, I'd been driving Eric's Jeep ever since, and he'd have a stroke if he found his beloved Wrangler in this condition. I did my best to keep it clean in deference to his health needs.

On the ride out to the resort, Conway and I exchanged information about the case. He knew about as much as I did—with the exception of the paper I'd found in Havermayer's floorboard—leading me to wonder who the source of his info might be. Turned out it was Havermayer herself. He'd gone to visit her right after I left, giving the detainee, who'd had no visitors to that point, two in one day. Add in clean clothing, and it had to feel like her birthday and Christmas combined.

Conway turned into the construction site and parked by the small trailer that functioned as the company office. Directly ahead lay the bones of the two incomplete buildings, adjoined by the occupied one. Three vehicles sat near the completed structure. Not too bad for a resort with no facilities on a Wednesday in late October.

The grassy area between the lobby doors and the parking lot had been decorated with a grave, complete with a fake tombstone and an assortment of witches, zombies, ghosts, and goblins. I doubted the Kirbys had any interest in Riddleton's tiny competition, but at least they'd tried to immerse their few occupants in the Halloween season.

I knocked on the trailer door, standing on the opposite side of the three wooden steps leading to it from Conway. After a muffled "Come in," drifted through the fiberglass, Conway tugged open the door, and I followed him up the rickety steps with no handrail.

Behind the desk facing the door sat a late thirties or early forties woman with platinum blond hair maneuvered into a French twist. Her tastefully applied makeup was topped off with berry-colored lipstick that matched her silk blouse. Someone I'd expect to find in a bank rather than on a construction site. However, since this was the first time I'd ever been in a construction trailer, my assumptions were likely based more on movie and television portrayals than reality.

Standing at a desk to our left were two other women, and Conway included them when he introduced us and told them how sorry we felt for the ordeal they were going through. As he spoke, I watched the blonde behind the desk, Stephanie Robinson, according to her nameplate, scowl, then quickly cover it with a toothy smile that missed her eyes by miles.

The other two women exchanged a glance, then turned back to us, wearing the same fake smile as Stephanie's. Conway had the right idea coming here. It seemed all three had secrets they'd prefer to remain uncovered. Or perhaps they all had the same secret. Regardless of which it might be, nobody seemed happy to see us.

Stephanie introduced herself and offered us seats and coffee. Conway declined both. I followed his lead. She introduced the other two women as Simeon's wife, Virginia Kirby, and Marion Kirby Jenkins, his daughter. Smiles frozen in place, they each nodded, but as I turned away I caught Virginia glaring at Stephanie out of the corner of my eye. Secret number one presenting itself. Now, I only had to figure out the details of why Virginia

didn't like her. Given Stephanie's appearance, I suspected I already knew.

Conway rubbed his hands together as he spoke, as if the temperature in the trailer had plummeted since we entered. "Thank you for giving us a few minutes of your time, ladies. I know you're as anxious to learn what happened to Simeon as we are, and I appreciate your willingness to help."

Marion put her shoulders back and her chin forward. "I'm not sure I understand, Mr. Conway. The police have someone in custody. Why do you need to speak with us? We've already answered their questions."

"Yes, ma'am, but there are a few loose ends that need to be tied up."

She crossed her arms over her multicolored diamond-print blouse. "But why did they send *you* for that? Why aren't we speaking with Detective O'Malley? He's in charge of the case, isn't he?"

I was beginning to understand what Eric meant when he said the daughter was difficult to deal with. The steely resolve in her eyes made my skin itch.

Conway glanced at me, then said, "He is, and he's handling other aspects of it at the moment. The department is shorthanded for reasons you seem to be aware of. I'm helping out until the situation is resolved. As an unpaid consultant, so to speak."

"Still, I see no reason—"

Virginia Kirby snapped her head toward her daughter. "Oh, for goodness' sake, Marion, just talk to the man. We have nothing to hide."

Marion pressed her lips into a line, dart-throwing eyes firing first at her mother, then at Conway, who returned fire without blinking.

On my right, Stephanie was doing the same thing with less success. A black puddle formed beneath her lower eyelid. Marion remained stone-faced, making it seem Stephanie was more upset about Kirby's death than his own daughter.

"Do any of you know of a reason someone might want to harm Mr. Kirby?"

All three women shook their heads. "Everyone loved my husband," Virginia replied.

I disguised my snicker with a cough.

Conway opened his mouth to ask another question.

I put my hand up to stop him and stepped back so I could see both Virginia and Stephanie at the same time. "Mrs. Kirby, how was your marriage? Did you ever suspect your husband of having an affair?"

Stephanie's head dropped at the same time Virginia's chin came up.

Perhaps I should've been more specific and asked if he was having an affair with his executive assistant.

Virginia started and stopped, eventually saying, "My husband loved me. And I loved him. There were no problems in our marriage."

Which didn't answer my question. She should've been a politician.

I exchanged a glance with Conway.

Marion's smirk gave it away as much as Stephanie's head-drop. Kirby was cheating on his wife, and his daughter knew about it.

Time to find out what else she knew. "Mrs. Jenkins, what's your function in the company? In other words, what do you do here, and how often do you do it?"

She glanced at her candy-apple-red fingernails. "I'm the chief financial officer. Mostly, I handle the books."

"And how often are you here in Riddleton?"

"A couple of times a month. Sometimes more when reports are due. I prepare them for our accountant."

"Do you mind telling me what your brothers do?"

After exchanging looks with her mother, Marion replied, "Sim . . . Simeon Jr. handles the investors and scopes out new development opportunities. Elliott supervises the actual construction projects."

Conway took over the questioning. "Mrs. Jenkins, would you consider allowing us a look at the books? There might be something in them that could give us a clue as to why someone murdered your father."

"What are you accusing me of? I've done nothing wrong."

I exchanged another glance with Conway. Rather than exonerate herself, Marion had just vaulted to the top of the suspect list. "Nobody's accusing you of anything, Mrs. Jenkins," I said, trying to defuse the situation. "Someone could be doing something improper without your knowledge. An impartial set of eyes on them might ferret out the culprit."

And locate where the corner of a page I found in Havermayer's house came from.

She shook her head. "I'm sorry. I can't give you that information without a subpoena. We have board members and investors to answer to."

"I understand." Conway suppressed a smile. "I'll relay your concerns to Detective O'Malley so he can make arrangements for the subpoena."

Marion's face turned a sickly shade of green, similar to that of the ledger I sought. I looked for a handy trash can in case she couldn't make it to the restroom. When she stepped out from behind the desk, I got my first glimpse of her five-inch heels, the same color as her nail polish. How did she walk on those things? I'd probably break my ankle just trying to put them on. Actually, thinking about putting them on would likely break something or other.

But more important, could those heels be what left the mysterious holes in the soft ground at the crime scene in the park?

CHAPTER FIFTEEN

As intriguing as I found Marion's high heels, Stephanie had also worn heels today, and I could safely assume Virginia owned at least one pair herself since the Kirbys seemed to make frequent public appearances. Stilettos were a common wardrobe staple for most women, so really the killer could've been any one of 50 percent of the population of Riddleton. *If* the odd little holes found at the crime scene were made by high heels sinking into the soft ground. I'd have to run it by Eric and see what he thought.

When I returned to the conversation from my mental dissertation on the history of high heels, Conway was once again asking Marion to show us the books. When she demanded a subpoena for the second time, I asked her about the scrap of paper that resembled a corner from a ledger sheet.

"Mrs. Jenkins, do you do your bookkeeping on the computer or use ledger books?"

She laughed. "We may be a small company, but we live in the twenty-first century like everyone else. Of course we use the computer."

So much for that idea. The scrap was probably a

corner of the paper Havermayer used to wrap her glassware when she moved that stuck to her shoe like toilet paper and ended up wedged in the crack between floorboards. Only a red herring.

I handed out Eric's business cards in case the women thought of anything else useful, and we left, me feeling like we'd wasted our time. We'd learned nothing new that might help the police solve the crime or even get Havermayer freed from suspicion.

As we reached Conway's Bronco, a black Chevy Suburban pulled up beside us with a man with caterpillar eyebrows perched over Neanderthal brow ridges in the passenger seat and Elliott Kirby behind the wheel. Was it safe for him to drive in his current condition? Apparently, he'd remembered how, if nothing else. With luck, though, he'd remembered something about the events of Friday night, too. We waited for them to exit the vehicle.

The Neanderthal seemed familiar. Logic told me he was likely Simeon Kirby Jr. Where had I seen him before? Then it came to me. He was the guy who'd scowled at Savannah in the bookstore the day we found Elliott in the park. Now I had a perfect excuse for not liking him.

Elliott cut the engine and climbed out of the Suburban, smiling at me. "Hey, I'm glad you're here. I wanted to thank you for all you did the other morning. I was in pretty bad shape."

I returned his smile, a twinge of guilt for believing him capable of murder creeping into my chest. "You're welcome. How are you feeling?"

"Much better, thanks. My headache's finally gone, and I'm starting to remember a few things from before. Nothing about the attack yet, but I'm getting closer."

"That's terrific. The sooner you remember what happened to you, the sooner the police might figure out what happened to your father."

He pinched his eyebrows together. "You think they're related?"

Clearly, he recalled nothing important yet. Like the fact he was covered in his father's blood. Reminding him might not be a good idea, though. It might shock him back into total amnesia. Or the shock might return his memory. Since I had no expertise on the subject, I took the safe way out. "It's possible."

Elliott frowned, chewing on his lower lip as if that would bring back his memory. When I looked up, his brother was watching him with an odd expression on his face. Was he concerned about what Elliott might remember? Or had his breakfast given him heartburn, and the connection was purely my imagination? Could go either way, but my bet landed on Elliott's memory.

While I chatted with Elliott, Conway questioned Junior about his whereabouts Friday night. No surprise, he claimed to be home with his wife. If all the people with motives were telling the truth about being home alone with their spouses, Simeon Kirby must've shot himself three times because there remained nobody left to do it for him.

Somebody had to be lying about where they were that night.

We got back in the car and Conway cranked up the Bronco and headed us back toward Riddleton. "So, what do you think?" he asked, turning onto the main road.

"Well, for starters, I think Simeon Kirby was having an affair with his executive assistant, and his wife knew about it. That gives them both motives to kill him. The wife because he cheated on her and the assistant because he wouldn't leave his wife for her."

He nodded and changed lanes to move around a creeper blocking the lane ahead. "Good. What else?"

Why did I suddenly feel like I'd ended up back in college? "Elliott Kirby's getting his memory back. If he remembers what happened to him that night, we might learn what happened to his father."

"True, but for the moment it's a long shot. What else did you learn from our interviews?"

"Are you training me to be a detective, Detective? I already have a job, remember? Two, in fact."

"I know, but that doesn't stop you from getting involved in these investigations. I figure I might as well help you out where I can so you won't waste so much time doubling back on your own trail."

Huh. "I didn't realize I was. I thought I'd been doing pretty well so far."

He chuckled. "You have, which is why we're even having this conversation. I thought you might like some help being more efficient instead of relying on luck so much of the time. I'll stop asking you questions if you want."

Did I want him to stop? No. Learning from a real detective would help in my writing, too. Why didn't Eric ever offer to help me? I'd have to ask him the next time I saw him.

Although, I'd be risking a fight. Perhaps I'd wait until after he solved the case.

"I want to learn, thank you. What was the question again?"

"What else did we learn besides Kirby was cheating

and Elliott's getting his memory back? We have a big discrepancy hanging out there for you to grab. What is it?"

I had no idea. What had I missed? Staring out the window at the passing scenery, I replayed the interviews in my mind. It was all basic stuff: where were you Friday night, do you know anyone who might want to hurt your father slash husband slash boss, can we look at the company books? Marion had said "no" to that one. Was that what he was looking for?

"I'm not sure this qualifies as a discrepancy, but Marion refused to let us see the books without a subpoena. Seems like she might have something to hide there."

"That's good, but there's more. Keep working on it."

Okay, I was looking for a discrepancy. Something one person said that didn't jibe with someone else's statement. Wait a minute. Didn't Virginia tell us that Junior was at an investor meeting with Elliott Friday night? Junior told Conway he was home with his wife when his father was murdered.

Looked like we'd found our first liar, but which one?

I relayed my thoughts to Conway, and he grinned. "I knew I wasn't wasting my time with you. What do we do now?"

It only took a second for me to see the obvious solution. "Since everyone but Elliott claimed to be home with their spouses, and they all live in Spartanburg, I'm thinking maybe we need to go to Spartanburg and check out some of these alibis. Starting with Junior."

"I agree." He made the turn toward the interstate, which would have us there in roughly an hour and a half to two hours, depending on traffic.

156

I settled in for the ride and called Eric so he wouldn't worry.

"Hey, babe, where are you? I stopped by the store, and they said they hadn't seen you."

"I'm on my way to Spartanburg." I briefed him on our visit to the resort. After that, the trip to the Kirbys' hometown became self-explanatory. "I think you need to have another chat with Elliott Kirby, though. With a little help, he might remember something useful. And get a subpoena for the company's books. They're definitely hiding something there."

"You might be right. I'll try to set something up before they get their lawyers involved. Assuming they aren't already. The subpoena's a whole other story, though. We need evidence of wrongdoing to show the judge. Your intuition isn't going to mean anything." He took a deep breath, then said, "Jen, what are you doing going to Spartanburg? I've already spoken to all those people. That's what they make telephones for. You're wasting your time."

"Maybe, but you know as well as I do it's a lot harder to lie to someone face-to-face. Plus, you only spoke with the people the Kirbys told you about. The ones they wanted you to hear. I'm a little surprised you didn't take this trip yourself."

"I will when I know enough to make the trip worthwhile." He blew air into the phone. "You don't have any authority. They probably won't even talk to you. Or Conway. He turned in his badge when he retired. And contrary to what he might've told you, he isn't working for us."

I switched the phone to my other ear and lowered my voice. "Look, babe, I understand you think this is a bad idea. Conway seems to know what he's doing, and he thinks we need to do this. I promise we won't involve you in any way. I'd never do anything to get you into trouble. If people don't talk to us, we'll leave, okay?"

"It's not me I'm worried about, it's you. Conway's known to be a little loose with the rules. He used to do stupid and dangerous things sometimes when investigating. I don't want him dragging you down with him. Or worse, getting you hurt or killed."

Since Conway had broken into my apartment twice, I couldn't argue with Eric's assessment of the retired detective's methods. However, my boyfriend would have to learn to trust my judgment on these things. I could take care of myself. Most of the time. "I'll be fine. I won't let him do anything that jeopardizes our safety. I promise."

After a couple more reassuring exchanges, Eric hung up, unconvinced but resigned to the fact I'd do whatever I thought best, no matter how he felt about it. I hated being that stubborn, but if it were up to him I'd spend my life at home or the bookstore encased in bubble wrap. I couldn't live in fear of what might happen. Sometimes, I just had to do what needed to be done and hope for the best.

I sat with my phone in my lap, watching the miles speed by out the window.

"Everything all right?" Conway asked. "Do you want me to take you home?"

"No, we have work to do. Somebody has to figure out what the Kirbys are hiding."

"Are you sure? I don't want to start any trouble for you."

Shifting in my seat to face him, I said, "You're not starting any trouble. It's the same conversation Eric and I have any time I try to do something like this. He's overprotective, that's all. And it's annoying sometimes."

"Sounds like he cares about you. Is that so bad?"

"No, of course not. I love him, too, but he can't protect me from everything."

"All right. It's your decision." He reached over and turned on the radio.

I turned toward the window to take a nap. We had a long day ahead of us.

When I awoke, we'd stopped for gas. Conway slid back into the driver's seat.

I rubbed my eyes and stretched my arms overhead. "Where are we?"

"Just got off the interstate. We're about six miles from Converse Heights, where all the Kirbys live."

"They all live together?"

"In the same subdivision."

I found that strange since Marion clearly hated her father so much. I presumed she'd want to live as far away from him as possible. Maybe she loved her mother enough to want to be close despite her feelings for her father. "Okay, who are we going to hit first?"

"I was thinking we'd go straight to the source first. Simeon Kirby's house. It's unlikely anyone's home, so the neighbors might talk more freely."

"Or better yet, maybe they have a housekeeper. They usually know everything that goes on. The trick will be getting her to talk. Some of them are very loyal."

Conway laughed. "Given Kirby's sunny personality, I doubt anyone who deals with him on a regular basis is all that attached."

"True, but they might want to protect his wife."

Ten minutes later, we halted in front of a two-story brick Colonial with three dormer windows on the roof and a two-car garage off to one side. The freshly cut lawn bordering the driveway was divided by a concrete walk leading to a pillared porch, which didn't seem to ever be used. No tables, no chairs, no porch swing. *Why bother?*

Conway knocked on the door. No response, as expected. Unfortunately, that also meant no disgruntled housekeeper to spread the dirt, either. No problem, though. A man as bristly as Simeon Kirby had to have made some enemies somewhere. Now, we only had to find them.

When we received no answer to the second knock, Conway shrugged and led the way next door to a ranch-style house with no porch. Loud music played inside, but I couldn't tell the song or the artist. Something recent, though. Definitely the preferred listening of a teenager.

Conway elbowed me as he rang the doorbell. "Hey, we might luck out and get a teenage girl. They love to gossip!"

"Sometimes. Sometimes, they're moody and uncommunicative. It could go either way."

"True, but let's hope for the former. If we don't get some information from somebody, we came a long way for nothing."

Assuming nobody could hear the bell over the music, Conway pounded on the door. The music volume lowered to a whisper, and a young girl about half Conway's height, dressed all in black and with stringy black hair brushing her shoulders, opened the door. Shouldn't she be in school? Maybe she took time off for Halloween. Looked like she was already trying out her costume.

She brushed her hair back out of her eyes, which flicked back and forth between us, unable to rest in one place. "What?"

Oh boy. Moody and uncommunicative. It figured I'd be right on this one.

Conway towered over her. "My name is Jeremy Conway." He jerked a thumb toward me. "This is my associate Jen Dawson. We're consultants with the Riddleton Police Department, and we'd like to ask a few questions about your neighbors. Are your parents home?"

She peered suspiciously at us. "Why?"

"We need some information." He shifted his gaze from the Queen of One-Word Answers to me, then back to her. "Mr. Kirby is dead. We need to speak to your parents."

"They're at work. Come back around six." She started to close the door.

Conway stuck his foot in the opening. "Wait a minute. You might be able to help us."

Her lips twisted. "I doubt it. I barely knew the guy. He was in a bad mood all the time. Totally mean. Especially to his wife."

"In what way?" I asked.

She shrugged. "I don't know. He just wasn't very nice to her. Putting her down all the time, you know?"

"Can you give us an example?"

Catching her lower lip between her teeth, she stared at the house across the street. "One time, they were going somewhere, and she wanted to drive—I think 'cause he was drinking, but I'm not sure. Anyway, he got all nasty with her. Told her she couldn't drive a go-cart, whatever that is, and she wasn't touching his Mercedes. He yelled at her for a long time, but I don't remember what else he said. She was crying."

"What happened then?"

She smiled. "He backed out of the driveway into his trash cans. Dumped garbage all over the ground. Didn't even stop to pick it up. Just burned rubber down the street. I laughed so hard I almost peed myself."

Sounded like Kirby's temper was even worse than I'd imagined. "Can you tell me if you saw the Kirbys last Friday night? Were they home?"

"No idea. I stayed at a friend's house. Went there straight from school. Her parents weren't home, and we partied all night."

Conway asked, "Is there anything else you can think of we might need to know?"

The girl started to shake her head, then stopped. "Oh yeah, there is one thing. Another time, they were arguing in the driveway, and he hit her. Just a slap. I mean, he didn't beat her up or anything. Does that help?"

I wonder if Virginia thought it was "just a slap."

CHAPTER SIXTEEN

Conway thanked the girl for speaking with us. She went back inside, and the music was back up to rock-concert levels before we could get down the steps.

"That girl's gonna be deaf before she turns twenty-one at this rate," I commented.

"I bet you sound just like your mother right now."

Nope, not even close. My mother was never home. "No, my stepfather did all the complaining in my house." I poked him playfully. "And if you're telling me I sound like him, just shoot me now and get it over with. I couldn't stand him when I was growing up."

We crossed the grass to the neighbor on the other side. Still no signs of life at the Kirby house. Maybe they really didn't have a housekeeper.

"And now?" Conway asked.

"We declared a truce for my mother's sake. I don't live with them anymore, so no sense in having an adversarial relationship that makes my mom uncomfortable." Why was I telling him all this? I barely knew the guy. Guess some people are just easier to talk to than others.

The dwelling on the other side of the Kirbys' stood as tall as theirs but not as wide. Still a formidable place, though. Way out of my price range. A cardboard box under a bridge was probably out of my price range, too. Well, not quite, but close.

Conway knocked on the solid oak front door, avoiding the witch head staring back at us. No answer, so I reached over and tried the doorbell. Not as much fun as playing tag with a witch, but hopefully more productive.

As we were about to give up on anyone responding, the Kirbys' garage door rose. The mechanical rumble drowned out any chance we had of hearing someone inside their neighbor's house. I suspected nobody was home, so nothing to hear, anyway.

An older model blue Honda slipped into the available space in the garage, and we sprinted over to catch the driver before the door closed again. Conway's longer legs carried him there in time to detain a woman from Methuselah's generation wearing a plain black dress with a white collar, climbing slowly out of the driver's seat. I lagged about three steps behind him. Another reminder that my first growth spurt had also been my last.

Conway introduced us and asked her if she'd mind answering a few questions. He explained what information we sought, with her shaking her head the whole time, making it clear she had no interest in cooperating.

The woman popped the trunk and began unloading bags of groceries.

"Here, let me help you with those," Conway said, reaching for the bags. "It's the least I can do."

"No, thank you," she replied, throwing us a distrustful glance. "I do this every day. And the missus wouldn't like it."

164

"Why not?" I asked.

"She doesn't like strangers in the house when she's not home."

I reached for a bag. "We don't have to come in the house. Let us help you carry them to the door. Then, you won't have to lug them as far."

Her face relaxed, and she handed me a plastic bag full of canned goods. "You can help, not him. I don't trust him."

Smart woman. Exchanging a glance with Conway, I carried the bag to the inside doorstep and set it by the wooden door.

He stepped back out of the woman's way. "How long have you worked for the Kirbys?"

"Ten years."

"Do you like it here?"

"Obviously."

Terrific. Another one-word wonder. Conway got the teenager to open up. He might work his magic on the elderly, too.

"Have they gotten along well since you've been with them?"

She crossed herself and gave him the evil eye. "I will not speak ill of the dead."

I carried two more bags to the doorway. Though she didn't realize it, she'd told us something already. Clearly, Mr. Kirby was not high on her favorite-people list.

"Can you tell me if they were home Friday night?"

"No."

Conway pinched his brows together. "No, they weren't home, or no, you can't tell me?"

"I can't tell you because I wasn't here. The missus let me go at five since they were going out to dinner,

165

and I wanted to go to my granddaughter's ballet recital. Mr. Kirby wasn't home from work yet when I left." A hint of a smile twitched her lips. "My granddaughter was the best one there. She always is."

"You must be very proud." He waited a beat, then asked, "What about the children? Did they get along well with their parents?"

Her shoulders relaxed, softening her posture. "Mr. Elliott is a good boy. He still lives at home and works hard to please his parents. The other two?" She shuddered as if that would explain everything.

"Is there any scenario you can think of that might make Elliott shoot his father?"

She vehemently shook her head. "He would never do such a thing. He idolized his father. Wanted to make him proud."

"But you don't like Simeon Jr. and Marion?"

"Marion is a witch, and that husband of hers is just as bad. He treats her like dirt, although I can't say she doesn't deserve it sometimes. She starts an argument with her father every time she comes here."

"What about the older son?"

"I have nothing to say about him. My mother always said, 'If you can't say anything nice about someone, don't say anything at all.'"

Since she'd just called Marion a witch, that rule must only apply to men. Not unusual for women of her generation. I retrieved the last two bags and closed the trunk, signaling the end of our conversation. We had learned little other than the dislike of the elder Kirby males seemed universal. Our goal now was to find out why.

Conway thanked her for her time and offered again

to help her carry the groceries into the house. She declined and flipped the switch to close the garage door. We scrambled to get out before it sank to the concrete floor.

"So, what do you think?" Conway asked on our way back to the car.

"Are we going to play twenty questions again? Because, so far, I don't think we've learned much we didn't already know, other than Kirby liked to hit his wife."

His lips twitched. "You sure?"

Apparently not. "What do *you* think about what they said?"

"I think there's more to Marion's story than 'she didn't like her father'. I'd like to know more about her husband, too. And how she ended up married to him."

"According to Charlie's rampage through her social media, Simeon pushed Marion into marrying the guy because he invested in the company. No love necessary on her part. That's one of the reasons she hated her father so much."

"Sounds like it turned out to be a match made in hell. Perhaps Marion's husband also had a reason to hate Kirby. Either way, I think that should be our next stop. We know Marion's in Riddleton, and her husband's probably at work, but maybe we can find a chatty neighbor or two. We had pretty good luck here. I hope it holds."

As we settled into the Bronco, Conway asked, "How's the suspect list looking? Who's on the top of yours?"

Here we go again. When did my training period end? "I can't make up my mind. My first thought is Junior. He has the most to gain from his father's death, and he has the strength to knock out his brother with one blow. But I can't come up with a motive for him to kill his father."

Buckling his seat belt, Conway said, "It's my understanding that Kirby was grooming Junior to take over the company. That's a motive."

"But he'd still only get a percentage, the same as everyone else."

"True, but I expect Kirby was well insured. He probably had a substantial life insurance policy. Keyman insurance for the business as well. Junior had a lot to gain when his father died. Maybe he needs the money now. Or maybe he just got tired of waiting for his father to step aside so he could run the business."

"Okay, I'll buy that, but what about the wife? Shouldn't we be looking at her, too?"

Conway started the engine and eased away from the curb. "Sure. She has as much to gain as everyone else in the family besides Junior, and she gets rid of her cheating husband. I just don't think she's strong enough to overpower both her husband and her younger son."

"Kirby was shot, remember? It doesn't take much strength to pull a trigger."

"What about hitting Elliott hard enough to knock him out? She'd have to be pretty strong to do that. Even if she caught him by surprise. And what about having to lift Kirby into the back of Havermayer's car? Forget about carrying him there."

He had a point. "Virginia said her husband dropped her off at home before coming to Riddleton, but nobody can verify that. However, she also said that Junior went to that investor meeting with Elliott Friday night. Junior told us he was home with his wife."

"Maybe we'll get lucky, and his wife will be home to verify that when we get there." He turned at the corner and again at the next, bringing us to the next street up from the Kirbys. "Then she can tell us who's telling the truth. Assuming she gives us an honest answer."

I chuckled. "Which would be a big assumption. Almost as big as assuming Elliott didn't kill his father because somebody hit him with the gun. Only Elliott knows what really happened that night. I wish he'd get his memory back."

"Me too. What motive did he have to kill his father, though? He seems to be the only one who gets along with everybody." Conway rolled to a stop at a Cape Cod-style house with two dormers and no porch. "And all he gets out of his father's death is his share of the company. Junior gets all the power, and I suspect Elliott wouldn't consider working for his brother a bonus."

"Maybe, but he *did* have his father's blood all over him." I studied the Jenkins house, which looked deserted as we expected. "What about the girlfriend, Stephanie? Kirby might've tried to break things off, and she killed him in a fit of anger."

He cut the engine and opened his door. "We'll have to look into that when we get back. Right now, let's see what we can find out about Marion and her husband."

I followed him up the walk between a ghoulish graveyard on one side and a witches' coven on the other. The front door had a black-and-orange wreath covered with skulls in the middle, and a werewolf's head obscured the doorbell. I stuck my hand in the wolf's mouth and pushed the illuminated button. Spooky music chimed through the house. Safe to assume the Jenkinses loved celebrating Halloween. Or maybe Marion wanted to feel

169

more at home. Her parents' housekeeper *did* call her a witch. Perhaps she was more accurate than she realized.

No ghouls appeared in response to the bell. Ditto Conway's knuckle rap on the door. The house was as empty as it appeared. We looked at each other.

"Neighbors?" I asked.

"Neighbors."

Unfortunately, checking out Marion's neighbors didn't amount to anything, either. Nobody home in any of the houses, including the ones across the street. No parents, no housekeepers, no kids playing hooky. I'd call it a wasted trip, but, since it was only around the corner from where we were, that seemed a bit harsh.

"What now?" I asked Conway on the way back to the Bronco.

"Lunch, then Junior. He's the only one left. If we don't get any new leads at his place, we might as well head on home."

My rumbling belly seconded his decision to get something to eat. I'd skipped breakfast and now had a full-fledged insurrection going on in my stomach. "Sounds good. Where did you want to eat? Do you know any places around here?"

"The last time I came here was over twenty years ago. Spartanburg's changed a lot since then. How about we just hit a fast-food place?"

"That works. I'm not dressed for anything fancy, anyway. And I couldn't afford it, even if I was."

"I know the feeling. Cops' pensions don't go nearly as far as they used to when I first started. If I'd known, I might've made a different choice of what to do with my life."

170

I looked at him over the top of the car as I opened my door. "No, I don't think so. Obviously, I don't know you very well, but you were born to be a cop. I can tell."

The skin around his eyes crinkled. "Then I guess it's a good thing my folks couldn't afford to send me to college. Cops don't make very good doctors. Lousy bedside manner."

"Really? You wanted to be a doctor?"

"Long as I can remember. I got a medical kit for Christmas one year and practiced constantly on my dog. Listening to her heart with my plastic stethoscope, bandaging her paws. That kind of stuff. Poor thing thought she was a guinea pig by the time I outgrew it."

He pulled onto the street and drove toward downtown, negotiating the heavy traffic. A couple of blocks in, he pointed to a McDonald's. "How about Mickey D's? That work for you?"

"Fine with me. I haven't had a Big Mac in forever. And I think they have the best fries."

"Good. I didn't want to get too far away from where we're headed next. I hate driving in this kind of traffic. Guess I got spoiled working in Riddleton all those years."

"I know what you mean. That's one of the reasons I despised Kirby's development ideas so much. They would bring too much traffic to town."

He parked his Ford in the sole empty spot by the side door, and we went inside. The line filled the serpentine outlined by poles and cords to keep customers who hadn't ordered yet away from the people eating their meals. We took our place at the end and inched forward with everyone else.

Fifteen minutes passed by the time we reached the

counter and placed our orders. Another ten went by while we stood at the drinks station, waiting for our food. It was almost two when we finally sat down to eat. The day had flown by, and we had little new information to show for it. Hopefully, we'd learn something at Junior's house. Otherwise, it really would be a wasted day.

Conway inhaled his Quarter Pounder with Cheese combo as if he'd never eaten before. One thing I loved about Eric was he didn't choke down his food like a ravenous wolf. I could take my time and enjoy my meal without having to worry about him being bored, waiting for me to finish. Not so with Conway. He was fidgeting and checking his watch before I'd made it halfway through my sandwich.

I wrapped up the remains of my half-finished lunch for Savannah. "You ready to go?"

"Are you done already? You haven't eaten much."

"Guess I'm not as hungry as I thought. Let's go catch us a bad guy."

The trip back to Converse Heights took twice as long as the drive to the restaurant because the traffic grew heavier as the day progressed. Fortunately, as far as we knew, we had only one more stop to make. Simeon Kirby Jr.'s house.

We pulled up by a Georgian-style white-brick edifice with two dormers and two chimneys, at least a third larger than Kirby Sr.'s Colonial. Yup, Junior would do anything to escape his father's shadow. Including building a home he couldn't afford? Possibly. As far as we could tell, his wife didn't work, but perhaps her family had money they contributed to the cause.

Both doors of the two-car garage were closed, so no way to know if anyone was home. Given the late hour,

172

we divided and conquered. Conway would try Junior's house, while I visited the neighbors. With luck, we'd end the day on a high note and learn something important.

A car pulled into Junior's driveway, and Conway turned back to talk to the occupant, who, with any luck, would be Junior's wife. I trudged across the grass to the A-frame on the left, with a vehicle in the driveway. No Halloween decorations to entertain me on my journey. Perhaps they waited until the last minute or didn't bother. When I rang the doorbell, the faux-mahogany door opened almost immediately, sending me back a step in surprise.

A mid-forties blonde wearing jeans and a sweatshirt with her hair drawn back in a ponytail asked, "Hello, can I help you?"

Finally, a rich person I could relate to. Her fashion sense, anyway. I gave her the rundown on why I wanted to speak with her, and, as soon as I mentioned Junior's name, she rolled her eyes. I suppressed a smile, not wanting to skew the direction of the conversation. "I take it you're not fond of your neighbors?"

She smirked instead. "That's the understatement of the year."

"Do you mind if I ask why?"

"It's complicated." She studied me for a moment, then continued, "Actually, we used to be quite close. We did a lot of things together. You know, the usual: barbecues, dinner parties, hanging out on Sunday afternoons. We spent a lot of time together when Sim was in town."

Sim? That's what Marion had called Junior before she corrected herself. "So, what happened?"

"My husband had the brilliant idea of starting a weekly poker game. A guys' night. No women allowed, which I had no problem with. He invited Sim, of course, and everything was fine at first." She hesitated, meeting my gaze. "Then Sim began to take it all way too seriously. We'd gotten the impression by then they were having money problems, and it almost seemed like Sim thought he could fix it by winning at poker. It was ridiculous, of course. The guys didn't play for pennies, but they weren't playing for thousands of dollars, either."

"What made you think that?"

"He became aggressive. Betting big, then accusing people of cheating when he lost. It got so bad my husband finally asked him to stop coming. Sim took it personally, and it ended our friendship. I heard he found some other poker games with higher stakes ."

Huh. Gambling debts sounded like a good motive for murder.

CHAPTER SEVENTEEN

Elliott Kirby swung the butt of his gun toward my head just as Fleetwood Mac's "Dreams" woke me Thursday morning. Sweat covered my forehead and armpits. My hands shook, and my heart hammered, breaths coming in sharp gasps. The nightmare was only another in a series that had plagued me through the night, but at least it would be the last. For today. Unless someone confessed to Simeon Kirby's murder, tonight would bring more of the same.

The dreams started when I was a kid, and, while I understood even then that all children had nightmares, mine always seemed to relate to something going on in my real life. No phantom monsters or indecipherable hints from my subconscious for me. My father died in a plane crash when I was six, and I dreamed of being in one every night for two years. No need to guess what that was all about.

Nowadays, my dreams seemed sedate when I remembered them unless I found myself embroiled in another murder investigation. Then, the victim, the prime suspect, or both haunted me in my sleep until the crime was solved. And the nightmares I always recalled in vivid detail despite my inability to remember what I had for dinner last night.

It didn't bother me the way it used to, though, once I recovered from the initial shock of waking up surrounded by a mishmash of dead bodies. I considered it motivation to wrap up my involvement in the case posthaste. Unfortunately, I could never do it in one day.

We'd returned from Spartanburg late last evening after having uncovered little that helped with the investigation into Simeon Kirby's death. Junior's wife had stuck to the story that her husband was home with her Friday evening despite his mother's assertion he'd attended the investor meeting with his brother Elliott. She claimed he'd changed his mind and decided his brother could handle it by himself. "It was time he grew up" were his exact words, according to his wife. True or not, it sounded like something he would say from my experience.

Savannah shifted her head to my chest and blinked her sleepy brown eyes at me. Yesterday had been a long day for her, too. She'd been on guard duty all day, which interfered with her nap schedule. The poor thing found it hard to sleep while surrounded by fierce threats like leaves blowing across the sidewalk below and the mailman.

I considered letting us both go back to sleep, but I had to compare notes with Eric. I'd called him when I arrived home, but it went straight to voicemail. Then I went to sleep, leaving my phone on the coffee table.

The smell of coffee brewing in the automatic coffeemaker lured me into a standing position, but my German shepherd remained unconvinced. She scooted into the warm spot I'd left behind to resume dozing in my scent. I went on to the bathroom to begin my morning routine, feeling my way along the walls until I could convince my sleep-sticky eyelids to open completely.

By the time I'd splashed water on my face and made myself semi-presentable, Savannah had moved to the front door and sat holding her leash in her mouth. I retrieved my Nikes from under the coffee table and checked my phone. No call from Eric. He'd told me he had plans to reinterview Elliott Kirby. If Elliott had regained his memory, their discussion would've lasted for hours.

The coffeemaker gurgled and hissed, and I longed to pour a cup for the road. I'd learned my lesson, though. If I poured too soon, the rest of the pot would be as weak as dishwater, while my first cup would taste like battery acid. Better to wait until the whole thing was done.

I leashed the dog, and we plodded down the steps to the oak tree adorned with red, brown, and yellow leaves. Savannah scratched some that had fallen around the base of the trunk into a pile, then christened the dirt below. No idea why she had to move the leaves first. Another doggie idiosyncrasy I'd never understand. I'd asked her once, but she refused to say. Typical.

The sun crested the roof of the Piggly Wiggly as we turned the corner of Oak toward Riddleton Road so Savannah could finish her business by the church—her favorite number-two spot. When she hunched, I shivered in the early-morning autumn chill, looking around to ensure nobody was watching. Not that it mattered. I had a plastic bag with me to retrieve her leavings, but it still made me uncomfortable for some reason. Strange, since I had no religious background to speak of.

The coffeemaker had hissed its dying gasp by the time we returned, and I filled my mug, wishing for one of Eric's bacon-and-egg breakfasts. While perfectly capable of fixing my own meal—eggs being one of the few things I cooked that tasted somewhat close to the way they were supposed to—it wouldn't be the same. Eric had spoiled me. Guess I'd better keep him around, which would make my mother happy, too.

I snuggled on the couch with my sleeping girl as I sipped, debating on whether to phone Eric. I had little to report, and he was probably busy following up on whatever Elliott had revealed last night. But I missed him and wanted to hear his voice. We'd spent little time together in the past few days. Besides, I didn't need an excuse to call my boyfriend, did I?

The call went to voicemail, but he rang me back before I could leave a message.

"Hey, babe, what's up?"

"Nothing. You didn't call me back last night, so I wanted to check on you," I said, hoping I didn't sound accusatory. I wasn't upset about him not calling and didn't want him to think I might be.

"I'm sorry. My interview with Elliott Kirby ran late, and you sounded so tired in your message I didn't want to risk waking you."

"That's sweet of you."

"How did your day riding around with Jeremy Conway go? Anything happening there I need to be worried about?" he teased.

I laughed, pressing my lips together to keep from spitting coffee all over my sweatpants.

Savannah lifted her head, gave me a dirty look for disturbing her, and then went right back to sleep. Poor abused thing couldn't even sleep in peace.

"You absolutely have something to worry about. Haven't I ever told you I had a secret crush on Grandpa Walton? Conway could be his twin, so you'd better watch out."

"I'll take my chances."

Somebody's getting full of himself. He was right, though. He had nothing to fear. "What did Elliott have to say for himself? Has he remembered what happened Friday night yet?"

"He's getting there. He remembers most of the day, but he's still fuzzy about what happened that evening in the park."

"Does he recall anything about the investor meeting? Junior's wife is sticking to her story that he was home with her all night."

"Huh. Elliott was pretty sure his brother attended the meeting with him, but who knows how accurate his memory is at the moment. And a defense attorney would take him apart on the stand if it came down to his word against the wife's."

We needed a neutral third party to attest to Junior's whereabouts Friday night, but the only other person at the meeting was the potential investor. "Did Elliott say who the investor was? He could verify whether Junior was there or not."

"He wouldn't say. I suppose we could subpoena him for a deposition and get it out of him that way. He'd be under oath. Can't do that until we arrest Junior for the murder, though."

"Is he your prime suspect now?"

Eric cleared his throat. "We don't have one yet. We have bits and pieces of evidence against several people, but not enough to charge anyone."

He'd summed up the situation perfectly. We'd found at least one piece of evidence against every member of the Kirby family but nothing substantial on any of them.

"Speaking of subpoenas, did you have any luck getting the judge to sign off on one for the company's books? I think Marion's hiding something."

"No luck there, either. The judge said we didn't have enough evidence to justify it. Apparently, your gut feelings won't do it. Sorry."

Imagine that. "That's only because he doesn't know me. My gut's always right. Well, most of the time."

Eric snickered but wisely said nothing.

"Did Elliott give you anything else to go on?" I asked, giving him a pass on the laughter. To be honest, my instincts ran about fifty-fifty.

"Nothing we didn't already know, unfortunately. We'll have to wait for him to regain the rest of his memory, I guess." He hesitated. "Wait, he did tell us one thing we knew nothing about. His mother owns a thirty-two-caliber pistol. His father bought it for her for protection since he was gone so much."

Did we finally have some hard evidence? "Is it the gun we found in the park?"

"I don't know. That gun wasn't registered in the state of South Carolina, so we couldn't trace it back to anyone. She's supposed to bring hers into the station today, so we can verify she still has it. Otherwise, it might be sitting in the evidence lockup, which would mean she's our prime suspect."

"Yeah, but why would she kill him? All she gets is

a percentage of the company. Same as all the kids but Junior."

"Didn't you tell me you thought Kirby was cheating on her?"

"Yeah, but she probably would've come out better divorcing him. Besides, I have nothing to back up the theory. It's all gut, no facts, just like my thoughts on Marion."

"Maybe, but let's not forget the good old crime of passion. She might've learned of his indiscretion and confronted him. When he denied it, she lashed out and shot him, not meaning to kill him, but succeeding anyway."

Eric had a reasonable theory, but Kirby struck me as a serial cheater if there ever was one. He was someone used to getting whatever he wanted, and some women were attracted to a man like that. His affair with his assistant couldn't have come as a total surprise to his wife. "I don't know, babe. I'm thinking more 'enough is enough' than 'crime of passion.' A guy like Kirby probably had dozens of affairs throughout their marriage. She had to know about some of them."

"Could be. There's always the possibility we're both wrong, though. She might show up with her gun after all. That would take her off the suspect list altogether."

"How's Havermayer holding up?"

He shrugged. "Okay, I guess. Not happy about the way things are playing out. She hates having to depend on other people to begin with. Needing us to prove her innocence is driving her crazy. I wish we could let her out, but it would look bad, and she'd dive headfirst into the investigation. We can't allow her to compromise our chances of convicting the real killer."

"I understand how she feels. It's frustrating having your future in the hands of others. But at least she knows you're all on her side."

"Absolutely."

"Did we ever get ballistics back on the bullets in Kirby's body?"

"Sort of. They were all inconclusive."

All three inconclusive? How's that possible? "What do you mean?"

"Well, the thirty-two-caliber hit bone and shattered. Ingrid collected all the pieces, but none were large enough to match anything. They're trying to reconstruct it in Sutton, but I'd be surprised if they get anything useful. This isn't *CSI*. And, to make things worse, the techs think the barrel of the nine mil was filed. No rifling in the barrel means no striations on the bullets. Too bad we didn't find any shell casings at the crime scene. We could've matched them that way. As it stands right now, we're out of luck."

"You gotta be kidding me."

"Believe me, I wish I was."

A shower and clean clothes later, I leashed Savannah for a stroll to the bookstore, and we headed out. Dense clouds had joined the sun in the sky, portending what was to come. In the distance, a black wall rushed toward us, carrying a storm that would likely be upon us by lunchtime. The temperature had dropped into the low forties with the intensifying breeze, and I shivered in my sweatshirt. We were in for a miserable afternoon. *My favorite.*

We moved from a stroll into a trot and reached Ravenous Readers in record time, me wishing I'd opted to drive instead. Lacey had finished decorating the windows, and the Halloween-themed books on display would attract all our ghoulish readers. They turned out even better than I thought they would after looking at the sketches. Perhaps we should throw a Halloween party this year. I might get to dress up as Elvira after all.

Story Time had just let out, and several children carried copies of today's read: *How to Make Friends with a Ghost*. Lacey had a list of similar choices to read every day up to the holiday itself, and on that day everyone would be in costume, including all of us. The kids loved hearing stories about witches, goblins, and ghouls, and we loved feeding their imaginations. Their parents loved having someone else entertain their youngsters for a little while, so everybody wins.

Nerd Charlie had showed up for work today dressed in his long-sleeve white button-down shirt tucked into khaki pants and covered with a blue-and-white argyle sweater vest. He'd topped off his outfit with shiny brown penny loafers on his feet, heavy black eyeglass frames with no lenses, and a pencil tucked behind his right ear. He must be planning to do some serious research today. I'd have to see what I could do to help keep him and his laptop busy.

Savannah took off in search of Aunt Lacey, the walking treat dispenser, and I headed for the coffee bar for a hot drink to warm me up. My red fingers had stiffened in the cold, and the damp had chilled my bones. I wrapped my hands around my mug and sipped while watching Charlie clean up and restock.

Charlie finished filling the holes in the chocolate chip cookie tray. "Hi, Boss. It's turning into a nasty day, isn't it?"

I took another sip and relished the warmth traveling down my esophagus. "Definitely. Looks like we've got a wicked storm coming."

"Perfect day for people to curl up with a good book."

"Too bad it'll be a book they already own."

He pushed his fake glasses up on his nose. "Maybe, but if they read it today, they'll have to buy one to replace it, right?"

Leave it to Charlie to find the silver lining to every cloud. He and Lacey both. I envied their ability to see the good in all situations. No matter how hard I tried, I always seemed to find the negatives. I didn't let that stop me from doing what I needed to do, though. Most of the time. I gave myself credit for that.

"Have you found anything interesting on the Kirbys?"

I gave him an abbreviated account of everything we'd learned at the job site and in Spartanburg yesterday. Since we'd learned little, it was a quick and easy lecture.

"Sounds like you had a fun day," he said with a wry smile. "I haven't come up with much, either. That black SUV you mentioned belongs to Elliott. He's the only one in the family who drives an SUV. Everyone else loves their Mercedes sedans."

"Like the gold one Simeon had?"

"Different models and different colors, but yeah, like that one."

The black Suburban in the parking lot that Havermayer saw Friday night had to be Elliott's. Since we knew he was there, it only made sense. Unfortunately, it also meant we couldn't prove any other member of the family, besides Kirby himself, was present when Elliott got whacked on the head. The assailant could still be a random stranger, although I didn't believe that for a minute. I'd have to find some other way to prove a Kirby other than Elliott had been involved in Simeon's death.

"Charlie, have you done any checking into Kirby's financial situation? Specifically, his business? I have a hunch there might be something strange going on there."

"What makes you think that?"

"They refused to show us the company's books yesterday. Insisted we get a subpoena. I called Eric since Conway isn't actually law enforcement anymore, and he tried, but the judge won't give him one because there's no proof they're doing anything wrong."

Charlie withdrew the pencil from behind his ear and twirled it around in his fingers. "That stinks. What're you going to do?"

"There's nothing I *can* do."

A slow smile spread across his face like molasses. "Maybe there is."

"What?"

"We can go up to the construction site tonight after everyone leaves and take a look for ourselves. It shouldn't be too difficult to break into a trailer like that."

The keywords there were "break into." As in, breaking the law. I'd done my share of bending it before, but this was something even Eric couldn't get me out of if we got caught. "I don't know, Charlie. We could end up in jail."

"Only if someone sees us. I'll wear my ninja clothes like I did that time I helped you break into the property room at the police station." He offered a few karate moves. "I'll move so fast nobody will ever see me."

Oh, brother! "Let me think about it, okay?"

185

"Okay, but I'm telling you it'll be fine. And you'll get the info you need to see if you're right or not."

Either that, or I'd have plenty of time to think about things while serving my prison sentence.

CHAPTER EIGHTEEN

I spent the rest of the day in my office, alternating between moving the Davenport twins further along in their story and debating whether I wanted to commit a felony tonight. Even though I had no evidence that any members of the Kirby family were up to something suspicious, I couldn't shake the feeling that Marion was embezzling from her father's company. Without proof, or at least a hint of something pointing in that direction, there was nothing anyone could do about it.

It seemed foolish to believe in something despite all the evidence to the contrary. But over the past few years, I'd learned to trust my instincts. Not that they were always right, but, even when wrong, they always led me to where I needed to be to find the truth. After I found myself in a whole bunch of trouble, of course. Still, it was worth it in the end.

So, why did I have so much difficulty making the decision this time? Normally, I would dive into a situation headfirst and let whatever happened happen. This time, I hesitated. Very uncharacteristic for me. What held me back?

Maybe this time, for once, I had something to lose.

I actually felt like I had something worth living for. I had a family who loved me and had finally learned how to show it. I had a boyfriend I loved and who loved me and had no difficulty showing it. My career might grow into a success someday, and the bookstore showed promise. And I had friends and a furry child who needed me.

Did I want to risk throwing all that away for something that, if I stopped and thought about it, had nothing to do with me? Havermayer could take care of herself. The only reason they were still holding her was that Olinski didn't want to seem biased by letting her go. She was one of his detectives but had no alibi, and all the evidence pointed to her. Whoever had framed her had done a terrific job of it, and, so far, nobody had found any proof of her innocence.

I crossed my arms on the desk and rested my head on them, letting my jumbled thoughts roam freely in my mind like unattached atoms. Perhaps, if they collided enough, they'd form something useful. More likely, the process would give me a headache first.

A harsh throat-clearing sound in the doorway made me jerk my head up to find Eric leaning against the doorjamb, arms crossed with a smirk on his face.

"Have a good nap?" he asked.

At the sound of his voice, Savannah leaped out of her bed and charged the door. Eric put his hands out to protect himself from her attack.

"I wasn't sleeping, just thinking," I replied.

Eric took a seat across the desk from me, and Savannah did her best to climb onto his lap. He gently pushed her down and stroked her head. "What were you thinking about?"

Did I dare tell him about Charlie's suggestion that we break into the construction trailer? No. If we got caught, that would make him an accomplice, and I couldn't do that to him.

"Nothing important. I was just trying to figure out what to do with this stupid book of mine." Not a fib exactly, but not the whole truth, either. "What've you been up to?"

He sat back and crossed his arms again. "Mostly getting my butt chewed by Olinski."

"Why, what did you do?"

"Not what I did. What *you* did."

My brain scrambled to remember what I could've done to get Eric in trouble but came up blank. "What did I do?"

"You and your buddy Jeremy Conway pretended to be cops and interrogated Virginia and Marion Kirby."

"We did *not* pretend to be cops. Conway might've told them he was consulting on the case but never claimed to be a police officer."

"You're splitting hairs, babe." He leaned to scratch Savannah's chest in response to her paw swipe. "All they heard was Riddleton Police Department."

"It's not our fault they have selective hearing." I stood and came around to the other chair. "How did Olinski find out anyway?"

"Marion filed an official complaint with him. Said you were harassing them and trying to bully her into showing you the company's books."

Conway *did* get a little pushy when she refused the first time. Threatening her with a subpoena might've been a bit much. I could see how she might feel like he'd bullied her.

"Okay, so what now?"

"You need to stay away from them, Jen. You and Conway both. She said if she finds you up there again, she'll get a restraining order." He reached across the desk and took my hand. "Please don't bother them again. You'll get us both in trouble. If you find something noteworthy, let me know, and I'll look into it, okay? Don't get yourself arrested."

I grinned at him. "Why? You getting tired of bailing me out?"

"No, but in this case I might make an exception. Leave you in there just to teach you a lesson."

"Like that would work. Besides, I've already been in jail, so it wouldn't accomplish anything, anyhow."

"It might make *me* feel better." He smiled and kissed me. "I better get going. I still have to find Simeon Kirby's killer, although I feel like I'm wasting my time at this point. All I have are bits and pieces I can't seem to fit together into a working theory. The only thing I know for sure is Havermayer didn't do it, but I still have to prove it."

I drew him into a hug. "You'll figure it out. I have faith in you."

And I'd keep digging until I found something to help him. Guess I'd made up my mind. Charlie and I would break into that trailer tonight. If there were evidence of a motive for Marion to kill her father, we'd find it. For Eric's sake, if nothing else.

After walking Eric to the door, I turned to Charlie and said, "Have the ninja meet me in the parking lot at ten."

He nodded. "You got it, Boss."

* * *

190

I'd set my alarm for nine, hoping to get a couple hours' rest before the night's adventure, but never managed to fall asleep. Savannah enjoyed her bed nap, though, snoring into my ear for two hours, which might've contributed to my inability to doze off. I hit the button on the clock before it went off and threw the covers back. Time to get ready.

When I flipped on the light, my dog groaned, stretched, and covered her eyes with her paw. "Sorry to disturb you, kid, but I have to get ready to go."

She grumbled a response and stuck her head under the pillow. Sure, she acted like she didn't care now, but when the time came for me to leave she'd be wide awake and ready to go. The disappointed expression on her face would break my heart, but, as usual, I had no choice. No way she could attend this party.

I nuked a cup of coffee, then searched through my closet for an outfit that would match Charlie's. For once, he had the right idea—black clothing to make us invisible in the dark. After throwing black jeans, T-shirt, hoodie sweatshirt, and socks on the bed, I began to dress, covering everything except my face and hands.

In the old movies I used to watch with my stepfather, they used black shoe polish for this purpose. Good thing I had none. It would be a nightmare to wash back off again, and the discoloration impossible to explain tomorrow. I'd have to pull up my hood and take my chances.

Savannah poked her head out to watch, concern filling the brown eyes that tore at my heart. She could make me feel guilty for trying to use the bathroom without her. Not that my privacy lasted for very long. She followed within seconds, whimpering her indignation when I dared to close the door.

The nearer it came to go-time, the more my stomach tightened, twisting itself into a pretzel. Adrenaline surged into my arms and legs. My hands shook, making it almost impossible to tie the laces of my Nikes, and sweat broke out in all the usual places. An overwhelming urge to run invaded my lower extremities as my mind raced with all the possible outcomes, few of them good.

What am I doing?

What had seemed like a great idea only a few hours ago now had me trembling with fear. Since when did I shy away from an opportunity to find a murderer? I'd faced far more dangerous situations before. What was different about this one? I'd been in jail before and came out unscathed, and that would be the worst possible result if we got caught. It's not like any of the Kirbys would kill us for trespassing, right?

Unless one of them really did have something to hide.

Relax, Jen.

Deep breath in, slow breath out.

I had nothing to worry about. We'd break into the construction site trailer, snoop around a little, then get back out again. Maybe find enough evidence to make the risk worthwhile. If Marion murdered her father because he discovered her financial mismanagement, the proof had to be in that building somewhere. And we would find it.

Calmed by my internal pep talk, I donned my black leather jacket over my sweatshirt and took Savannah for a walk. Not the same as getting to go along with me, but the best I could do tonight. I'd try to make it up to her tomorrow, assuming I wasn't incarcerated or dead.

My stomach pretzel flipped, and dread crept into my chest. I'd been in this situation a million times before, but I couldn't shake the feeling something bad would happen this time.

My German shepherd dawdled on her trip around the block as if I might change my mind the longer we were out there. As much as I wanted to oblige, I couldn't pass on the opportunity to follow up on my instincts, which screamed that Marion was embezzling from her father's company, he caught her, and she killed him for it.

Havermayer was counting on me to help prove her innocence. And what about Elliott Kirby? If Havermayer was eliminated as a suspect, he was next on the list. The only reason he hadn't been jailed already was that he'd been knocked unconscious and presumed incapable of disposing of the body and all the physical evidence planted in the detective's vehicle and home. Take her out of the mix, and he became suspect numero uno. Especially since we only had his word that he'd been unconscious and could remember nothing.

I prodded my reluctant little girl up the stairs a few minutes before ten, surprised ninja Charlie hadn't accosted us. He'd be there in a minute, though. He was never late. Funny how I was surrounded by all these people who were never late, and I still couldn't make it anywhere on time. Too bad punctuality wasn't an infectious disease. I wouldn't make people mad all the time.

By the time I threw Savannah her chew stick and reached the bottom of the stairs, my phone screen read 10:01. Late again. I'd get it right one day.

Charlie, dressed in all black as promised, including a black balaclava to cover his face, popped out from behind the steps and whispered, "Boo!"

Tension pushed my heart into my throat. I took a deep breath, then plucked the old "knock, knock" joke out of my memory. "Boo, who?"

"Huh?"

Guess he'd never heard it. Not sure how since he'd definitely completed elementary school. "Never mind. Let's get going."

"You want me to drive?"

Charlie owned a white Ford Focus. Too difficult to hide in the dark. "No, I'm still driving Eric's Jeep. It's black and will camouflage easier."

"Makes sense," he said, climbing into the passenger side after I unlocked the door.

I slid behind the wheel and wiped my sweaty palms on my jeans. The drive to the resort took about a half hour, so that's how long I had to get my nerves under control. The biggest obstacle we had to worry about was the people staying at the resort. Any of them could be wandering around the grounds when we arrived. Fingers crossed, they were all tucked into their rooms for the night.

The Wrangler's engine turned right over, and I backed out of the parking space. Pointing the grille toward the lake, I said, "We need a good excuse for being out there in case someone sees us. Got any ideas?"

"Hmmm. Can't we just say we're guests at the resort?"

"Maybe, but dressed like this? Besides, I don't know how many rooms they're actually using. If it's only a few, everybody probably knows everyone else."

Charlie leaned across and turned on the radio. A mattress commercial filled the cabin. "I don't know. I think we'll be okay. Just because they recognize each other from the dining room or whatever doesn't mean they know if all the rooms are occupied. If a guest spots us, we can tell them we just checked in. By the time they figure out it's not true, we'll be long gone."

He made sense, but I still had my doubts. Probably a mixture of nerves and my overactive imagination. A bad combination in the best of situations. "All right, but we still need a cover story for why we're at the resort."

"We could always tell them we're on our honeymoon." He giggled and poked my leg.

Uh-uh. I wouldn't let that idea plant itself in his brain. He'd finally given up on any hope of a romantic relationship with me, and I wanted to keep it that way. "I got a better idea. How about brother and sister, and we're thinking about moving to the area."

"Together? That sounds a little creepy to me."

No creepier than us being married. "Fine. How about we're taking one last vacation as a family before we get married to other people? And our parents will be joining us later."

"That might work. What's the story with our betrothed?"

I chuckled. "I don't think we need to go that far. If we run into a Nosy Nellie, I'll fake a bathroom emergency or a heart attack or something, and we'll get out of there."

"You're a little young for a heart attack."

"Not with you for a brother."

We both laughed, and my tension eased. For the first time since I'd given up on my nap, I could breathe easily.

My grip on the steering wheel relaxed, and the dread that had plagued me since I'd decided to participate in this excursion faded. We could do this, and everything would be okay.

Maybe.

I stopped at the end of the gravel drive leading to the resort.

"Why are we stopping?" Charlie asked.

"We need to park someplace and walk up to the trailer so nobody will see the car, and I can't remember if there's any place to pull off along this road."

He blew air out between pursed lips. "I've never been here. Do you want me to get out and walk? I can come back and let you know if I find a place."

Glancing up at the overcast sky left over from this afternoon's storm, I said, "I'm not crazy about you wandering around by yourself in the dark. How about we both go?"

"Is it safe to leave the car on the side of the road like this? Eric'll kill you if you wreck his Wrangler. He loves this car."

"He couldn't love it too much, or he wouldn't have let *me* borrow it." I grinned to ease the tension. "I think it'll be fine. We haven't seen another vehicle in over twenty minutes."

We crunched down the gravel drive, slick from the afternoon rain, straining to see in the dark. Luckily, we didn't have far to go before we reached a cutout in the trees, just big enough to hide the Jeep.

I grabbed Charlie's arm. "You wait here so I don't miss it. I'll go get the car."

He nodded, and I trotted the hundred yards or so back to the road to collect the Jeep.

196

CHAPTER NINETEEN

I backed into the cutout, careful to avoid branch scratches on Eric's baby. This operation would be challenging enough without having to worry about what my boyfriend would say when he saw his car in the morning. I cut the engine and climbed out, closing the door quietly. So far, we'd noticed no signs of anyone around, but we were still a good ways away from the resort.

Joining Charlie on the gravel drive, I whispered, "I think we should stick to the woods. It'll be quieter than crunching on these rocks, and we can't be seen from the road in the dark."

He nodded, and we traveled as deep into the trees as we could without losing sight of the driveway. Soggy pine needles squished beneath our feet in the silence broken only by the occasional cricket's chirp. We worked our way tree by tree to the opening containing the construction trailer. Still no sign that any of the resort guests were roaming.

We stopped at the edge of the dirt circle and surveyed the area. A few rooms in the resort and the lobby had lights on, but everything else was dark, reducing the likelihood that the residents of the darkened rooms were outside in the chilly, damp air. I certainly wouldn't be out if I didn't have to be. I'd much rather be home in my warm, cozy apartment, curled up on the couch with my dog and a good book. In that order.

No vehicles sat in front of the trailer, and I whispered to Charlie, "It looks clear to me. What do you think?"

"I think we're good to go."

"Agreed. Let's work our way around to the back and get in that way so we won't be as exposed. The back door lock should be the same as the front, so if we can get in one, we can get in the other."

We edged our way through the wooded side until the back door came into view. No steps leading to the door, the bottom of which sat four feet off the ground. Reaching the doorknob to break in would be a challenge. At five-foot-six, the knob was too high for me, and Charlie wasn't much taller, if at all.

I gestured toward the door. "I didn't expect there to be no steps on this side. Should we try going around front?"

He shook his head. "Too risky. You think you can hold me up long enough for me to get the door open? I think we can climb in from there."

Charlie had at least thirty pounds on me. "It might be easier if you held me up."

He retrieved an object from his back pocket. It resembled a gun, but it had a long spike with a flat end sticking out the front instead of a barrel. "Have you ever used one of these before?"

"No, what is it?"

"It's a lock-pick gun. It'll get us in in about thirty seconds. Can you hold me up for that long? I'll work as fast as I can."

Why on Earth would Charlie have a lock-pick gun? No telling, knowing him. And we didn't have time for one of his long-winded explanations. "I can try."

We did a last check of the area, then scurried to the safety of the trailer. I bent at the waist and interlocked my fingers to create a pocket for Charlie's foot. "All right, let's give it a try."

He rested his boot in my hands, and I set myself against his weight. He stepped up, grabbed the doorknob with his left hand, and inserted the spike into the lock with his right. My arms vibrated, and my back fought against the unnatural position. I blinked away the sweat dripping into my eyes, dropped my chin to my chest, and gritted my teeth.

About the time I realized I couldn't hold him up much longer, Charlie opened the door and said, "We're in."

He dropped to the ground, and I stood with my hands on my knees, panting as if I'd just run a marathon. That was the first time since high school I'd tried to lift any kind of weight. And hopefully, it would be the last.

When I could speak, I said, "I think I'll skip the weight-training regimen from now on. I'm no weight lifter. I'll stick to running."

Charlie grinned, barely visible behind his three-holed balaclava. "From what I hear, you're no runner, either."

"Shut up and give me a boost."

I rested my hands on the floor inside the door. The dark interior limited my vision to about a foot ahead before everything else disappeared into the black. If my memory held, Stephanie's desk sat to my left and the other one across the room to the right. The leg of the desk on the left was visible and within reach.

With a little help from Charlie, I could grab it and pull myself up.

"You ready?" he asked.

"Yes. When you lift me, I'll grab the desk leg, and you can let go."

He moved behind me and wrapped his arms around my thighs, resting his cheek against my butt.

I glanced back over my shoulder. "Don't get too comfortable down there."

His chuckle evolved into a grunt when he straightened his legs, hoisting me into the office. I reached for the desk, gripped the leg, and pulled. It slid straight back toward the doorway. The momentum carried me backward, and Charlie lost his balance. He landed on his back, and the air rushed out of his lungs. I thumped on top of him, pain shooting through my shoulder when it hit the ground. I bit my lip to keep from crying out.

Safe to assume that wasn't the desk leg.

I lay there for a minute. My ribs hurt, but everything except my shoulder seemed intact. My barista made a terrific crash mat.

Charlie eased his hand out from under me and tapped me on the arm. "Excuse me. I'd like to get up now."

"Yeah, sorry." I groaned and rolled over onto the dirt. "Are you okay?"

He sat up and massaged the back of his neck. "I think so. What happened?"

"I grabbed the chair, not the desk. Hard to tell the difference in the dark."

"We'll have to get you some glasses." He clambered to his feet and brushed his hands together to clear the dust. "Shall we try again?"

I stood and shuffled back to the doorway. "Might as well. It's the only way in."

"We could always go around the front where the steps are."

"Somebody might see us."

He bent at the waist and formed a pocket with his hands the way I'd done earlier.

Probably should've done it this way in the first place. I stuck one Nike in and bent my other knee. "Ready whenever you are."

"Here we go. On three." He shifted his feet for better balance. "One . . . two . . . three!"

He straightened his knees and heaved me into the doorway, where I lay half in and half out, my legs dangling. The edge of the floor cut into my belly, and I struggled to breathe. I dug my forearms into the thin carpet and heaved myself forward until I could prop my knee on the edge. A minute later, I was in.

Charlie boosted himself up, and I grabbed his arms to pull him the rest of the way. We lay on the floor—he on his belly, I on my back—and regrouped. I started to laugh.

"What's so funny?" he asked.

"Us, thinking we're some kind of super spies or something. Stuff like this always looks so easy in the movies."

"Too bad we don't live in the movies. The actors have stunt doubles. Besides, I'm not a spy. I'm a ninja!"

I rolled to my knees and stood. "That's right. Sorry, I forgot."

He reached up a hand for me to grab and scrambled to his feet. "No problem. Don't let it happen again."

"You got it." I retrieved my phone from my back

pocket and switched on the flashlight, careful to keep the beam away from the windows. "You want to check the computer while I go through the desks?"

Charlie did the same with his phone. "What exactly are we looking for?"

"Proof that Marion Kirby Jenkins is embezzling from her father's business. If we find that, we're one step closer to proving she murdered him."

"I'll see what I can do. Hopefully, the files aren't encrypted. They'll take a lot longer to get into. More time than we want to spend here—that's for sure." He started typing on the keyboard, then sneezed three times.

"Bless you. You all right?"

He sniffed. "Yeah, it's just really dusty over here."

"Same here. I guess it's the cleaning staff's year off." While he worked on breaking the password, I started going through Stephanie's desk drawers. I'd finished with the top center drawer when headlights swept across the front windows. They disappeared, and a car door slammed.

"Crap, Charlie, somebody's here!" I glanced toward the back door. I could leap out and roll under the building, but no way Charlie could reach it in time. I couldn't leave him to take the heat by himself. "Hide!"

He dove under the desk. "You get out while you can. I'll catch up with you later."

"I'm not leaving you here."

Footsteps sounded on the steps by the front door. Besides, it was too late for me now too.

I squeezed under the desk with my knees against my chest and tugged the chair in as far as I could. A key rattled into the doorknob, and the door creaked open. I held my breath.

Heavy steps lumbered into the room, and the

overhead lights blinded me. Keys clattered onto the desk, and a familiar woman's voice said, "Well, what do you want me to do about it?"

Marion. Who was she talking to?

Silence, then: "I'm sorry, Sim. I have no idea where your whatchamacallit is."

Whatchamacallit? That sounded interesting. And irrelevant to us.

More silence. "Do what you have to do. I have to go."

Her phone joined the keys on the desk, and I froze, waiting for what she did next and wondering how Charlie was holding up. He didn't have the experience with situations like this that I did, and *I* struggled not to freak out. I could only imagine what he was going through.

I slowly shifted my position so I could peek around the desk. Marion gave no sign she heard me moving, so I risked poking my head out a bit more. She squatted in the corner, but her body blocked her actions. What had I seen in that corner yesterday? No idea. I'd been too busy watching the interactions between Virginia, Marion, and Stephanie to pay attention to my surroundings. No wonder Olinski thought me an amateur.

Finally, Marion stood, and I could see a small safe she'd opened. How did I miss that? In her arms, she held a green ledger book, which she carried to the other desk. Was that where the scrap I'd found in Havermayer's floor came from? I'd have to get a look at the pages to know for sure. If one of them was missing a corner, we might have our killer.

As she approached the desk, I hoped she planned to work standing up. If she tried to sit in the chair, she'd find Charlie. I willed her to stand in my mind.

Please don't sit. Please don't sit.

It didn't work.

When she pulled out the chair, Charlie scrambled out from under the desk. As he tried to squeeze past her, Marion grabbed the collar of his jacket, and his feet went out from under him, flipping him backward to the other side of the desk. Marion lost her balance and landed on the floor beside him.

I jumped out to help him.

She crawled to the safe and removed a gun, waving it back and forth between us. "Don't move. I'm calling the cops."

With my hands up, I said, "Don't do anything foolish, Marion. We'll just leave. No harm done."

"The hell you will. Move around to the front of the desk and hand me that phone."

Slowly, I did as she asked. Charlie started to move toward her, and I shook my head. No way I'd risk him being injured or killed. I'd rather go to jail.

Rising, Marion waved Charlie over to stand by me, and she watched us while talking to the 911 operator. Her voice never cracked; she showed no sign of emotion. The more she spoke, the more I could see in her eyes a cold, calculating killer. A shiver ran down my spine.

I asked Charlie if he was all right, and he nodded, his eyes imploring me to let him use his imaginary ninja skills. I shook my head again. Just because he'd dressed like a ninja didn't mean he *was* one. No convincing him of that, though. Better to take our chances with the police. Safer, anyway.

The moment the first set of tires crunched on the gravel outside the trailer, Marion put the gun back into the safe and closed the door. No need for us to try to run;

the cops were already here. Eric showed up about the same time the county sheriff's deputy did. My shoulders relaxed at the sight of him, even though we were in the deputy's jurisdiction. He could talk them out of taking us in. Maybe.

Eric met my gaze, shock followed by disappointment flitting across his face. I'd done it again. How long before he tired of me always putting him in difficult situations?

He replaced his disappointment with a neutral mask and approached the Sutton County Sheriff's Deputy who'd also responded to the call. After chatting with the deputy for a few minutes, Eric drew me to the side. "Are you all right? What are you doing here?"

"I'm fine. We came to find the evidence you need for the judge to grant you a subpoena."

Anger turned his face an overripe apple color. "Good grief, Jen! You have to stop doing these things. You're going to get yourself killed."

I stared at the cracked leather tops of my Nikes. "I'm sorry. I was only trying to help."

"I don't need your help. Not like this. Now I'm going to have to take you in."

"You, not the deputy?"

He glanced at the deputy, who was talking to Marion. "I convinced him to give me jurisdiction since this trailer is part of an active investigation of ours."

At that point, Marion said, "I want them arrested right now! I don't care whose jurisdiction it is, as long as they go to jail where they belong!"

The deputy looked at Eric and shrugged. "You need me for anything else?"

Eric shook his head. "No, I got it from here. Thanks for your help."

The deputy waved and left.

Marion stepped into Eric's personal space. "So, are you going to arrest them?"

Eric clenched his jaw, then let out a long breath. "I think we can work this out civilly, don't you? After all, they haven't stolen or damaged anything. What would be gained by arresting them?"

Eric's words ricocheted through my head. If he arrested us, the trailer would become a crime scene, and he could search it. "Eric, wait. I think you should arrest us. Marion's right. We committed a crime, and we should be punished for it."

He pulled me to the side again, eyes throwing flames in my direction. "What are you doing? You want to be arrested?"

"If you arrest us, you can search the trailer." I jutted my chin toward the other desk. "That ledger has incriminating evidence in it. I know it!"

"That's a stretch, Jen. You're in enough trouble already, don't you think?"

Ignoring Charlie's puzzled glance, I said loud enough for everyone to hear, "I confess to breaking into this trailer with the intention of stealing that ledger book." I whispered to Eric, knowing I might've just done permanent damage to our relationship. But this was too important. I could only hope he'd understand in the end. "There, that makes it evidence."

Marion's eyes widened. "Wait! I think you're right. We can work this out. I'd like to drop the charges."

I walked over to the desk and opened the ledger full of accounting entries. "Look at this," I said to Eric. "She told us yesterday she did the company books on the computer. This looks like a second set of books. Proof she's embezzling from the company."

Eric looked at Marion. "Are you sure you want to drop the charges?"

"Yes, absolutely. No harm was done, and I think you should let them go with a warning."

"All right, if you're sure."

She nodded emphatically. "I'm sure."

Eric retrieved his handcuffs from the case clipped to the back of his belt. "In that case, Marion Kirby Jenkins, I'm detaining you for questioning."

Marion stepped back and snatched her hands away from him. "Questioning about what?"

"Suspicion of embezzlement and murder."

I flipped through the pages until I found the one with the missing corner left at Havermayer's house. Satisfied, I closed the cover and handed the ledger to Eric.

CHAPTER TWENTY

The tots filed out of the store clutching their copies of *Me and My Dragon: Scared of Halloween* to their chests. Their parents smiled and thanked me, leading the little ones out the door. Another successful Story Time in the books. Lacey had worked wonders with the program. One more thing for me to be grateful to her for.

I closed the door and stepped into my book display table behind me, knocking it back into the cardboard cutout standing beside it. I couldn't wait until *Twin Terror* came out, and Lacey took the display down. *But if the book never came out, it couldn't fail*. My stomach jumped, and I swallowed hard. Nope. I refused to think like that. The book would soar as high the first one.

Lacey came up as I retrieved the cutout. "Admiring yourself again?"

"Yeah, 'cause that's what I do."

She straightened the books on the table while I set the stand back into place. I considered turning it around to face the wall but knew Lacey would only fix it as soon as I left her sight.

"I heard you and Charlie had an exciting night last night."

"Bad news travels fast. How'd you hear already?"

"How do you think?"

I rolled my eyes. "Angus. How did he find out?"

"Who knows? Maybe somebody from the department stopped in for coffee this morning on the way to the station."

"You know, that's what I used to hate about this town. I couldn't sneeze without somebody starting the rumor I had a cold."

"And now?"

After a moment's thought, I said, "Now, I've realized the good outweighs the bad. I'm still not crazy about being fodder for the rumor mill, but I know people will be there for me when I need them. Sometimes, they even know I need them before I do, courtesy of you know who. It's a fair trade-off."

Lacey smiled. "I'm glad to hear it. I'd hate for you to turn tail and run like you did before."

"Turn tail and run? I went to college, for Pete's sake. Gimme a break!" I said, a little irritated even though I knew she was only teasing. Apparently she'd poked a sore spot of mine. I'd have to work on that.

Cowboy Charlie moseyed up to us with thumbs hooked in his gun belt, empty holster slapping his thigh. He tipped his ten-gallon hat back on his head and pretended to spit. "Howdy, ma'am. When did you get here?"

"A few minutes ago. You were busy cleaning up after Story Time."

He glanced down at my side. "Where's Savannah?"

Silly question. We all turned to find her in the kids' section, licking cookie crumbs off the carpet. I pointed toward her. "Where else?"

"You really should feed that dog once in a while," he said with a grin. "She can't live on cookie crumbs alone, you know."

"Don't forget, I give her treats, too!" Lacey said.

I dropped a hand on Charlie's shoulder. "See? She's fine."

He shook his head, eyes pointing toward the ceiling. "Did you tell Lacey how I used my ninja skills last night?"

"I don't remember that. I *do* remember you hiding under the desk, though."

"Only because you made me!"

"Of course! I didn't want you to get arrested or worse. Sorry if I cramped your style, but you're standing here unscathed, so I can live with it."

"What exactly did you do last night?" Lacey asked.

Charlie began an elaborate, embellishment-filled story full of heroes—us—and villains—them. I went for some coffee so I wouldn't steal his thunder by interrupting with the truth. I kind of liked his version better, anyway. It was certainly more exciting. Maybe Charlie should be the writer instead of me. He'd handle the stress better, without a doubt.

I mentally returned to the coffee klatch in time to hear Charlie say, "And Jen handed Eric the book, and he hauled Marion off in handcuffs. Wasn't that awesome?"

Lacey chuckled at Charlie's enthusiasm. "Sounds like it." She turned to me. "You're lucky you didn't get hurt. Why would you take a chance like that?"

I shrugged. "I know I should be more careful, but I didn't think I had a choice. I knew Marion was stealing from her father, but Eric couldn't get the evidence he needed legally, so I had to help him."

"Well, one of these days, you're going to get yourself into a pickle you can't think your way out of. Then what're you going to do?"

She was right, of course. I turned toward the kids' section, pretending to look for Savannah since I had no reply.

"That's all right," Lacey continued, trying to lighten the mood. "Just make sure your share of the bookstore comes to me in your will."

My will? I didn't have one. Another one of those grown-up things I'd given no thought to. Guess I should, though. As things stood my half would go to my mother if something happened to me. That wasn't fair to Lacey and Ben. I put it on my mental to-do list. The one I immediately forgot about as soon as I added anything to it.

"You got it, Boss!" I said, stealing a line from Charlie. He fired a mock glare at me.

I wandered over to our decorated windows. "Hey, Lacey, are we getting any response to the decorations?"

She joined me. "Some. Not as much as I'd like, though. Maybe I should've added more zombies and fewer witches. Try to get the younger crowd."

"I think it's fine the way it is. In fact, it's more than fine. Everything looks fantastic. It might be drawing people in who don't mention it. You never know."

"Possibly. I definitely don't think it's a contest winner, though. We need another trophy. The one we won for Christmas the year before last is getting lonely."

Good thing Lacey didn't know we hadn't won that one, either. Veronica had kept her word and not told anyone we only came in first because the winner dropped out of the competition. And I wouldn't tell Lacey now.

"Don't worry too much about it. The competition is supposed to be about community togetherness, not a cheap plastic award."

She sighed. "I know, but my competitive side takes over now and again. Guess I'll just have to outrun Eric on Saturday to make up for it."

"Gee, thanks. Put him in a bad mood for *me*, huh?" I crossed my arms in faux irritation. "And you claim to be my friend."

"Don't worry—you'll get over it." She winked and went to the stockroom.

I grabbed the feather duster from behind the cash register counter and went to work on the bookcases, wondering how we might get Lacey another win. It didn't seem important to me, one way or the other. I took it all in fun. But if it mattered to Lacey, it mattered.

I might need to chat with Veronica about the situation. Even though the town council judged the contest, not the mayor, she probably knew what they were looking for and might share it with me. It wouldn't be cheating since I wasn't asking her to encourage them to vote for us. Only gathering information. I'd call her later.

The bells over the front door jingled, and Eric came in looking about as tired as I'd ever seen him. He must not've slept much, if at all. Had his interview with Marion lasted all night? I went to the coffee bar and poured him a large cup. With luck, it would help smooth things over between us.

He came up behind me and rested his chin on my shoulder. "Hi, babe. I hope that's for me. I sure could use it."

I handed him the cup, then wrapped my arms around his waist with my head on his chest, relieved that he'd

212

recovered from being angry with me. "Long night? I missed you."

"I missed you, too."

"How'd it go?" I took his hand and led him to a table. "Did Marion give you anything helpful, or did she lawyer up?"

"Both." Running a hand over his orange buzz cut, he sipped his coffee. "She confessed to the embezzlement but insisted she had nothing to do with her father's death."

"Do you believe her?"

He sighed and rocked his chair back. "I think so, yes. Her husband verifies she stayed home with him Friday night, and there's nothing else pointing in her direction."

My eyebrows dropped to my nose. "What about her motive?"

"What motive? She says her father never knew about her stealing, and we can't prove otherwise. She insists she planned to pay it all back before he ever found out. He was a development guy. He never looked at the books. Too bad his daughter wasn't as trustworthy as he thought."

Either Marion was very convincing, or Eric was tired enough to want to believe. She had to be the killer. She had motive, access to the gun—assuming the weapon found in the safe was the murder weapon—and the opportunity. Home with her husband was a flimsy alibi no jury would believe. The trial would be the proverbial slam dunk.

However, Eric had excellent instincts as a rule and had learned to trust them. And I needed to trust him. If he believed in Marion's innocence, I should direct my attention elsewhere. For now. "Did Marion have anything to say about the corner of the ledger sheet we found in Havermayer's house?"

"I asked, but she didn't know anything about it. Said she's never been in Havermayer's house. Didn't even know where she lived."

"So, where does this leave Havermayer?" I asked him.

"Olinski's releasing her this afternoon. We've already held her way too long without charging her, so she'll be on administrative leave until we get this all sorted."

"Are you worried about her skipping town?"

He shook his head. "She's determined to clear her name. No way she's going anywhere. It's killing her not to be able to help with the investigation."

"I know the feeling."

"I figure you two have a lot in common right about now. Maybe even enough to base a friendship on."

When you-know-what freezes over. But I had to try for his sake. Especially since I'd upset him last night. "You think?"

"Maybe. It depends on what you each decide to do now. What are your plans?"

"As far as Havermayer is concerned? Take baby steps, I guess. You think she'd like a ride home when she gets out?"

The skin crinkled beside his eyes. "She might. Want me to call you when she's being processed?"

Was I ready to end the feud between us? Maybe not, but for Eric's sanity, I should at least make an effort. "Yes, that would be nice."

He leaned over the table and kissed me. "I'm glad."

"You're just happy you might not be stuck in the middle anymore. You know this isn't going to be an easy

214

process, right? Some habits are hard to break. Especially when someone is as stubborn as your partner."

"You're right. I only know one other person as stubborn as my partner."

Suspecting I already knew the answer, I asked, "And who might that be?"

"You, silly."

I stuck my tongue out at him, then retrieved his empty cup and refilled it along with mine. When I set his in front of him, I said, "You need a nap, not more coffee, but I know you won't take one, so here you go."

"I'd rest if I could, but if Marion isn't guilty, the killer's still out there."

"I know. Who's your prime suspect now?"

He blew the steam off his cup and sipped. "We're back to Elliott Kirby. We know he was there, we know he touched his father's body after he was shot, and his blood was on the thirty-two caliber, so he fired at least one of the shots."

"I don't know, Eric. Did you find gunshot residue on his hands?"

"That's one of the things that troubles me. We found it on his palms but not on the tops of his hands or his sleeves. Like he touched the gun after it had been fired, but if he's the one who fired the shot, there should've been blowback on the tops of his hands and his arms, and there wasn't any."

"What's your explanation?"

"Don't have one."

I crossed my arms. "Have you considered the possibility he didn't do it?"

Eric slapped the table in frustration. "Then who did? Who else is there?"

"What about his brother?"

"We can't find anything connecting him to the crime. Not one shred of evidence. No indication of a motive other than his inheritance. There just isn't anything there!"

"Well . . ." I reached over and took his hands. "That brings us back to Marion, doesn't it?"

"Or his wife, but we have nothing on her either. Money can't be a motive for her because of the way Kirby's will is structured. She gets the same share as the kids, so she actually ends up in worse financial condition than she was before her husband died unless he has insurance and she's the sole beneficiary. We haven't found that policy yet, so what else is there?"

"He cheated on her. Maybe she'd finally had enough."

Eric stood and stretched his arms overhead. "No proof of that and no proof she knew about it, even if he was cheating." He drew me in for a hug. "And no, your hunches don't count."

I opened my mouth to reply, and he put his forefinger over my lips. He leaned down to kiss me. His phone rang, and he groaned.

He retrieved the cell from his pocket and swiped the screen. "O'Malley."

After a minute of listening, he met my gaze. "Yup. Be right there."

"What's going on?" I asked when he disconnected.

"It looks like you were right." He massaged the nape of his neck. "Elliott Kirby's body was just found in the park, in the same spot we think his father died."

216

CHAPTER TWENTY-ONE

I leaned on the brick pillar beside the Riddleton Police Department steps, waiting for Detective Havermayer to come out. I doubted she expected me to be here unless Eric told her I intended to offer her a ride home. Since he was likely to still be at the park, processing Elliott Kirby's crime scene, I'd catch her off guard, if at all. She might've already slipped out the back door, for all I knew.

The overcast sky had me shivering in the sweatshirt that had been more than adequate before the clouds cloaked the sun, and I questioned my decision to extend this hand of friendship to someone who'd been my mortal enemy only a few days ago. But Eric wanted us to be friends, or, at a minimum, friendly. It would make his life much easier if Havermayer and I got along, at least a little. Being trapped between the two of us for over a year had made a stressful job even worse for him. I needed to do my part.

I would do whatever it took to keep this relationship alive. An odd sensation for me. Usually, I took off like a jackrabbit at the first sign of trouble. Not this time. No guarantee Eric would be my forever love, but for once

I wasn't actively trying to sabotage things. My mother would be proud.

I'd made up my mind to give up when the door opened, and Havermayer stepped out, carrying her little suitcase and looking like she'd just spent a month in the backwoods of West Virginia with no supplies. Hollowed cheeks dominated a sallow face, and dark purple circles accentuated her eyes. Sandy blond hair stuck out around her head despite obvious efforts to tamp it down. And worst of all, her clothes had wrinkles all over, as if she'd slept in them, which she probably had. That alone had to be killing her.

She narrowed her eyes at me. "What are you doing here?"

I gestured toward Eric's Jeep parked at the curb. "Your chariot awaits, madam."

Lowered eyebrows of confusion were her only reply.

"I thought you might want a ride home. You've had a rough week."

"It's only two blocks, Jen. I can handle it."

Despite Eric's hopes, little had changed. Havermayer would continue to refuse my help if she were neck-deep in quicksand and I had the only stick within a hundred miles. "Suit yourself. I thought we might talk a little, that's all. Just because they let you out doesn't mean they've cleared you."

"Why do you care?"

"Simple. Eric cares about you, and I care about Eric."

More confusion as if she'd never heard of that concept before. "So, you're telling me you're willing to help me because your boyfriend wants you to?"

"Pretty much."

"Why does *he* care?"

"He respects you. You're the best detective in the department, and he wants to earn that title someday. You can only be the best if you learn from the best, right?"

She glanced up at the solid gray sky, then back at me. "Fine. You can drive me home."

I bit my tongue to distract my mouth from the sarcastic reply soaring into it. "Great!"

Havermayer squeezed into the passenger seat, holding the case with all her belongings in her lap. She stared out the windshield, clenching and unclenching her jaw.

As I buckled up in the driver's seat, I asked, "Are you okay? Do you need to stop for anything?"

"I'm all right." She hesitated. "Thanks."

Progress. Hopefully, she'd chill out a little more by the time we arrived at her house. I'd hit a dead end on her case, and she might have some ideas on where I could go next. Of course, that would mean admitting I might be the amateur she'd always accused me of being. And swallowing my pride.

I merged into Main Street traffic, crossed Pine, and drove a block to make the left on Oak. One more block and I rolled to a stop at her tiny dwelling.

"Thanks for the ride." She bolted from the Wrangler before the engine stopped.

Poking my head over the roof, I said, "Wait a minute."

She stopped and turned. "What?"

"I thought we could talk about your case."

"What about it?"

I closed the car door and walked toward her. "Well, with Elliott Kirby's death, we've basically run out of suspects other than you. Maybe we can brainstorm."

Her eyes widened. "He's dead? When did that happen?"

"Last night or early this morning. I don't know exactly. A jogger found him in the park. They didn't tell you?"

"No. Last I heard, he'd regained his memory and was coming in this morning for another interview. I had no idea he was dead."

She set down her suitcase and fished her keys from her pocket. "Come on in. I'll make some coffee."

I followed her into the kitchen, and she opened a door and slid the case into what I could only assume was the laundry room.

"Hey, do you mind if I take a quick shower first?" she asked.

Surprised at her willingness to leave me unattended in her home, I replied, "Not at all. Take your time. I'll start the coffee." Maybe she really *had* softened toward me.

I understood her need to wash, though. It wasn't dirt she was concerned with; more like she needed to send the whole experience down the drain. I'd only spent one night in jail, and the first thing I did when I got home was take a long hot bath. I couldn't imagine how dirty she felt after almost a week. Inside and out. Taking care of the outside was easy. The inside would take a while. I hoped she had someone to talk to.

Havermayer had never spoken of friends or family. Not even to Eric. I had to wonder if she had any. With her bristly personality and apparent inability to let anyone in, let alone reveal her innermost secrets, it wouldn't surprise me if she didn't. Given our shared experience, I'd offer her the opportunity to discuss what she went

220

through. Doubted she'd take advantage of it, though. But she might. What if I ended up being her only friend?

I'll have to kill Eric.

The coffeemaker sat on the counter beside the sink. I searched the cupboards, finally finding the coffee and filters in separate cabinets on the other side of the room. And people said *I* was disorganized. At least I kept my coffee supplies where they were used. Perhaps she let down at home because she felt she had to be perfect everywhere else. Or perhaps I'd spent too much time with my shrink, Dr. Margolis.

The shower sang backup to the coffeemaker's gurgling lead, and I considered taking a peek into the rooms Eric barred me from when we were here gathering clothing for Havermayer. I shook the idea out of my head. She'd trusted me in her home, and I'd respect that, no matter how much I wanted to search for clues missed by the crime scene techs.

I had good reason to wonder if there wasn't something left to find, though. I *did* locate that scrap of ledger paper they'd overlooked. Without that, we might never have learned Marion was embezzling from her father's company. Still, I'd wait for her to get out of the shower and ask her about it then. She'd probably turn me down, but maybe it would put the idea in her head, and she'd look for herself.

The water shut off, taking away the option of exploring the rest of the house. I found the sugar bowl in yet another cabinet and some vanilla creamer in the refrigerator and set them on the table. By the time a barefoot Havermayer made it into the kitchen, wearing jeans and a Riddleton Police Department T-shirt and toweling her hair dry, the coffee was ready to drink.

I first met her a year and a half ago, and she finally seemed like a regular person. Not a superstar detective, not even a cop. An average human with faults and doubts and insecurities just like the rest of us. I felt my body relax, though I'd never realized I was tense. An unconscious reaction to the Detective Havermayer I'd grown accustomed to dealing with. I had to come up with a new game plan for the person I faced now.

Havermayer draped the wet towel across the back of the chair and settled into a seat across from me. She fiddled with the fringes of the maroon placemat on the table while she studied her coffee—black, no sugar, like Eric. Guess she'd become used to the lack of supplies in the break room, too. Although, why would she have creamer in her refrigerator if she drank her coffee black? Maybe she had other friends after all.

She took a sip, grimaced, and put the cup down.

Uh-oh. I made lousy coffee. "Sorry, I didn't know how strong you liked it, so I just made it the way I drink it."

She said, "No, it's not you or the coffee. I think I'm just in the mood for something stronger." She rose and took two strides to the cabinet over the coffeemaker beside the sink. Reaching onto the back of the top shelf, she retrieved a bottle of Jameson Irish Whiskey and wiped the dust off it.

Show-off. "You trying to tell me I'm short? I'd have had to climb up on the counter to get that bottle."

Havermayer laughed. Another first for me. I couldn't remember ever having heard her laugh before. "I never said that, but since you brought it up . . ." She shrugged.

She returned to the table, took a large swallow of

coffee, and made up the difference in the cup with whiskey, then offered me the bottle. "You want some?"

Drinking hard liquor had never been my thing. Wine got me into enough trouble by itself. I didn't need anything stronger to make a fool of myself. But it felt like Havermayer had offered me an olive branch. An opportunity for a glimpse into her inner self, even if only a small crack in the starched and pressed armor.

I accepted the bottle and topped off my cup, the alcohol smell curling my nose hairs. A small sip burned my throat. I needed to take it slow since I'd eaten little today. The booze would hit me like a tractor-trailer with failing brakes barreling down a mountain, and I'd be in no condition to walk or drive by the time I finished this cup of coffee. I'd have to call Eric to take me home tonight.

Havermayer emptied her cup and replaced the coffee with a couple of fingers of straight whiskey. I'd better talk to her now while she remained coherent. "Have you learned anything new about your case since we spoke last?"

She held her drink near her mouth with both hands. "Look, Jen, I appreciate what you're trying to do for me, but you don't seem to be getting anywhere, so maybe you should just let it go. I'm out now, and I can take it from here."

Here we go. Some things would never change. "They're letting you work on a case you've been a suspect in? That's a surprise. Especially since Eric told me you're on administrative leave."

Her eyelids narrowed. "Eric talks too much."

"Maybe. Or maybe he realizes you need all the help you can get right now."

"That's ridiculous." A large swallow of whiskey went down. "They've got the daughter on embezzlement. It's only a matter of time before she admits to the murder, too."

I took another sip. This time, my stomach burned, too. "Could be, but I doubt it. I don't think she killed her father or even knows for sure who did."

"Based on what?"

"Eric's gut."

She cackled and tipped more whiskey into her mouth.

Now *I* needed a drink. I swallowed a fair amount and splashed a refill into my cup. "I thought we got this all straightened out when I visited you in jail. What changed?"

"I came to my senses."

"Doesn't sound like it to me." Perhaps more alcohol would help loosen her up. I needed to know what she knew. I grabbed the bottle and added a dollop to each cup.

Time to try another tack. "Did they tell you I found a scrap of paper wedged in your floor the crime scene techs missed?"

"Yeah, Eric mentioned it." Her upper lip curled into a sneer. "I guess now you're going to tell me that's how you caught Marion Jenkins?"

"I think you know the answer to that." I took a swallow of more whiskey than coffee, and my nose crinkled. "Eric wouldn't let me search the rest of the house while I was here. You think maybe we should? Who knows what else they might've missed."

She shook her head. "I'll look around tomorrow, but I doubt I'll find anything."

"That's what Eric said, and then I did."

"Dumb luck."

"Sometimes it's better to be lucky than good."

"I'm both."

She drained her cup and reached for the bottle. She had to be feeling the effects of the alcohol by now, but she didn't seem fazed by it. I, on the other hand, fought the nausea generated by the room swirling around me. Nope, not driving home tonight. In fact, I was almost happy she refused to let me search. I wasn't sure I could stay upright long enough.

After refilling her cup, she said, "I gotta say, though, those Kirby kids are real spoiled brats. The absolute worst."

"What do you mean?"

She snickered into her drink. "I could hear Marion going off when they brought her in last night. Man, she wouldn't shut up. I wanted to go out there and read her the Miranda again, just to remind her she had the right to remain silent."

Seemed like Havermayer was finally feeling the drink. I had to take advantage, though I wondered if I'd remember anything she said in the morning. "What was she going on about?"

A snort rather than a snicker this time. "You name it. Everything from who killed her father to her brothers arguing all the time to her eldest brother whining about losing his lucky charm. It was nuts. I felt sorry for Eric."

Me too. "What did she say about her father?"

"Nothing that made any sense. I think she named everyone who lived in Riddleton by the time she was through."

No help. "What about her brothers? Why were they fighting?"

225

"She didn't say. Just went on and on about it. That and the stupid lucky charm."

Could that be the whatchamacallit she mentioned on the phone? "What was the charm, anyway? Did she say anything specific?"

"No idea. The whole thing sounded ridiculous, and I was glad when they got her into an interview room. At least they're soundproof."

She'd begun to slur her words, so I took a chance. "Are you ready to tell me why you *really* hate me so much?"

For a moment, I thought I'd lost her. An internal struggle contorted her face. Finally, she came to a decision, took another gulp of whiskey, and said in a voice I could barely hear, "When I was in school, I wanted to be a writer someday. My teachers told me I had talent, and I had a chance to make it. It was my dream."

Not what I'd expected. Havermayer had an overactive imagination, too. Who knew? "What happened? Why aren't you writing?"

She shared a sad half-smile. "My father died three months before I graduated high school. He'd been sick for a long time, and my mother was drowning in his medical bills. And she had to take care of my two younger brothers on top of all that. She worked two jobs and still couldn't manage everything. I had to get a job to help support my family, so I worked a series of low-wage gigs for a few years. When I turned twenty-one and saw the department was hiring, I applied. Went to the first available class at the academy."

Apparently, there was a lot about Havermayer I didn't know. Things that explained how she came to be the person she was today. I'd misjudged her badly. "I'm so sorry. How is your family doing now?"

"They're doing well. Mom's retired, one brother's in law school, and the other graduates college this year. It was all worth it in the end."

"That's wonderful. Have you considered picking up your writing where you left off?"

Shaking her head, she said, "I still write now and then, but it's not the same. I've learned to think like a police detective. My brain just doesn't work that way anymore."

How her brain worked had been one mystery I'd been unable to solve to this point. And I still had to wonder what she really thought now. Was any of this story true? Or was she trying to manipulate me in some way? Given our history, I wouldn't put anything past her.

I decided to go with the proverbial flow and see what happened. "You should write mysteries. You know how things are from the inside. You'd probably put me to shame."

More whiskey went down. "Nah. That ship has sailed."

"Not necessarily." I sipped my drink. "I still don't understand why you have so much hatred toward me, though. I think this gives us a common interest and we should be friends. Or at least friendly."

"Don't you see?" She leaned forward to prop her elbows on the table. One slipped off, and she replaced it. "You already have the career I wanted. I resented you for that from the time you came back to town. I should've received all the accolades, not you."

She sat back in her seat, rocking to one side. "I knew it wasn't your fault I had to abandon my dream and go to work, but I couldn't help myself. Then, when you started interfering in our investigations, it was like you were trying to take that away from me, too."

The detective was full of surprises today. "That's not true! I only got involved because I had to defend myself against your accusations. I didn't want your job. I wanted my freedom."

Havermayer covered her face with her hands. "I know that now, and on some level I knew it then. It's just taken me a while to understand what I was doing. By the time I did, I had no idea how to fix it without telling you the truth. It was easier to just keep pretending I hated you until I figured a way out."

Strangely enough, her story made sense. It also explained why she'd never tell Eric the source of her hostility either. Now, the truth was out, if it *was* the truth. Time for us to move on. "Okay. I vote we put it all behind us and start over."

She lifted an eyebrow. "Can you do that?"

"I think I can. You've been pretty awful to me, but I gave as good as I got, right? Except the part about you accusing me of murder every time I turned around. I never tried that one."

She upended her cup and shook the last drops onto her tongue. Slamming the cup down on the table, she said, "Look, you better get out of here. I'm going to bed."

With that, she left the room. A moment later, I heard soft snoring coming from her bedroom. I stumbled in there through the brain fog and dragged the comforter over her.

I inched down the front steps with both hands on the rail to the Jeep. It took four tries for me to get the door unlocked, but, finally, I slid into the driver's seat and called Eric for a ride.

The last thing I remembered was how unhappy he sounded.

Oh well, I'll straighten it out tomorrow.

CHAPTER TWENTY-TWO

The sun streaming through the open blinds Saturday morning hit my closed eyelids like laser beams. Guess I deserved it, being too drunk to remember to close the blinds before I went to bed. I should give myself a pass on that, though, since I didn't even remember *going* to bed. I assume Eric had taken care of that process for me. My personal valet, but only when I'd had too much to drink. And I loved him for taking such good care of me.

I hoped he wasn't angry about having to come get me. I hadn't intended to get drunk last night. Only to give Havermayer a ride home and maybe convince her to talk about what she knew. How was I supposed to know it would take half a liter of Jameson to pry anything out of her? And what she finally *did* say wasn't particularly helpful. The Kirby boys were arguing a lot, and Junior had lost his lucky charm.

Big deal.

At least I'd remembered something. Now I understood in a small way how Elliott had felt last weekend in the park. However, I'd been through this type of amnesia before. Every time I drank too much. Everything important found its way back into my memory eventually, as far as I knew. I felt comfortable with the assumption that, if I never remembered something that happened when I'd been drinking, it wasn't important.

Construction workers jackhammered in my head, demolishing concrete to repair a water main break or some such disaster. I peeled my sticky eyelids open with my fingertips and reached for Savannah to get my morning hug, but my sidekick had abandoned me. The bed was empty. Eric's side hadn't been slept in. I couldn't remember the last time I woke up alone. Must've been drinking that time, too.

Where was my baby? Eric's absence meant she wouldn't be in the kitchen, dripping saliva, waiting for him to drop bacon on the floor. Maybe I'd kicked her in my sleep one too many times, and she'd spent the rest of the night on the couch where she could get some uninterrupted rest. No problem when she almost pushed me off the bed, but let me disturb her even once, and she took off on me.

So much for woman's best friend.

I called her name, the sound of my voice reverberating through my skull. No response except from the jackhammers. Maybe she found her dreams too entertaining to pay attention. No doubt chasing an imaginary squirrel up a tree or digging a pit to bury a *Guinness Book of Records*-sized bone would be more fun as far as she was concerned.

Easing back the comforter, I swung my legs over the side of the bed, sitting up in one fluid movement. The demolition went on, but my headache was unusually tolerable for a hangover. More manageable than I'd expected. Perhaps because I hadn't had very much of the whiskey, most of it being diluted with coffee. I wasn't used to the higher alcohol content, though. Wine was at most 10 percent, whereas the Jameson was more like 40, so it didn't take much to send my world into a spin.

I dropped my feet to the cold floor and shuffled out to the living room to roust my lazy dog off the couch, but she wasn't there. No sign of her. A rush of adrenaline zinged down my spine, and my stomach bunched into a bowling ball as panic crept in. I checked the kitchen and the bathroom. No Savannah. My dog had disappeared. I had no idea where she was, and I didn't like the feeling one bit.

Eric had picked her up from the bookstore before collecting me because I remembered her sitting in my lap in the car, trying to lick my face. She definitely came home with us. Did she slip out the door while he put me to bed? No way. He'd never leave the door open. Not on purpose, anyway.

Accidents happen.

Anxiety spread through my chest. I had to find her. I opened the front door and called her name. "Savannah? Savannah!"

No German shepherd. I ran back into the apartment, ignoring the pain shooting through my head, and snatched my phone off the coffee table. I swiped the Valentine's Day picture beside Eric's name, and the phone rang four times before he answered.

"Good morning, sleepyhead! I wasn't expecting you to call so soon." His breath came in short gasps, telling me he was running.

"Where's Savannah? Do you have her?"

"Yeah, she's right here having a ball. She loves running with me. She actually gets some exercise. Unlike with someone else I know."

"Are you crazy? You scared the heck out of me. I thought I'd lost her. I've been going out of my mind with worry."

He chuckled. "Yeah, like that would ever happen. This dog sticks to you like a burr in the spring. It took me ten minutes to convince her to come with me this morning. She wouldn't leave you. I had to bribe her with a treat. Didn't you see my note?"

"What note?"

"The one I left on the refrigerator."

I dashed back into the kitchen and, stuck to the freezer section under a magnet, I saw Eric's piss-poor excuse for handwriting looking back at me. I pulled the scrap of paper down and squinted to focus on the vibrating words. It read:

Good Morning!

I have Savannah. We'll meet you at the park when you get there.

Love you,
Eric

I breathed slowly, trying to calm my galloping heart. "Oh, thank you! Next time, leave the note on the pillow or something so I'll see it right away. I'm shaking."

"I will, sorry. I didn't mean to scare you. I just figured you wouldn't make it for our run this morning and didn't want Savannah to miss out. You know how much she loves the park."

"That was sweet of you. I'm sorry I got so upset. What time is it, anyway?"

"Eight fifteen," he said.

"Oh, crap! I have to get ready."

"You're all right. You had a rough night. Get some rest. We can talk about what you learned from Havermayer later."

"No, I need to sweat out some of that whiskey. Besides, she didn't say much, even after she added the Jameson to her coffee. I'll see you in a few minutes."

"Okay, if you insist," he said and hung up.

I chugged a bottle of water and took some pain reliever to pull the plug on the jackhammers. The repairs could wait forever, in my opinion. I needed to function today. As long as Simeon Kirby's killer remained free, Havermayer would still be under suspicion. While we hadn't done a lot to solidify our friendship last night, we'd made some progress. I refused to let the effort go to waste, even if she refused to help.

I slid the Jeep in beside Eric's Suburban in the parking lot and made my way to the wrought-iron gate guarding the park entrance. The sun rested at the treetops, not yet warming the air, and what remained of the overnight dew dripped from the tree branches onto the ghosts, goblins, and ghouls planted beneath. Halloween was only a few days away, and I still hadn't picked out a costume. Maybe I'd get to it this afternoon if I had time.

My friends ran together as a group on the other side of the park, and, when Eric looked in my direction, I waved. Savannah spotted me, and he had to let her go to avoid losing his arm when she lunged toward me. She galloped at full speed, paws barely touching the ground, tongue flopping from side to side. I braced myself for the onslaught, knees bent, hands out. She screeched to a halt at my feet, spinning in place. Guess she missed me, too.

"Easy, girl," I said, searching for a stationary spot to pet. After a moment, she sat, and I scratched her neck while we waited for the others to catch up with us. I relished the feel of her fur between my fingers, and her scent wafted up to my nose. Grateful that she was safe, I squatted for a full neck hug. She squirmed away, prancing. My girl wasn't big on hugs.

Eric and Lacey sailed by, waving, and I eased into a trot beside Angus and Ingrid with Savannah at my side, where she belonged. "Hey, guys, whatcha been up to?" I asked.

Ingrid elbowed me in the arm. "We've been getting our exercise, unlike you, Miss Slugabed. I heard you fell asleep before Eric even got you in the house. He had to sling you over his shoulder like a sack of potatoes."

"My hero," I said with a grin. "I had to pry some information out of Detective Havermayer last night, and that required getting up close and personal with Mr. Jameson."

"Mr. Jameson?" Angus asked.

"Yes, as in Irish Whiskey."

His mouth formed a circle, and he shook his head. "I had no idea Havermayer was a drinker. Never thought she was the type. Too straitlaced, if you know what I mean."

"I don't think she's much of a drinker, really. She had to blow dust off the bottle when she took it out. I think she needed to put the last few days out of her mind for a while, and I happened to be there trying to make her think about it." I peeked around Ingrid to catch Angus's eye. "So, don't you go starting any rumors, okay?"

He put his hands up. "Who me? I never start rumors. I only pass along interesting stories I hear from others."

Savannah towed me toward the grass, so I dropped back and slipped in on the other side of Angus. She never sniffed while we ran but loved to be near the lawn. I could only guess she liked knowing it was nearby if we passed something fragrant.

I peered around Angus this time to talk to Ingrid. "Have you finished Elliott Kirby's autopsy yet?"

She nodded. "It was pretty straightforward. Two gunshot wounds to the chest. He died quickly, I suspect."

"Were you able to retrieve the bullets?"

"I did, but I'm not sure they'll be much help. They're from the same nine millimeter that killed his father. No usable markings."

"Maybe not, but that seems like evidence enough by itself. The sets match each other. That's something, right?"

"Once we find the gun."

My leg muscles tightened since I hadn't stretched before I started running. Guess Eric and Lacey had it right. Stretching first mattered. I'd never tell them that, though. Our resident speedsters had big enough heads already from running circles around the rest of us every week. No need to feed the monsters. I plowed on, determined not to show my discomfort to Ingrid and Angus. No need for a round of "I told you so" either.

As much for distraction as information, I asked Angus, "Have you heard any interesting stories lately? Anything useful?"

"First of all, all my information is useful, but did you mean in general or about the murdered Kirbys?"

"Either, but let's start with the Kirbys. Whatcha got?"

"Not much, really. They've been arguing among themselves all week. Probably dividing the spoils before their father's even buried. Of course, Elliott's out of it now."

The same thing Havermayer had told me. "From what I heard, Kirby's will was pretty clear. Equal shares for everyone; Junior runs the show. What's to argue about?"

"Elliott's demise would complicate all that, wouldn't it, luv?" Ingrid asked.

I shrugged. "I don't know. He never married and didn't have any kids, so his parents would likely be his beneficiaries. Well, his mother now, and assuming he even had a will. A lot of people don't bother until they get married and have kids."

Angus replied, "Even if he didn't, his mother would be his beneficiary as his next of kin."

"Hmmm," Ingrid began. "I wonder if Kirby's will accounted for the death of one of his children. They might still divide equally, just have bigger shares."

"So, depending on which way the will's worded, Elliott's mother might benefit the most from Elliott's death, making her a suspect in his murder," Angus said.

"I don't know about that. Havermayer also told me he'd regained his memory and was supposed to come in for another interview this morning. That would make whoever killed his father a suspect in his death as well."

Ingrid moved ahead and turned around to face us, running backward. "So it could be the same person."

Could Virginia Kirby have murdered both her husband and her son to receive the maximum inheritance? As far as I knew, she wasn't on the suspect list for either death. Her husband supported her rather nicely, from what I

237

remembered of their home. What would she gain from his death? Other than being rid of him, of course. That might be worth any amount of lost income. Especially after he rubbed the affair with his assistant in her face.

"Have you made progress answering any of these questions yet, Jen?" Angus asked.

"Not much. I'm at a dead end at the moment." I glanced at him. "I'm open to suggestions, though."

"You've spoken with everyone in the family?"

Unfortunately. The Kirby family would never be accused of being overly social from my experience. "Yes, but we didn't learn much other than Kirby's daughter was stealing from the company. I thought that counted as a motive for her to kill him if her father figured it out, but Eric doesn't think so. She told him her father didn't know, and Eric believes her."

"Okay, assuming he's right and she didn't do it, what about other people in the company? Who else stood to gain from Kirby's death?"

"It was a family-run operation. The only people I saw who weren't related were the construction workers and his executive assistant whom he may or may not have been having an affair with. Stephanie something or other."

His eyebrows went up. "Stephanie Robinson?"

"That's it. Why—you know her?"

"Sure, she lives right here in Riddleton. Comes into the diner for coffee every morning on her way to work."

Finally, I might have another possible avenue to explore. "Do you know where she lives? I'd love to speak to her alone. The last time we met, the wife and daughter were both there. I had a feeling she had something she didn't want to say in front of them, but I could be wrong."

"I think she lives over on Walnut. Don't know the exact address, though. But she drives a dark green Toyota that she parks on the street. I know that because she's always complaining about bird droppings on her windshield. Apparently, the birds love hanging out in the old walnut tree in front of her house."

"Thanks, Angus. I'll head over there this afternoon. Hopefully, she'll have something interesting to tell me."

Maybe she'd even know who killed Simeon and Elliott.

CHAPTER TWENTY-THREE

Walnut Street was about two miles long, beginning at Riddleton Road and ending in a cul-de-sac on the outskirts of town. I made the right off Main and cruised slowly, searching for Stephanie Robinson's dark green Toyota. It should be easy to find if she parked it under the walnut tree she'd complained to Angus about. All I had to look for was a dark green car with bird droppings all over the windshield.

I rolled past block after block of almost identical A-frame houses, some decorated for Halloween, some not. The decorations ranged from went all out and covered every inch of available space to a strand of orange lights wrapped around the doorframe. Some people lived for that gold plastic trophy despite the likelihood they'd never win it. Of course, they couldn't possibly win the contest if they didn't try. That was Lacey's reasoning, anyway.

The vehicles available for inspection along the side of the road came in all shapes, sizes, and colors. None of them dark green Toyotas so far. Or dark green anything, for that matter. Mostly black, white, or one of a million different shades of gray. An occasional blue popped up now and again. Only one red, though. Only one person living on Walnut brave enough to drive a cop magnet. I couldn't blame everyone else, however. Unlike postage stamps, a speeding ticket collection had value only to the municipality where they were issued. And you couldn't sell them on eBay.

I swung around the cul-de-sac and headed back toward town. Hopefully, I'd missed something on the first pass unless Stephanie lived on the only block I hadn't covered yet. If not, I'd wasted time I could've spent exploring other avenues of investigation. What those might be, however, I had no idea.

Two houses from the end, at Riddleton Road, I spotted a dark green SUV sitting under a walnut tree the size of a house. According to Angus, Stephanie had described her vehicle as a car, but many people didn't make that distinction in casual conversation. I parked at the brick A-frame house with a black shingled roof and got out to check the make and model. A Toyota Highlander. Close enough.

I scooted down the concrete walk between two graveyards—one for the dead, the other for the zombies—to the three brick steps leading to the dark green front door, almost the exact same shade as the SUV. The knocker had a witch covering it, but the doorbell was clear, so I pressed the illuminated white disk.

A moment later, Stephanie opened the door wearing jeans, a loose white blouse tied at the midsection, and her platinum hair tied back in a ponytail. She held a broom in one hand and brushed unfettered hair off her forehead with the other.

"Can I help you?" she asked. Then, recognition

replaced the confusion on her face. "Wait, I know you. You're one of the detectives who came to the resort the other day to talk to all of us. What can I do for you?"

"Actually, I'm not a detective. More like an interested party. A friend of mine has been accused in Simeon Kirby's death, and I'm trying to help clear her name." Havermayer would have to forgive me for calling her a friend. At this point, I'd say whatever it took to get me in the door. "I was hoping we could chat for a few minutes so I could get a clearer idea of what happened that night."

"I don't know what I can tell you that's different from what we said the other day. Besides, I wasn't even there Friday night."

"You'd be surprised what might be helpful. And sometimes people remember things they didn't the first time we questioned them. May I come in?"

She hesitated and tightened her ponytail. "I'm cleaning right now. The house is a mess. Not ready for company."

Sounded like my place all the time. "I don't mind, and it'll only take a few minutes. Please, I could really use your help."

Stephanie stepped back and gestured for me to enter. The sparsely furnished living room seemed immaculate. No clutter, no dust, not a book on the bookshelf out of place. Apparently, her idea of a "mess" was a couple of magazines imperfectly aligned on the coffee table. How would she describe my apartment? I suspected I didn't want to know.

"Thank you. I'll try not to take up too much of your time."

"Would you like something to drink?" she asked, stepping toward the kitchen.

"No, thanks. I'm fine."

She shrugged and sat on the lime green couch. I perched on the edge of the matching love seat opposite. Safe to assume green was Stephanie's favorite color. Everywhere I looked, something in a shade of green looked back. It was like hanging out in a man-made forest full of parakeets, iguanas, and grasshoppers.

"So, what did you want to know?" she asked, impatience tingeing her tone.

Hopefully, I could get through this before she became irritated and threw me out. That tended to happen to me during these interviews. "Would you mind taking me through that day? Just tell me what happened."

Stephanie leaned her head back on the couch and stared at the ceiling as if debating how much to reveal. After a minute, she said, "It was a normal day. Nothing unusual happened at work. An investor meeting had been scheduled for that evening. Sim and Elliott took care of showing the guy around. And before you ask, I have no idea who the investor was. Simeon showed up later, and I left right after that. That's all that happened."

Junior's wife had sworn he was home with her all night, but he'd gone to the meeting just as Virginia said. Why would his wife lie unless they had something to hide? "Where did you go when you left?"

"I went to Blackburn. It was my parents' fiftieth anniversary and they threw a huge party. Everyone who's anyone was there. I had to go, or my mother would've pitched a fit. It was late by the time the last guest left, so I spent the night and helped clean up in the morning."

I assumed Eric had verified her alibi but asked anyway.

Sometimes, stories changed after a little time passed. "And people will vouch for you being there all night?"

"Absolutely. The police already checked with my parents. I was there all night."

They probably checked social media photos, too, to verify she hadn't left and come back. I'd have to ask Eric about it later. "And what happened next?"

"Nothing. The next day, Virginia called to tell me two different people had shot Simeon. She was hysterical, so I couldn't get much more out of her than that."

Interesting. We didn't know about two different guns being used until Ingrid did the autopsy Monday morning. How did Virginia know two shooters were involved on Saturday? She had to have been there when Kirby was killed. Or somebody who was had told her.

Time to switch tacks. "I've heard Simeon Jr. likes to play poker. Do you know anything about that?"

"Are you kidding?" She smirked. "Sim is the poster child for Gamblers Anonymous."

"You mean more than just poker?"

"Oh, yeah. Poker, blackjack, you name it. He likes to bet on sports, too." She leaned forward. "Last I heard, he owed a bookie over a hundred thousand dollars!"

A lot of money and possibly a motive for murder. "Does he have that kind of money?"

"I don't know for sure, but I don't think so. He and Simeon were arguing Friday morning. I couldn't hear everything, but I'm pretty sure it was about money. It was always about money with those two."

Perhaps Simeon wouldn't bail his son out with his bookie, so Junior killed him. "Do you think Sim murdered his father?"

Her eyes widened in horror. "Oh, no! He'd never do

244

anything like that. Sure, they disagreed sometimes, but Sim loved his father."

"Okay, then, who do *you* think did it?"

"I think that detective they arrested did it. Didn't they find his body in her car? And his stuff in her house?"

Actually, it was Elliott's wallet and phone the police found in her house. Better to go with her thoughts, though. She might let something slip. "Yes, but—"

"And she came around a few times to talk to him. I think they might've been having an affair if you ask me."

Havermayer and Simeon Kirby? No way. Although, Angus told Charlie they'd been seen together outside a motel. Perhaps there was something to the rumor, after all. Was I wasting my time trying to prove a guilty person innocent? Did Detective Havermayer kill Simeon Kirby?

But what about Elliott Kirby? I'd been assuming that whoever killed one killed the other. Havermayer was in jail when Elliott died, so that didn't track. Could the two cases be separate after all? Which would mean we had two murderers running around Riddleton. I found that hard to believe.

"What was *your* relationship with Simeon Kirby?"

She lowered her eyebrows and glared at me. "He was my boss. That's it! I am sick of hearing about the stupid rumors that we're . . . we were having an affair. It never happened! I wouldn't do something like that. And I couldn't convince Virginia nothing was going on between us. She made Simeon's life hell over it."

Funny, I'd said nothing about them having an affair. I put my hands up. "Okay, I believe you. Is there anything else you'd like to tell me?"

"No." She stood. "I think I've said all I'm going to say."

I followed her to the door. "Thank you for your time." I stepped out, and she closed the door behind me. As I got back in the car, it dawned on me that Stephanie had told Conway she was home with her husband all night when Kirby was killed. Which story did Eric verify?

It might be time for another trip to Spartanburg. Too many conflicting stories from too many people. And too many people having information they couldn't have unless they had personal knowledge of the crime. I had to discover the truth if I was ever to learn who'd killed Simeon Kirby.

Only one spot remained in my building's parking area when I arrived home, and I eased into it. Brittany had her mailbox open and her arm in it up to the elbow when I hit the bottom of the steps. I walked around to check my mail, too. Not that I expected anything important, but to keep the box clear for the next round of junk mail.

"How was work?" I asked Brittany when she'd finished sorting.

"Fun. I had a craft class for the kids. They made Halloween decorations to take home."

"That does sound like fun. For you. Worrying about a bunch of five-year-olds stabbing each other with baby scissors would make me crazy."

She laughed. "I precut all the pieces. No scissors required."

"That's why you're considered the smart one of us."

"Thank you." Brittany headed for the steps. "What're you up to today?"

We climbed side by side. "Oh, you know, the usual.

Butting into other people's business. It's a specialty of mine."

"I've noticed. Since the boys are busy saving the world, you want to do something this afternoon? Catch a movie or something?"

"Actually, I was thinking of going back to Spartanburg to talk to the Kirbys' neighbors again. You want to come? We haven't had a good road trip in a long time. It'll be fun."

We hit the landing, and she fished her keys from her purse. "Only you could consider spending the day interviewing murder suspects fun."

"Maybe not that part, but the rest of it. We can sing songs and eat junk food like we used to." In response to her less-than-enthusiastic expression, I said, "We can talk about the wedding."

Brittany smiled. "If you're willing to talk about the wedding, it must be really important to you. Let's do it."

"Does that mean we don't have to talk about the wedding?"

"Oh, no! That's all we're gonna talk about. Buckle up, sweetheart, we're going on a road trip!" She let herself into her apartment, closed the door in my face, then opened it again. "But no junk food. I have to lose ten more pounds before the wedding."

"What's that got to do with me?"

She closed the door in my face again.

I suspected I'd regret inviting her before we'd left the Riddleton town limits.

Savannah leaped her joy when I opened the door. Apparently, she'd heard a rumor I'd been lost at sea and would never come home again. She grabbed her leash and pranced around the living room to celebrate my return from the dead.

"C'mon, little girl, let's go for a walk." I grabbed the end of her lead and found myself in a tug-of-war to the death. When she refused to let go, I dropped my end. She skidded backward into the coffee table, knocking books and papers onto the floor, then sat with a confused expression on her face, the leash hooked around her lower incisors.

"I'm sorry, kiddo, we have to go. I have someplace I need to be soon."

She dropped the lead on her front paws and looked at me, her tongue hanging out the side of her mouth.

Goofball.

She let me clip the leash to her collar, and we headed out. She made her pit stop at the oak tree, then sniffed and squatted her way around the block. It took almost thirty minutes for her to read and respond to all her pee-mail. My German shepherd took after social butterfly Daniel Davenport without a doubt. Me? Straitlaced, analytic Dana, all the way. Sort of.

When we finally made it back home, I refilled her food and water dishes and tossed her a chew stick to keep her occupied for thirty seconds after I left. "All right, kiddo. I have to go, but I'll be back in a few hours. You be a good girl."

She watched me go with her chew stick wedged in her mouth like a cigar. When I peeked through the closing door, her devastated expression broke my heart.

I shook it off, tapped on Brittany's door, and let myself in. Brittany puttered in the bathroom. She'd changed from her work clothes into jeans and a sweatshirt.

I leaned on the doorjamb. "Hey, Britt, you ready to go?"

"Almost. Do you want me to drive?"

We had this discussion every time we went anywhere together. According to my best friend, I was a lousy driver with a car too messy for any civilized human to ride in. I gave the only response that wouldn't lead to an argument, playful though it may be. The result was always the same, so why bother? "Sure, that sounds great."

She came out of the bathroom, grabbed her keys and purse, and said, "Let's go."

CHAPTER TWENTY-FOUR

I settled into the passenger seat of Brittany's spotless Chevy Cruze. She was right about one thing. No clutter in her car. And the Cruze was more comfortable than Eric's Jeep. I knew I should shop around for another vehicle but couldn't muster the energy. It'd been months since I'd totaled my Dodge Dart when I was pushed off the road into a deep ditch.

Eric didn't seem to mind my driving his car, though. He said it would only sit in his driveway otherwise since the department had issued him the Suburban. Although, he might've changed his mind since I used it to commit a crime the other night. Either way, being a grown-up meant being independent, and driving someone else's vehicle didn't qualify. Unfortunately, at almost thirty-one, I still believed growing up was overrated.

Brittany backed us onto the road, and we headed out.

"So, where are we stopping for snacks?" I asked, grinning.

"I told you, no snacks! Ten pounds overweight, remember? I don't want my wedding dress stitched closed in the back like I'm the guest of honor at a funeral."

It hadn't occurred to me she was serious about losing weight for the wedding. She'd never had the body issues many women suffered from, and she looked fantastic. Maintaining her weight had been effortless for her in the past. Although she was thirty-one, too. Perhaps she struggled more now and had just never mentioned it.

"You look fine, Britt. Olinski loves you just the way you are."

"So, you're saying I look fat, but it's okay because he loves me anyway?"

Oh, boy. This was a side of Brittany I'd never seen before, and I had no idea how to handle it. It had to be the stress of the wedding. "What? No, that's not at all what I said. I think you look wonderful, and if you asked Olinski he'd say the same thing."

"Sure, he'd say it, but would it be true?"

"Of course it would. He loves you. You're going to be a beautiful bride."

Her knuckles whitened on the steering wheel. "You think so?"

"I know so."

Blood flow returned to her hands. "I'm sorry. The big day is still months away, but the pressure is already killing me."

"How can I help? Taking the pressure off you is my job, right? Let me do my job."

"You're doing everything you can do. It's not only the wedding. I'm stressing about getting married, too."

"Are you getting cold feet?"

Brittany stared out the windshield, taking deep breaths. "Possibly. I don't know. I love him, and I can't imagine my life without him in it. So, what's the problem?"

251

I'd never encountered an indecisive Brittany before, but, given my history with commitment, I was in no position to judge. Unfortunately, I also had no idea what to say that would make her feel better. "Why don't you tell me what you're feeling?"

"Honestly? I'm terrified. How do I know he's the one? What if I'm making a mistake? After all, you wouldn't marry him."

"Uh-uh. That's not a fair comparison. He was a different guy back then, and I wasn't ready to settle down, remember?"

"Yeah, but—"

"No buts! He's not the person he was in high school. None of us are. And you're not me. You know what you want. I was just a kid with a dream that didn't include cleaning house and making babies."

"And what about now? When are you going to be ready to settle down? Eric would marry you tomorrow if he thought you'd show up for the ceremony."

Nice subject change, Britt. "We're not talking about me."

"Well, maybe we should be."

"Eric and I are happy with the way things are between us."

"You sure about that?"

"Yes." Where was this coming from? "Has Eric said something to you?"

Brittany shook her head. "No, but I see the way he looks at you. He loves you, Jen."

"I know he does. I love him, too. That doesn't mean we're ready to get married and live happily ever after."

"Why not?" She merged onto the highway. "What's holding you back?"

"Well, for starters, he hasn't asked me to marry him."

She barked a laugh. "Only because he knows you'd say 'no.'"

"Not necessarily. I could live with a long engagement."

The statement brought me up short. It was the first time I'd ever considered marrying him. Did my subconscious override my mouth? Did I really want to marry Eric and only refused to acknowledge the feeling? My chest tightened as my heart raced into panic mode.

Calm down, Jen.

Deep breath in, slow breath out.

Brittany interrupted my freak-out. "How long we talking here? Ten, twenty years?"

I released a final breath. "I don't know. I didn't even know I felt that way until I said it."

"Sounds Freudian."

"Ha. Sometimes, a cigar is just a cigar. Also Freudian." I looked out my window as the buildings and billboards zipped by. None of them had the answers. "What happened to our fun road trip, anyway?"

Brittany squeezed my arm. "We're not kids anymore. We have more important things to worry about these days."

"What, so grown-ups aren't allowed to have fun?"

"Sure, but maybe we define it differently."

"Baloney!"

She took her eyes off the road long enough to meet my gaze, and we both burst into laughter. I reached over and turned on the radio.

I guided Brittany into the Converse Heights subdivision, and we went to work. Simeon Kirby's two-story brick Colonial appeared abandoned when we parked at the

253

curb. Newspapers piled up at the front door, and the mailbox was stuffed to overflowing. What happened to the housekeeper? Had she abandoned her post?

Brittany looked at me and shrugged. "I guess nobody's home."

"I wasn't expecting anyone to be living here since Simeon and Elliott are dead and Virginia's in Riddleton making arrangements to bring home their bodies, but the housekeeper's obviously gone too. Very strange."

"Let's try the neighbors."

We headed for the house next door where Conway and I had met the teenager. No loud music blasting through the door this time, so perhaps we'd get an actual adult this time. Brittany rang the bell.

A tall, thin man pushing fifty and wearing khakis and a white polo shirt opened the door. "Hi, can I help you?"

I explained who we were and that we'd spoken to his daughter a few days earlier and had a few more questions about his neighbors.

"I'm sorry, she's not home, and she never mentioned speaking with two women she didn't know."

"Actually, I came down with a man last time. A retired police detective. We're trying to gather information that might help catch Mr. Kirby's killer."

"I don't see how I can help with that. I barely knew him."

Since I wasn't getting anywhere, Brittany took over. "We understand that. We were hoping you might have noticed if either or both of the Kirbys were home last Friday night. Or if anything unusual happened."

He rubbed his bare cleft chin. "Last Friday night?"

"Right. Not last night, but last week."

"Hmmm. Let me think a minute." He rubbed his chin again as if he'd recently shaved off a beard. "You know, now that you mention it, I do remember something strange."

"What's that?" I asked.

"They went out for a while, then after a couple of hours he came back and dropped her off without going in the house with her. I thought it odd at the time."

The housekeeper had mentioned the Kirbys had gone out to dinner with friends that night. This must've been when they came back.

"Then what happened?"

"Well, about ten minutes later, his wife left. He left her alone all the time, but usually she just stayed home. This time, she went out, too."

Brittany asked, "How is it you happened to notice what they were doing?"

"My wife and I were going to a movie, and she went back in the house for her purse. It took her a few minutes to find it. By the time she did, we had to wait to pull out until Virginia drove by. I saw the whole thing. Didn't think much of it at the time, though."

"Can you think of anything else you've noticed lately that seemed strange or unusual?"

"No, not really. Why? You think she killed him?"

"We don't know who did it yet. Thanks for your help. We appreciate you taking the time to speak with us."

He nodded and closed the door. Brittany and I trudged back to the car.

After we climbed in, I turned to Brittany and asked, "What do you think?"

"I think Virginia wasn't home like she told the police."

I couldn't imagine Eric hadn't verified her story. Perhaps somebody lied for her. Another thing I'd have to ask him about later. "Kirby went to his meeting, but where did she go?"

"Great question." Brittany started the car. "Where to now?"

"Let's see what Junior's neighbors have to say for themselves. Go straight down the street. I'll let you know where to stop."

She shifted into drive and took off. A few minutes later, she stopped at the Georgian-style white-brick house I pointed out. Nobody home. Disappointed, I led Brittany to the house next door. I'd hoped to have a conversation with Junior's wife since she'd stuck to her story that Junior was home with her the night Kirby died. And give her the opportunity to tell the truth now that we could prove she lied, but I'd have to settle for a neighbor again.

Instead of the blonde, we got her husband this time. He told the same story about Sim's problems at the poker games and expressed his disappointment at having to ask him to stop coming.

"So, you're convinced Sim had a gambling problem?"

"Absolutely. No doubt in my mind."

I remembered Marion's comments about the item Sim lost. "Did you ever hear him talk about a lucky charm of some kind?"

After a laugh, he replied, "Oh, yeah. He had a poker chip he carried everywhere. Swore it brought him luck. Except, he had a bad losing streak before I had to toss him out. Guess it wasn't so lucky after all."

It could amount to worse than bad cards if it turned out that poker chip was the one we found in the park the morning Elliott approached us. "Do you have any idea where Sim might've been the night his father died?"

"He told me he had a meeting to go to, so I assume that's where he was."

Our third confirmation he'd gone to the investor meeting. I'd leave it to the police to figure out why his wife lied and said he was home with her. "Thank you for your time. I appreciate your help."

"My pleasure. Have a good day."

"You, too. Thanks."

He went back into the house and closed the door.

I turned to Brittany. "One last stop, and we can head home."

"Lead the way."

I gave her directions to Marion's house, but it turned out to be another failed attempt to reach anyone in Marion's life who'd provide us with information. We walked slowly back to the car. On the bright side, Marion was already in jail, so, if it turned out she was the culprit, they wouldn't have to go far to make the arrest.

Brittany opened the driver's door.

I looked over the top of the car from the passenger side. "Do you want me to drive back? You must be pretty tired by now. You had to work this morning."

"No, I'm fine."

I laughed. "I'm not that bad a driver, you know. I've never even had an accident."

"I know," she said. "I just like to tease you."

"So, do you want me to drive or not?"

"No, I'm not tired. Besides, you have more reason to be worn out than I do after your party with Havermayer last night."

257

I opened the passenger-side door and got in while she joined me on the driver's side. "How'd you hear about that?" I asked.

"I have my ways." She winked. "Actually, I ran into Eric on my way to work this morning."

"He stayed with me last night? It didn't look like he'd slept on his side of the bed."

"He told me he slept on the couch. You were so restless he didn't want to disturb you."

"You mean he didn't want to get kicked like he did last time I had too much to drink? Smart man. He stayed out of the line of fire."

"Yeah, probably. That too."

Brittany made the U-turn to head back to the main road and asked, "You think we accomplished anything today?"

"I think we've narrowed it down to two suspects. We're either looking at Virginia or Junior. They both had motive and opportunity."

"You think?"

"I do. I mean, think about it. Virginia lied about being at home when her husband was killed. From the look of it, she followed him to Riddleton. We know from the way she and Stephanie acted when Conway and I went up to the trailer and the trusty rumor mill that Kirby and Stephanie were probably having an affair. Or at least Virginia believed it, so I'm thinking, when he left her on that Friday night, she jumped in the car and followed him to catch them in the act."

Brittany nodded. "Okay, that's plausible, although unsubstantiated, so why are you still looking at Junior?"

"Well, Junior had a gambling problem, according to everyone, and according to Stephanie he'd racked up a hundred-thousand-dollar debt to his bookie. It's possible he asked his father for the money, and his father turned him down, so he killed him to get his inheritance."

"All right," Brittany said, merging onto the highway. "You have two plausible theories. How are you going to narrow it down? You don't have any hard evidence to prove either one."

"The last place Kirby was seen alive was at the construction trailer, right?"

"Right."

"Maybe that's where we need to go to find the evidence."

"But what about Elliott? Haven't you been assuming whoever killed Kirby killed his son, too? Do you really think Virginia has it in her to murder her son, or Junior has it in him to take out his brother? And don't forget, the last time you went there you got caught breaking and entering. You sure you want to take that chance again?"

I had no intention of getting caught again. There was no way to convince her of that, so I chose to ignore her last question. "I don't know if any of the Kirbys are capable of murder, but it's the only story that makes sense. And maybe I'm wrong about the one-killer theory. Maybe there are two different killers. Who knows? Maybe Virginia shot her husband, Elliott witnessed it, Junior smacked him on the head to keep him from going to the cops, and then, when Elliott regained his memory, Junior killed him to protect his mother."

"That's plausible, too, but I haven't gotten the impression from you the family was close enough to kill for each other. If anything, it seems to me Elliott was closer to his mother than anyone else. Junior was closer to his father, so wouldn't Junior want his mother punished for murdering his father?"

I dropped my head into my hands to beat back the burgeoning headache. The situation was so complicated, and there were so many possibilities I couldn't think straight anymore. "I don't know, Britt. Maybe you're right, but I think the only thing we can do right now is head out to the trailer. There's a gun in the safe that might be the murder weapon. We have to find it and bring it to the police."

Brittany glanced at me. "Didn't the police already search the construction trailer after they arrested Marion?"

"I don't think so. I think Marion dropped the charges against Charlie and me, so the place was no longer a crime scene. Eric found the ledger sitting out for anyone to see while he made the arrest for embezzlement. They may not have been allowed to search the rest of the premises or the safe."

"But if they arrested Marion for embezzlement, wouldn't that make the whole trailer a crime scene? Including the safe?"

"Oh, yeah. I forgot about that. So maybe they found the gun after all."

"Why don't you call Eric and ask him? Then we won't be wasting a trip."

Because he'd probably tell me to forget my plan. "I can't imagine he wouldn't have mentioned finding the murder weapon, can you?"

"What if the gun you saw wasn't used to kill Kirby or Elliott? Then he'd have no reason to mention it."

Try as I might, I couldn't think of an argument. "All

260

right, I'll call him. I don't want to go out there if we don't have to, either."

Brittany put her hand on her arm. "Wait a minute. How are you going to get into the safe, anyway? Do you have the combination?"

"When Marion put the gun back after the cops came, she never spun the dial after closing it. That means it's unlocked."

"Unless the police locked it after they emptied it."

I blew out a loud sigh, irritated at Brittany's logical responses I couldn't answer. "Assuming they searched it in the first place, why would they? They probably left the door standing wide open if they found it unlocked."

"Fine. Make your call."

I phoned Eric and told him about our discussion. He said the judge had issued a warrant for the computers and anything else related to the company finances. He didn't mention a gun in the safe. Perhaps someone else removed it before the search. Maybe we'd luck out and they put it back afterward.

When he tried to tell me to abandon our plan to visit the trailer again, I pretended we had a bad connection and hung up. The gun had better be the murder weapon, or he'd never forgive me. Either that, or I'd have to come up with a spectacular apology gift for him. Unfortunately, I had no idea what that might be, but I'd think of something.

Brittany glanced at me, then turned back to the road. "So, are we a go?"

Despite the price I knew I'd have to pay with Eric, I replied, "Yup."

"All right. Let's do it," Brittany said, sounding excited about the prospect for the first time.

My enthusiasm level had diminished a bit after my conversation with Eric, but finding the murder weapon to solve the case had to be my first priority right now. And, if I was right, that's exactly what we were about to do.

If I was right.

CHAPTER TWENTY-FIVE

We sat in a parking spot in the lot of our apartment building while Brittany argued against going to the construction trailer tonight.

"You were fine with this an hour ago, Britt. What changed?"

"I've had an hour to think about it. It's foolish and dangerous. You've already been caught once and got away with it. You really want to risk going to jail this time?"

"It's seven o'clock on a Saturday night. It'll be eight before we get there. Who's going to be around to catch us?"

"Who caught you last time?"

"Marion, and she's in jail. That only leaves Junior and Virginia, and they'll probably be having a fancy dinner somewhere."

Brittany lifted her eyebrows. "Listen to yourself, Jen. Those are your two prime suspects. You really think they're not going to be keeping an eye on the crime scene?"

I took a beat so I wouldn't say something to cause a rift between us. "Okay, let's say you're right. What's the alternative? Letting whichever one of them murdered Kirby get away with it? Eric can't search that trailer again to look for the gun. The murder weapon might as well be encased in concrete at the bottom of the ocean. What would you do in my place?"

"Why is this so important to you?"

"Eric needs my help. His hands are tied and mine aren't. I know it doesn't seem like much, but he's given me so much. I want to give something back."

"Let me ask you this," she began, a thought bubble floating over her head. "Do you think Eric will be able to use the gun as evidence if you obtain it illegally?"

"He will if he doesn't know where it came from."

"Right. Like he'll have any doubt."

I crossed my arms and planted my feet on the floorboards. "I'm still waiting to hear what you would do."

Brittany studied her manicure.

After two full minutes of silence, I said, "All right, then. I'm going to get the lock-pick gun from Charlie, and then I'm going out to the trailer. If you don't want to come, I understand completely. I promise I won't be upset."

I got out of the car and walked down the hall to tap on Charlie's apartment door. Muffled beeps and explosions from whatever game he was playing filtered out. When he didn't respond, I knocked harder, eventually pounding with my fist. He must've had headphones on.

The doorknob turned under my hand, and I stepped in. Charlie sat on the couch to my left staring at an HD TV that covered most of the wall in front of him, bare

264

feet propped on the coffee table cluttered with empty snack bags and drink bottles. "Charlie?"

I waved my hand to get his attention. No reaction, as if he were a hologram. I could see him, but he couldn't see me. Either that or he had no peripheral vision at all.

He spoke into the microphone, hovering near his lips.

"Charlie!"

He blew up a tank.

Oh, for Pete's sake!

I walked over and rested my hand on his shoulder. He jumped up and fell over the coffee table.

Extending a hand to help him up, I asked, "Are you all right?"

"Jeez, Jen, you scared me. What're you doing here?"

"I came to borrow your lock-pick gun. I'm going back out to the trailer."

"Oh, boy! Another adventure! Let me change my clothes."

I shook my head. "Not this time, Charlie. I'm going by myself. It's too dangerous, and I can't put you at risk again." Charlie was still an amateur when it came to these things. Brittany was a pro, and I trusted her. But she didn't want to go this time. I couldn't blame her. We'd faced so many challenges together, and she had too much to lose if things fell apart, as they had a tendency to do.

"But—"

"No! If you don't give me the gun unless you go, I'll find another way to break in."

He scowled and went into the kitchen. "You never let me have any fun."

I pressed my lips together to hold the laughter in. "Believe me, jail is no fun."

"I still think you should let me back you up," he said, handing me the lock pick and the tension tool.

"Thank you, but I'll be fine," I replied, hoping I didn't have a severe case of wishful thinking. Brittany and Eric would say I did, without question.

Pursing his lips, he retrieved his headphones and returned to his game.

I let myself out. Charlie would get over it. Come Monday, he'd probably be his old chipper self again. Or so I hoped.

As I neared the steps leading to my apartment, I hesitated. Should I take Savannah for a walk or leave her be? If I took her out then immediately left again, she'd be upset. On the other hand, it'd already been a long day for her. Perhaps Brittany would walk her for me and maybe hang out with her for a while afterward. She'd never take her irritation with me out on my dog.

I trotted upstairs and knocked on her door. No answer.

Seriously? "C'mon, Britt! Don't be so ridiculous."

Still no response.

I turned the knob and found it locked. She really didn't want to see me. I opened my apartment door, expecting the typical Savannah greeting, but nothing happened. Great, now my dog was missing again.

"Looking for someone?"

I turned to find Brittany and Savannah coming up the steps. "Not anymore. Thanks for walking her. Would you mind letting her hang out at your place for a while? She's been alone all day."

"Sure, but I'm not going to be home, either."

Unleashing Savannah and letting her into the apartment, I said, "Oh, okay. No problem." I retrieved a chew stick from the bag on the counter. "Where are you going?"

"With you, silly. You don't think I'm going to let my best friend get into trouble by herself, do you?"

Tears pooled in my eyes. I dabbed at them. "Thank you. I hate when we fight."

"You call that a fight? Give me a break. Why are you crying?"

"I don't know. Just stressed, I guess. Charlie's mad at me, and I really wasn't looking forward to going out there by myself. But I would have if I had to." I hugged her. "Thanks for not making me have to."

"Let's get going before I change my mind."

I tossed Savannah her chew stick and closed the door.

On the way down, Brittany asked, "Why's Charlie upset with you?"

"He wanted to go, and I said 'no.'"

"Why'd you say he couldn't go? I thought you didn't want to go alone."

Why didn't I want him to come with me tonight? It's not like he'd get in the way or cause more trouble than Brittany. He was actually quite adept when he wanted to be. So, why was I willing to take Brittany and not Charlie?

"I'm not sure. Maybe it's a trust thing. I've known you all my life. I know you have my back, no matter what. I don't really know how Charlie will react if we get caught this time. It's a much more dangerous situation." I opened the car door. "I feel like I can trust him, but I don't *know* it yet. Does that make sense?"

"Actually, it does. I get it. And if you try explaining it to him, he will, too."

I slid into the passenger seat and buckled my seat belt. "I don't want to hurt his feelings. He's a great kid, and I love having him around."

Brittany cranked the engine. "Maybe that's your problem right there. He's not a kid; he's a grown man. You just have trouble seeing him that way because of how he acts."

"And how he dresses. Let's not forget that."

"You know people could say the same things about you. Did you ever consider that?"

No, and it was a good thing I didn't have time to think about it now. I gave Brittany directions to the resort and stared out the window into the dark, trying hard not to think about anything.

I had Brittany park in the same cutout I'd left Eric's Jeep in the other night. Her pockets wouldn't hold anything more substantial than a matchbook, so I stuffed the car keys in one of mine. Then, we maneuvered through the woods beside the gravel drive, following the same path as before. This time, though, we found a Suburban parked by the construction trailer and a light on inside.

Havermayer's or Elliott's?

We hunkered behind a tree, and Brittany whispered, "Who do you think is in there?"

"Well, if that's Elliott's car, I'd wager it's either Junior or Virginia. The two people we didn't want to see tonight."

"Who else's could it be?"

"If they released Havermayer's car from evidence, she could be up here investigating for herself."

"I thought she was suspended?"

I snickered. "Yeah, and? What's your point?"

"True." She shook her head. "What do you want to do?"

"Let's hang out for a few minutes in case they leave." I lowered my bottom to the ground and wrapped my arms around my knees. "Might as well get comfortable. It could be a while."

Brittany mimicked my position, and we watched the trailer from either side of the tree.

What seemed like an eternity later, the light went out, and someone exited through the front door, but I couldn't see who. I leaned toward Brittany. "Can you tell who that is?"

"Not really. It looks like a man, but I can't be sure."

"Me either."

We ducked behind the tree while the Chevy headed down the gravel road.

"What now?" Brittany asked.

"I think we should hang for a bit to make sure he doesn't come right back."

We waited another fifteen minutes, but nobody appeared. Adrenaline building in my muscles had me ready to explode. "I can't wait anymore. Let's take our chances."

Brittany nodded, and we weaved our way through the trees to the back door.

"This is how we got in last time. Charlie took about thirty seconds to get the door open, but it'll probably take me longer. Wait here and keep an eye out. I'll wave when I'm in."

"Okay. Hurry!"

I sprinted across the small clearing between the woods

and the trailer, then leaned against the building to catch my breath. When I glanced up at the door, I realized this was the side with no steps. I'd forgotten. No way I could reach the doorknob without help. Especially since a shiny new deadbolt lock had been installed as well. I scuttled back to Brittany.

"What's wrong?" she asked.

I pointed toward the door. "No steps. You're going to have to hold me up so I can reach."

"Holy cow! How did we miss that?"

"Too worried about getting caught, I guess. I should've remembered from the other night, though. I'll kick myself later."

"No need. I'll do it for you if we can't get in."

I glanced at her and smiled. "No doubt. Do you think you can hold my weight long enough for me to get the door open?"

"You said it took Charlie thirty seconds?"

"Yeah, but I've never done this before. And they added a deadbolt. No telling how long it'll take to get that open."

Brittany thought for a minute. "Maybe we should try the front door instead."

"That side is out in the open, and it's only eight fifteen or so. We'd have to wait until all the resort guests are asleep. That could take hours."

"What if we carried the steps from the front back here?"

"It's risky, but it might work. If someone sees us, we're through, though."

She stood and stretched. "How long do you think we can sit here before someone spots us? I vote we get caught doing something proactive."

"All right, let's do it."

We scurried to the side of the trailer facing the woods. I inched to the end and poked my head out far enough to see the entrance to the resort. Nobody in sight. Almost half the rooms I could see had lights on. No telling how many guests occupied rooms on the back side, but none were strolling around the grounds at the moment.

I waved Brittany forward. "All clear."

Scooting around the front, we dove under the building behind the mini staircase. Still nobody around. I duckwalked out into the open, squatted by the steps, and waited for Brittany to follow. I reached up and tried the doorknob while I waited. It didn't open, of course. My luck never ran *that* good.

When we were both in position, I stood, bent at the waist, and grabbed my side.

Brittany did the same, met my gaze, and said, "On three. One. Two. Three!"

We heaved simultaneously, but the steps didn't budge.

"They must be heavier than we thought," I said, looking around to make sure we didn't have company. "Try again, on three. One. Two. Three!"

I grunted as I yanked on the wood, a splinter digging into my finger. Still no movement, though. "Crap! What's going on? They can't weigh that much."

"Jen, maybe it's time to give it up. The longer we're out here, the greater the chance we get caught. If I get arrested, I'll lose my job."

Brittany loved her job. It's why she came back to Riddleton after graduation. I couldn't let her risk losing it. "I'm not quite ready to quit yet. You should go back and wait in the car, though. I can handle it from here."

"I'm not leaving you here."

"It's okay. I don't want anything to happen to you. Olinski would never forgive me. And we both know how long he can hold a grudge."

She glanced back and forth between me and the road leading to the car, obviously torn between retreating to safety and helping me. Eventually, she shook her head. "I'm not going. We'll both get out of here faster if we work together."

"Thank you."

"Look, why don't we just try getting in this door? We stand a bigger chance of getting caught messing with these steps."

"All right. Let me know if you see anyone moving around."

She nodded, and I retrieved the lock-pick gun from my pocket. I inserted it and pulled the trigger as I'd watched Charlie do, but nothing happened. The knob still wouldn't turn. I tried again, squeezing the trigger several times in succession. Still nothing.

"What's going on?" Brittany asked.

"I don't know. I'm doing exactly what Charlie did, and it's not working."

"What do you want to do now?"

"Gimme a minute." Perhaps I'd been wrong about the front and back door locks being the same. Or, more likely, I wasn't doing it right. Either way, we weren't getting in this door.

I dropped to my haunches and examined the base of the staircase. The bottom was buried in dried mud. "It looks like the rain the other day made the ground muddy, and the steps were pushed down into it. When the mud dried, the bottom became encased. We have to loosen them up somehow. Then they should lift right out."

"We could rock them back and forth like we did last winter when my car was stuck in the snow," Brittany offered.

I pushed hard on my side, putting my weight behind it. No movement. "That won't work. They're stuck fast. I'm going to crawl underneath and see if I can kick them loose."

Once in position, I rolled over onto my back and placed one foot on each side. Then I curled my knees up to my chest, counted to three in my head, and catapulted my legs forward. Pain shot up my limbs into my hip joints. I clamped both hands over my mouth to keep from crying out and giving us away. I panted through my nose until the throbbing subsided.

Rolling out far enough to see Brittany, I asked, "Did it work?"

She gripped with both hands and tugged. From my position on the ground, I could clearly see the steps remained stuck. "No dice, Jen," she said. "Maybe if I get under there with you, we can get it out."

I massaged my aching legs. "I'm not sure I can handle another jolt like that. If it doesn't work, you might have to carry me home." Brittany's keys dug into my thigh, giving me an idea. "Let's try digging some of the dirt away. I think car keys are solid enough to do some damage."

I handed Brittany my keys, and we each took a side to scrape at the dried mud. It was like trying to chisel concrete with a nail file, but it was all we had to work with. I wrapped my hand around the plastic top and pounded the dirt as if I were chipping ice for a party. My knuckles collided with the wooden base, and my wrist ached, but after about fifteen minutes I had the beginnings of a channel running alongside the base.

"How're you doing over there, Britt?"

"I'm getting there."

I belly-crawled over to her side to see for myself. She'd had the same idea I did. Chip the mud away at the base to create room to rock. With luck, the staircase wasn't sunk too deep.

I looked up at her, squatting beside me. "You ready to try rocking it?"

"Sure. Should we go side to side or front to back?"

"Let's try side to side first. If it doesn't work, we'll go the other way." I slithered out from underneath and took my side. "Let's give it a shot."

We alternately pushed on our sides, creating more space with each shove. When we'd created a half inch of room on each side, I said, "Let's pull it up."

Brittany counted, "One. Two. Three!"

We jerked on the top step, and the staircase flew out of the hole. Brittany let go, and I stumbled, landing on my back with the stairs resting on my chest. The air in my lungs exploded out, and pain shot through my rib cage.

Brittany moved the steps off me and put them back in front of the door. "Are you all right?"

"Yeah, just give me a minute to catch my breath."

A voice coming from the resort drifted in our direction.

"We may not have a minute," Brittany said, peering into the darkness.

I rolled onto my belly, ignoring my screaming ribs,

and spotted someone on the phone walking down the path leading to the trailer. When the person stepped under one of the incandescent lamps lining the walk, I could clearly see who it was.

Virginia Kirby.

And she'd spotted us.

Oh, crap!

CHAPTER TWENTY-SIX

We exchanged glances as disaster moved closer with each of Virginia's steps. "What're we going to do, Jen?"

"I need a minute to think."

"We don't have a minute!"

"I can't let her see my face. She'll recognize me."

Virginia reached the edge of the dirt circle. A few more steps, and we'd be toast.

Brittany grabbed my arm. "I have an idea. Quick, sit on the steps and cover your face with your hands. Pretend you're crying, and let me do all the talking."

I followed instructions, trusting her instincts. My sniffles and whimpers sounded fake to me, but maybe Virginia would fall for it. Our fate was in Brittany's hands.

From a few feet away, Virginia said, "Ladies, this area is off-limits to guests. You'll have to leave."

I split my fingers slightly to watch the action unfold.

Come on, Britt, work your magic!

Brittany came through. "I'm so sorry! We didn't know." She drew Virginia off to the side and lowered her voice. "My friend has just received some very bad news. We only wanted a quiet place for her to digest it. I'm sure you understand."

To punctuate her words, I let out a wail, and Virginia stepped back, flustered.

My buddy went in for the kill. "If you'll just give her a few minutes to pull herself together, we'll go back to our room. I promise."

Virginia looked back and forth between us. "Well, I guess it's all right. Is there anything we can do for her?"

"No, ma'am. She'll be okay in a minute. Thank you for understanding."

"Of course. I've suffered some losses myself recently."

Losses of her own making?

I held my breath until she finally turned back to the resort.

When she could no longer hear us, Brittany squatted beside me and whispered, "Just a few more minutes, and we'll be clear."

"I hope it's fast. My hands stink like mud, and I think I've inhaled enough dirt to fill in a swimming pool."

A minute later, Brittany said, "Okay, she's gone. Now let's get out of here."

I dropped my hands and stood, lifting the end of the steps. "Are you kidding? You think I'm going to leave without that gun after everything we've had to do to get it? No way!"

Resignation covered her face. "Fine. No point in arguing with you when you get like this. Grab your end." She reached down and picked up her side of the staircase.

We scuttled to the back door, and I fished the lock-pick gun out of my pocket and inserted it into the doorknob. I squeezed the trigger and tested my work. It turned easily.

Halfway there.

I inserted the gun into the deadbolt and fired it. The door remained locked. I tried it three times in quick succession. Same result. "I'm going to have to use the tension tool."

"Have you done that before?"

"I've never done any of this before. Keep your fingers crossed. If it doesn't work, this whole episode has been a waste of time."

Brittany crossed the fingers of both hands and held them up for me to see.

I retrieved the tension tool from my back pocket and inserted it into the deadbolt. Then, I pulled the trigger again, testing the door after each attempt. On the third try, the door swung open, almost knocking me off the staircase. I held on to the doorknob for balance, looked back at Brittany, and smiled. "We're in!"

"All right! Let's find this gun and get out of here."

We scrambled inside. The flashlight on my phone revealed the safe in the corner. The door was closed.

Please don't be locked.

I used the bottom of my sweatshirt to cover my fingertips and tugged on the handle. The door opened easily, and the gun Marion had pointed at me and Charlie lay inside the safe. Finally, something went as planned, making all the trouble worthwhile. We had what we needed to put the killer away. And the fingerprints on the weapon would tell us who that person was.

Pinching the bottom of the trigger guard between two of my sweatshirt-covered fingers, I held the pistol up for Brittany to see. "Got it!"

Brittany retrieved a plastic bag from her pocket. "I thought we might need this."

"Good thinking! It never occurred to me to bring something to put the gun in."

"That's why you need me," she said, holding out the open bag.

I dropped the potential murder weapon in, and she sealed it up, saying, "Now, can we go? I've had enough fun for one evening."

"Same here."

We turned toward the doorway and froze.

Simeon Kirby Jr. smiled at us from the top of the steps, holding a gun. He held out his hand. "Good evening, ladies. I'll take that."

Are you kidding me? How many guns did this guy have? I should've left Brittany behind. Now, I've gotten her in trouble again. I'd just have to make sure we got out of it. Again. Olinski was gonna kill me when he found out, though.

Brittany handed him the bag, and I put my hands up.

"Now, give me your phones."

I pulled mine out of my back pocket and handed it to him.

He looked at Brittany. "Come on, yours, too."

"I don't have it with me. I left it in the car." She showed him her empty pockets.

Again? She never had her phone when we might need it the most. At least this time we'd have access to it when we got away from Junior.

He flipped the light switch and stepped into the trailer. "Mother told me we had visitors, so I decided to see for myself."

"Lucky us," I replied.

"Well, lucky for me, anyway. I'm not so sure about you, though."

"You have what you want. Just let us go, and you can get rid of the evidence."

Junior withdrew a length of rope out of his pocket. "I don't think so." He handed the rope to Brittany. "Tie her up and make it tight."

Brittany drew her hands back. "I won't do that."

He shrugged. "Tie her up, or I'll shoot you both right here. I have the whole lake to dump your bodies in. Nobody will ever know what happened to you."

I swallowed against the fear clogging my throat. "It's okay, Britt. Tie me up."

She looped the rope around my wrists, quaking behind my back, and tied it in a loose knot.

When she finished, Junior said, "Turn around and let me see."

I did, and he tested Brittany's work. "Tighter! If you try that again, I'll shoot her."

Brittany redid the knot, leaving the rope cutting into my wrists. I showed it to him, and he grunted, apparently satisfied. He pointed to the desk chair. "You sit there and don't move."

I complied while he pulled more rope out of his pocket and handed it to Brittany. "Now, tie her to the chair."

Brittany ran the rope through my arms around the back of the chair and secured it without bothering to try anything this time. I sat there, trussed like a Thanksgiving turkey.

He waved Brittany over to the other desk chair. "Don't try anything stupid, or I'll kill your friend. Understood?"

Brittany nodded. Junior laid the gun on the desk and tied her hands behind her back.

I could see the fear in her eyes, but she never let it show. Her bravery gave me strength. I tried to distract him in the hope she'd figure out what I was doing and try to get away. "Why are you doing this?"

No answer.

I tried again. "Why did you kill your father?"

"I don't know what you're talking about."

Like I'd believe that. If he didn't kill Kirby, then who did? Elliott, maybe, but then who killed him? And why? Ditto Marion. If she killed her father, then who murdered her brother? She was in custody when he died. That only left Virginia and her eldest son. My bet was on Junior.

I tried again, desperate for Brittany to get away. "I don't believe you. Why did you kill your father? Did you hate him that much?"

He snickered. "Yes, but that had nothing to do with it."

"Then what was it?"

He pushed Brittany into the chair and tied her to it. "You need to shut up."

"Why won't you tell me? We're going to die anyway, right? We at least have the right to know what we're dying for, don't you think?"

"You're dying because you don't know when to mind your own business."

Brittany jumped in. "You didn't mean to kill him, did you? It was an accident, right?"

Two shots to the chest and another to the gut an accident? Not likely.

Nice try, Britt.

"No. When Mother shot him, I saw the chance to . . ."

He'd messed up, and he knew it. The whole story fell into place. Virginia shot Kirby with the thirty-two, probably in a jealous rage. But that wound didn't kill him. Junior finished him with the nine millimeter.

Three shots from two different guns.

Unfortunately, now he had to kill us. There was no way out of it. Unless we escaped before he finalized his plans. But how to get away? We were both tied to chairs, and he held us at gunpoint. Our chances didn't seem very favorable at the moment.

I had to keep him talking while my brain worked on a plan. "How did Elliott fit into all this? Did he see you shoot your father? Is that why you had to get rid of him?"

Junior's angry mask cracked for a moment. "Elliott was the perfect one in the family. He cared about people, and he loved us all despite our faults." The mask hardened again. "And he was a foolish child. He saw good in us where none existed. I tried to tell him, but he wouldn't listen. He thought our father was an upstanding man, and all he needed was a little direction."

He laughed and fire shot from his eyes. I'd poked the beehive, which could be bad for us.

I caught Brittany's fear-filled gaze. I smiled to reassure her, but we both knew there was nothing behind it. I was as much at a loss as to what to do as she was.

Brittany took over the questioning, which gave me time to think. "Sim, why did your mother shoot your father? Was he cheating on her?"

Anger flashed through his eyes. "Of course he was. He always had someone on the side somewhere. Stephanie was just the last in a long, long list. I'm not surprised my mother shot him. I'm only surprised it took so long."

"Perhaps she loved him. Women put up with a lot to keep their families together."

"She was a fool. He never loved her."

"You can't know that."

He curled his upper lip. "Sure I can. He told me as much. The same time he told me they had to get married because she was pregnant with me."

An odd mix of anger and sadness drifted across his face. Maybe a little disgust too. With his father or himself? Was his frustration based in the knowledge he'd been unwanted? That his mother had suffered through a loveless marriage because of an accidental pregnancy? Because of him? I momentarily pitied him, but his feelings about his birth weren't my most pressing problem right now.

While Brittany had him distracted, I began working on the knot that held my hands. If I could get loose, we might have a chance. Especially since he'd become distracted by his emotions. The cold, calculating Junior who'd interrupted our search was on the edge of becoming erratic and emotional. We could use that to our advantage.

I nodded to Brittany so she'd continue to distract him while I worked at the knot.

She drew his attention again. "So, if he'd been cheating on her all along, what made her shoot him now? And why not just divorce him if she was fed up with it?"

He looked at his phone as if expecting a call, then shoved it in his pocket in frustration. "She didn't plan to kill him," he snarled. "When she drove up here and found him walking around the park with Stephanie instead of being at the meeting or home with her, she just lost it. She took out the gun to scare them. To make Stephanie leave him alone. It was Stephanie she tried to kill, not her husband. Father jumped in front of her."

He snorted and shook his head. "It was the first selfless thing he'd ever done in his life."

"Where did your mother get the gun?"

"That's the real irony. Father bought it for her so she'd feel safe when he was gone. And he was always gone."

My ears perked up. "Was that the thirty-two caliber we found at the scene?"

Junior jerked his phone out of his pocket and glanced at it again. "Yes, my mother shot my father with the gun he bought her."

I'd created a bit of space between my wrists by the time his phone actually rang. He answered, then went outside.

"Hang on, Britt, I'm almost loose." I jerked my wrists back and forth, ignoring the burning. He was likely making arrangements for us, which wouldn't take long.

I had almost enough space to slide one of my hands out.

"Hurry, Jen," Brittany whispered. She could see him through the doorway. "It looks like he's almost done. He stopped waving his hands around." She inched her chair away from the desk toward me. "I'd like to be out of here before he finishes making plans for our demise, if you don't mind."

I gritted my teeth and tried to pull my hand out of the loop. "And, I'd love to accommodate you. I'm trying my best."

"I know you are."

My hand came out, and I shook the rope off just in time to hear Kirby right outside the door. If I held my hands behind me and didn't move the rope binding me to the chair, he wouldn't know I'd freed myself. I held my breath when he came back inside.

"Everything okay?" Brittany asked to keep him from looking in my direction.

He showed her a closed-lip smile, more frightening than friendly. "It is now. You two will be out of my hair shortly."

We were running out of time. As it stood right now, we had him outnumbered and might take him by surprise. Once he had help, we lost that advantage. Since I had no idea how long "shortly" might be, it was now or never.

Junior still faced Brittany, so I risked showing her my free hand. I used my eyes to tell her she needed to keep his attention on her. I could only hope she understood, though. She might just think I had a weird tic or something.

I eased the rope around my chest over my head.

Brittany started talking. "Sim, is there any way I could go to the bathroom, please?"

"Forget it."

I stood and crept around the far side of the desk, careful not to bump anything.

"But I really have to go."

"You can hold it. You're a big girl."

I crouched behind him and prepared to spring.

"I know, and I'm really embarrassed to say this, but I have a bladder infection. If you don't take me to the bathroom right now, I'm going to have an accident. You don't want that to happen, do you?"

I uncurled my legs and jumped onto his back. He

shook me off, throwing me against the wall like a rag doll, driving the wind out of me. I could see Brittany struggling with her bonds. If I could keep him busy for a few more minutes, she could help me overpower him.

Bracing myself, I pushed off the wall and rammed into his knees, bringing him toppling down on me. I was pinned under his weight.

"C'mon, Britt. I could really use some help here."

He drove his knee into my belly, and all the food I'd ever eaten threatened to come back out.

I punched him in the throat but couldn't get much on it.

He coughed and grabbed his neck but didn't move.

Out of the corner of my eye, I saw Brittany yank off the rope binding her to the chair. The cavalry was coming. She bolted around the desk and threw herself at him.

He grunted and fell on his side. I scrambled to my feet and grabbed for the bag with the murder weapon in it he'd left on the corner of the desk.

Before I could reach it, a familiar voice came from the doorway.

"What's going on here?"

Virginia had returned. She must've been Junior's backup plan.

The distraction sent Junior back into action. He threw Brittany to the side and lunged for the gun that had slid across the floor when I jumped on him. He reached his at the same time I reached mine. It was a standoff.

Unfortunately, Virginia had brought one too.

CHAPTER TWENTY-SEVEN

We walked toward the resort four abreast. Junior had his arm around my shoulder as if we were a couple heading back to our room for the night. He kept his gun under his jacket, sticking into my ribs, forcing me to keep up the façade. My brain raced, searching for a way out of this mess and wondering if Eric would get worried and come looking for us.

Virginia held Brittany's hand, her weapon in the other hand, down by her side. She didn't need it. Brittany knew if she tried to run Junior would shoot me. Once again, I'd dragged my best friend into my problem and put her life in danger. It didn't matter if I survived because, if Junior didn't kill me, Olinski would.

Junior led us into the empty main lobby, and I surreptitiously scoped out all the potential escape routes. I'd never been inside the resort before and had no idea which doors remained open all night and which were locked. It made no difference if we couldn't escape our captors, though. And that depended on what Junior planned to do with us. I couldn't imagine he'd kill us here in the lobby. Too many potential witnesses, although I saw nobody around at the moment.

We took a right into a long hall with doors on either side. Guest rooms, most likely, but how many were occupied? Maybe we'd luck out, and someone would need to refill their ice bucket from the machine at the end of the hall. Not sure how I would get the message to them even if they did, however. I supposed I could blink an SOS in Morse code. But the way my luck was going, the targeted recipient would probably think I had something in my eyes.

Junior unlocked a door on the right marked *Authorized Personnel Only* at the end of the passageway. He glanced back down the hall to ensure we remained alone, then shoved me into the dark room. Brittany quickly followed. I stumbled and fell to the tiled floor, and she landed on top of me. He closed and locked the door.

We untangled ourselves and sat on the cold floor, waiting for our eyes to adjust.

"Are you all right, Britt?" The smell of disinfectant and paper goods wafted in the chill air. I suspected he'd stashed us in the supply room until he could figure out what to do with us.

"I'm fine. Physically, anyway."

"Okay, sit tight. I'm going to try to find a light switch so we can see what we're dealing with. Maybe we can find a way out before he comes back."

I reached out into the black and smacked Brittany on the shoulder. "Sorry."

"No problem. There doesn't seem to be much room to maneuver in here."

Switching hands, I tried the other side and almost immediately rapped my knuckles on something not Brittany. I felt around the cold metal and encountered a softer and warmer item resting on top. Okay. It was a shelf of some sort.

Picturing where Brittany sat in relation to where I stood, I said, "I'm going to follow these shelves along the wall and hopefully find a light switch somewhere. Don't move, okay?"

"Got it. I'll just do what I usually do. Sit in one place while you save my life."

Uh-oh. Always-positive Brittany was sliding into my territory. "That's not true. Don't say things like that. We'll never get out of here without your help. You know that. Besides, I'm the reason we're in this mess to begin with. It's my responsibility to fix it, but I can't do it without you. Got it?"

"Got it. Now, get the lights on. I can't see a bloody thing, as Ingrid would say."

"Aye, aye, Captain."

I slid sideways down the racks. From what I could tell in the dark, it seemed like a series of metal racks holding supplies lining the wall. I couldn't wait to see what we had to work with. When I hit the end of the line, I turned the corner toward the wall. Sweeping my hand up and down the Sheetrock, I moved forward one step at a time until I reached the front corner of the room. No light switch yet, but there had to be one somewhere near the door.

Standing in the corner, I slid my left arm up and down, covering about two feet in each direction, beginning at shoulder level. Another step brought my hand to the doorjamb. I felt for hinges likely to be on the inside where we could get to them since the door opened inward. When I ran my hand up the inside edge of the doorjamb, I found them exactly where they should be. First problem solved.

I eased across the painted wooden door to the other side. There had to be a switch on the wall on the side where the door opened. It didn't make sense for it to be anywhere else. The room didn't have automatic lights, or I wouldn't be doing this in the first place. I repeated my sliding motion and busted my knuckles against a metal rack. Apparently, they ran all the way to the front wall on this side of the room.

Sticking the offending knuckle in my mouth, I thought for a minute. I'd felt nothing during my sweep. It had to be there, though. No way a brand-new resort like this would expect its employees to grope around in the dark looking for a string hanging from a light fixture in the ceiling. For insurance reasons, if nothing else.

I faced the wall and slid both hands together up and down slowly. I didn't care if it took all night; I would find the light switch. I took a deep breath and exhaled my frustration. If something this simple was this difficult, how hard would it be to escape? It didn't matter. If we didn't get out, we'd die.

On the third pass, I felt a narrow, flat plate under my palm. I ran my fingers over it and pushed on the top. The room flooded with light from three overhead fixtures stretched across the ceiling. It was a rocker switch set so close to the wall as to be almost invisible. It figured. Only the best for the Kirbys.

When I turned around, Brittany grinned at me, squinting against the sudden glare. "I knew you could do it."

I reached out a hand to help her up. "All right, now we just have to get out of here."

"There are rooms all along this hall. Why don't we just pound on the door and yell until somebody hears us?"

"I doubt Kirby would've put us in here if it was that easy. I suspect these rooms are empty or soundproofed. For what people will be paying to stay here, they won't want to hear everything that goes on in the rooms around them."

She pressed her lips together, nodding. "You're probably right, but it's worth a try."

"Let's do it, then."

We pounded and yelled for help until our voices became hoarse, and we ran out of breath. No response. At least we attracted no negative attention, either. I had no idea where Junior and his mother were, and we'd risked drawing them back to us. But Brittany was right. We had to try.

My breathing slowed to a manageable rate. "If anyone heard us, we'd know by now. Time for phase two."

"What's phase two?"

"Breaking out of here. All we need is a hammer and a screwdriver to pop those hinges out. Then we take the door off, and we're on our way."

She looked around the narrow room lined with racks full of cleaning supplies, towels, miniature soaps, and tiny bottles of shampoo. "I don't see any tools. They must store those in a maintenance room or something."

At the far end of the room were two cleaning carts used by the housekeepers. "Maybe there's something we can use in one of them."

We headed that way.

Brittany stopped and picked up a shampoo bottle. "Hey, if we can't find a screwdriver, maybe we can douse them with shampoo, and the hinge pins will slide out."

I laughed. "We'll keep that idea as a last resort, okay?"

She shrugged and put the bottle back. "Okay, but when it works, just remember who thought of it."

"You got it." I rolled one cart away from the wall. "I'll gladly give you all the credit. In the meantime, see what you can find in this cart."

I searched the second, pawing through shampoo and cleaning products and toilet paper on the top shelf. The bottom held sheets and towels. I opened a small drawer behind the handle and found it full of little soaps. No tools of any kind. I looked over at Brittany. "Anything?"

"Nope. The same stuff you've got. I'll bet that shampoo idea is sounding pretty good now, huh?"

"Better, but I'm not quite there yet."

I went back up front for a closer look at the door. I still had the lock-pick gun in my pocket, but the doorknob was solid on this side. The only access to the lock was on the outside. Could I use the end of the flat tension tool to remove the screws holding the knob to the door? I removed it from my pocket and examined the end. It might be thin enough to fit into the Phillips screw head. But was it wide enough to grip? Only one way to find out.

Brittany came up behind me. "What're you doing?"

"I'm going to try to take the doorknob off using this." I held up the tension tool.

"It looks kind of small. You think it'll work?"

"It has to. I don't know what else to do."

I inserted the flat end of the tension tool into the screw and turned counterclockwise. It slipped out immediately. I tried again, only this time putting pressure on the tool as I turned, hoping it would hold. The tool remained in place, but the screw wouldn't budge. Did they insert it with an electric screwdriver?

How would I get the stupid thing out? And even if I managed to remove this one, there was another on the other side. I clenched my fists at my sides.

Deep breath in, slow breath out.

"Are you all right, Jen? Is there something I can do to help?" Brittany's concerned face appeared in my field of view.

"I'm fine. Just frustrated. I'll get it—don't worry."

I reinserted and leaned in, hoping the added weight wouldn't bend or break the tool. What difference did it make, though? It wasn't working anyway. I had to take the chance. I grabbed the end and turned with both hands. The screw rotated a fraction to the left. I turned and grabbed Brittany for a hug.

"It's working! We're gonna make it!"

Going through the process again, I turned the screw a fraction at a time until it finally broke free, and I could remove it with my fingers. I dropped it into Brittany's palm. "Okay, your turn. I did this one. You get the next one."

Brittany cocked an eyebrow. "Are you kidding? You barely got the screw out and you're much stronger than I am."

"Nonsense. Come on, my hands hurt. Give it a shot."

She took the tension tool from my hand.

I showed her where to put it and helped her hold it in place. "Now, just put some weight into it and turn to the left."

She tried it, and the tool slipped out.

We set her up, and she tried again. The screw stuck fast.

"No problem," I said. "Just lean in a little more. Use both hands the way I did."

I inserted the tool into position and put pressure on it. "Now grab your end, lean your weight into it, then turn with both hands."

It worked. The screw gave up its first fraction of an inch.

A clap on the shoulder brought a smile to her face. "See? I told you you could do it. Now, do it four hundred and seventy-two more times, and we'll be out of here."

We both laughed, and Brittany went to work. A few minutes later, she held up the screw like it was a fresh-cut diamond, and the plate hung loose around the doorknob. I removed the knob, and the one on the other side clattered to the floor. I reached into the hole in the door and removed the latch.

I took a deep breath and turned to Brittany. "You ready?"

She nodded.

"Okay. We just walk out of here like we have every right in the world to be here."

"Then what?"

"We run like hell to the car and use your phone to call Eric while we're driving away."

"Sounds like a plan. I'm ready."

I opened the door and peeked out. No signs of life in the hallway. "Let's go."

We stepped out of the supply room and strolled down the hall. My legs itched to run, but I forced myself to act casual. Halfway down, we heard a noise from one of the rooms. Brittany froze like a possum on the road at midnight.

I took her arm. "It's all right. We belong here,

remember?" I prodded her into motion again, searching what I could see of the lobby for any activity. So far, so good.

When we reached the end of the passageway, I pressed against the wall and peeked around the corner. The main desk, along with the rest of the lobby, remained vacant. The path to the front door was clear.

My heart jumped into overdrive, and sweat broke out, well, everywhere. This was it. Thirty more feet, and we were out of here. We made it halfway, and I peered out the door into the darkness. The entry had overhead lighting, making it difficult for me to see what lay beyond. If either of the Kirbys were out there, they'd see us long before we could see them.

Movement in the left side window drew my attention. I pushed Brittany back against the desk. "Wait here," I whispered.

I slithered on my belly toward the window, staying below the level of the sill as much as possible. The carpet scraped against my elbows and knees. I'd have rug burns tomorrow and no fun story to go along with them.

When I reached the corner where the window met the wall, I lifted my head to peek out. Junior and Virginia were standing on the side of the patio, having a strident discussion. Probably arguing about what to do with us. I was determined not to give them the opportunity to act on whatever they decided.

I slithered back to Brittany and led her into the hall we'd just escaped. "The Kirbys are out there. We have to go out the back door and go around through the woods."

We kept to the wall this time and followed it all the way around to the rear exit. I swung the door open, and we sprinted into the woods that skirted the area. Safely hidden from view by a thicket, we caught our breath.

"Are we going to be able to find our way back to the car staying in the trees?" Brittany asked, doubled over with her hands on her knees. "I'd hate to get lost in here."

"We'll be fine if we keep the road in sight. All we need is enough cover so they can't see us. And only until we get back to the gravel drive."

"It would be easier if we had a flashlight. Too bad Kirby took your phone."

I squeezed her shoulder. "We can do it. I promise. But we better get going before they decide to wander back here for some reason."

We picked our way through the trees, freezing every time one of us stepped on a stick to listen for someone searching for us. Fortunately, most of the trees were pine, so no crunching leaves beneath our feet. The needles weren't nearly as loud.

It felt like hours had passed by the time we sighted the construction trailer. Almost there. It shouldn't take long to skirt around it to the road. I couldn't believe they hadn't discovered us missing yet. I didn't want to push our luck, though. It was bound to run out. I urged Brittany on, and we scrambled through the trees to the road.

As soon as the first piece of gravel rocked under my foot, I took off running. Brittany followed close behind. We finally reached Brittany's well-hidden car, and I puffed at the passenger side, waiting for her to let me in.

She patted all her pockets, then looked at me horror-stricken. "I can't find the keys. They must've fallen out of my pocket."

"Are you sure? Check again!"

She did.

Then I remembered and dug them out of the front pocket of my jeans. "I have them."

I let myself in and reached over to unlock her door. She jumped in. I handed her the keys.

"Where's your phone?" I asked as she started the engine.

"In the charger under the dash."

She tore down the gravel road, and I dialed Eric's number.

We'd made it. We were safe.

CHAPTER TWENTY-EIGHT

I moved carefully through the crowd, holding my drink over my head to avoid spilling Angus's eyeball punch on my Elvira, Mistress of the Dark costume. I'd claimed the right to wear it months ago in a discussion with Lacey, who'd tried her best to discourage me. Given the level of discomfort I suffered from thickly applied makeup and ample padding added to each side of my bra to fill out the dress, I decided she was right. I'd have been much happier dressed as a butterfly or something. Lacey didn't have to know that, however.

Ravenous Readers wore its costume of party decorations much better than I did mine. Lacey had outdone herself, creating a festive Halloween atmosphere. She'd even helped me dress Savannah as a werewolf and let her attend the party as well. However, with the loud music and raucous atmosphere, the poor dog had spent most of the evening in her bed in the office. Turned out parties weren't her thing.

Brittany, wearing a Tinker Bell outfit, waved me over from her perch on the couch by the front window.

"Having fun?" I asked when I dropped down beside her.

"Great party," she replied, offering her cup in a toast. "You did a terrific job with the decorations. Really spooky!"

"That was all Lacey's doing. She has a real eye for these things." I sipped my punch, wishing I had something stronger. "Where's Olinski?"

"He'll be here in a minute. I think he's thinking up reasons not to wear his costume."

"Oh? What is it?"

She giggled. "Peter Pan to match my Tinker Bell."

I laughed. "No wonder he isn't here. He never even wears shorts. A dress with green stockings will drive him out of his mind."

"I know." She elbowed me in the side. "That's why I picked it. I wanted to see if he was brave enough for me to marry."

"I hate to break this to you, but you already said 'yes.' It's a little late now."

"Not really. The wedding's not for another eight months. Plenty of time to back out."

"Ha. You're not going anywhere, and you know it."

"True." She sipped her drink. "What's Eric wearing tonight?"

"He's supposed to be Dracula, but I haven't seen him yet. I hope he didn't chicken out."

The front door opened, and Peter Pan and Dracula joined the fun, looking none too happy about it.

I elbowed Brittany and pointed. "Looks like they're both braver than we gave them credit for." I stood and moved to a wingback chair to make room next to Brittany for Olinski on the couch, stopping to hug Eric on the way. "Hey, babe. Looking good!"

Eric covered the lower part of his face with the cape. "I vant to suck your blood!" he said in an awful imitation of Bela Lugosi.

I patted his black slicked-back-hair wig. "Be a good boy, and I might let you."

"Can't wait." He kissed me. "You ready for another drink?"

"I'm good, thanks."

He took the other chair and crossed his legs. "Well, I think we finally got the case all wrapped up. Simeon Kirby Jr. and Virginia Kirby have been arrested and are on their way to the Sutton County Detention Center."

"What charges did you finally settle on?"

"They confessed to the kidnapping, so Junior's going down for murdering his father and brother and kidnapping you and Brittany. We charged Virginia with attempted murder for shooting her husband and kidnapping."

"She didn't have much to do with kidnapping us. I think she was just going along with Junior to protect him."

Eric leaned over and took my hand. "As far as I'm concerned, she hurt my best girl, and she should have to pay for it. But honestly, I think they only threw that in there to encourage her to make a deal and testify against Junior."

I took a sip of my punch. "So, what's going to happen to Junior's wife? Are you going to press charges for her lying to you?"

"Probably not. She didn't lie to obstruct the investigation, only to protect her family's reputation. She thought he was gambling again and tried to cover it up."

"But once she learned her father-in-law was murdered, didn't she wonder if her husband had something to do with it?"

"Maybe, but we can't force her to testify against him, anyway, so why bother?"

I could see his point, but it still bugged me a little, letting her get away with obstructing justice. Especially when I'd been threatened with being charged with the same crime so often by Detective Havermayer. She'd never actually followed through on the threat, though.

"I get it. Besides, if you arrested everyone who lied to you, you'd have to build a bigger jail. Maybe it's punishment enough for her to have to live with knowing her husband's a murderer, and she tried to help him get away with it."

Eric stood. "I'm going to get a drink. You sure you don't want anything? Of course, you're probably still drunk from your night with Havermayer."

I narrowed my eyes at him, then smiled. "No, thanks. I think I've had all the eyeball punch I can stand, but, if you happen to run across a bottle of wine up there, feel free to bring back a glass."

"Eyeball punch?"

"You'll see."

Angus had cooked up a blood-red punch with gumball eyeballs floating in it. The sweet liquid tasted okay if I didn't think about the image too hard. I was ready for something less like melted gummy bears and more like alcohol, though.

Eric returned with two cups and handed me one. "Here you go. I passed on the punch, too. A little too realistic for a homicide detective, I guess."

"Thank you." I swallowed some wine, and it

went down much better than the punch. "Now that everything's settled, can you tell me exactly what happened the night Kirby died? Junior made a couple of references when he kidnapped us but never filled in all the blanks."

He took a deep breath. "It was a little weird, actually. Apparently, Virginia Kirby was convinced her husband and his assistant, Stephanie, were having an affair, so when he left her that night she drove up to the construction site. But he wasn't there when she arrived. Junior and Elliott claimed they hadn't seen him, so she drove around looking for him."

"That's strange. Stephanie told me he showed up for the meeting that night, and she left shortly after to go to her parents' anniversary party."

"Nope, not true. He did show up in Riddleton, but not at the trailer. He and Stephanie met in the park that night. Kirby liked the solitude, and they often walked there together. Virginia spotted his car in the parking lot and found them."

Another sip of wine burned its way down to my belly. "It was just the three of them? The other two weren't there?"

"Not at first. Virginia and Stephanie started arguing, and Virginia pulled out the gun her husband had given her for protection."

"That was the thirty-two we found at the scene, right?"

"Right, which explains why she never showed it to us like she was supposed to. Anyway, Virginia fired at Stephanie, but Kirby leaped in front of her at the last minute, which is how he was shot in the gut. It didn't kill him, though."

Brittany and Olinski joined the crowd to mingle, and Eric and I moved to the couch.

I snuggled against him, careful not to smear makeup on his cape. "What happened then?"

"Stephanie freaked out, and Virginia called her sons for help. When they got there, she tried to shoot Kirby again, but Elliott grabbed the gun, catching his hand under the hammer. Junior sent Virginia home in Kirby's Mercedes. Now, this whole time, Kirby's propped against that tree bleeding. Elliott picked him up to take him to the hospital, but Junior stopped him."

"That's how Elliott got Kirby's blood on him and left the hair on his chest. And how Elliott's blood ended up on the gun—from the cut on his hand."

Eric sipped his drink, almost losing his fanged false teeth. "Exactly. Now, here's where it gets interesting."

Funny, I hadn't been bored with the story so far. I wrapped my free arm around him and squeezed.

He continued, "At this point, Stephanie has calmed down some, and Junior negotiates a deal. He gives her his mother's car and promises cash if she'll keep her mouth shut. Then he grabs her hand and plants her fingerprints on the gun for leverage in case she changes her mind."

"I hate to say it, but that's brilliant. She can't turn him in without risking incriminating herself for accepting a bribe, and it's her word against his for the murder."

"After all that, Junior gets the bright idea to finish what his mother started. His bookie is threatening to harm his wife if he doesn't pay up, but he can put him off long enough to collect his inheritance. He pulls out his own gun, the nine mil, but Elliott won't get out of the way. When Elliott tries to pick his father up again, Junior whacks him on the back of the head and pumps two shots into Kirby's chest, killing him instantly."

"Okay, but how does the body end up in Havermayer's car?"

"Serendipity. Junior takes Elliott's keys, phone, and wallet and carries his father's body to the SUV in the parking lot, intending to let his brother take the fall. But when he pushed the unlock button on the key fob, he heard two answering beeps. One from Elliott's Suburban and one from Havermayer's across the street."

My eyes widened. "Wow, that's nearly impossible. But it still doesn't explain how Elliott's watch and wallet ended up in Havermayer's house."

"Junior was watching us the whole time Saturday morning. When Havermayer responded to the call, he climbed into an open window in the back of the house and planted the evidence."

"Did he know whose house it was?"

"I don't know, but I doubt it mattered to him."

"Jen!"

I heard my name being called over the din. I turned around, and Brittany tapped her watch. It was time for Veronica to announce the contest winner. I gave Brittany a thumbs-up and headed for the children's section.

I pushed a table into the middle of the store for Veronica to stand on. Somebody was going home tonight with a cheap plastic trophy and enough bragging rights to last until Christmas. Only a couple of months, but still better than nothing. Anytime you had a chance to crow in a small town like this, you took full advantage of it. You might never get another. I hoped it would be Lacey this time. She really wanted it.

With my help, Veronica climbed onto the table, balancing on her Princess Leia heels. I held my hands over my head. "Okay, quiet down, everybody! It's time for our illustrious mayor to tell us who won the Halloween Decoration Contest this year."

After much elbow prodding and shushing, the room went silent.

Veronica said, "Thank you, Jen! And thanks to Ravenous Readers for hosting this wonderful party."

A smattering of applause drifted across the store.

Veronica held up the trophy. "Wouldn't it be nice if this was real gold?"

Laughter replaced the applause.

When all was quiet again, she continued, "All right, drumroll, please! The winner of this year's Halloween Decoration Contest is . . . Angus Halliburton of the Dandy Diner!"

Applause and groans in equal measure filled the air. Not that anyone begrudged Angus personally. They just wanted it for themselves more. I turned in time to see Lacey in her bunny costume, masking her disappointment with a congratulatory smile directed at Angus.

I squeezed through the crowd to her side. "I'm so sorry, Lacey. I know how much you wanted to win this time."

"It's all right. We have three or four contests a year. We're bound to win one eventually."

"Christmas is up next. We'll go all out this time, okay?"

Angus approached us in his Weeble costume, holding the trophy.

Lacey stepped up and kissed his cheek. "Congratulations, Angus! You deserve it."

He shook his head. "Thanks, but I disagree. You did a much better job decorating than I did this time around. I think the council made a mistake." He offered the trophy to Lacey. "Here, I want you to have this."

Lacey scowled, shaking her head. "Absolutely not! You won fair and square." She tapped him with her elbow. "Don't worry, we'll take you down at Christmas."

"You know." He winked. "I bet you will."

A blast of cold air rippled by me, and I glanced at the front door. Somebody had left it open. I excused myself and headed over to close it. When I poked my head outside, I found Savannah rooting around by the drain, running from the gutter to just above the ground. How did she get out? I didn't even notice she'd left the office.

Way to go, Jen.

"Savannah! Come here, baby. Let's go inside where it's warm."

She ignored me, so I walked over to see what she was doing. I was two strides away when she trotted past me, carrying something in her mouth. "Savannah? Whatcha got there?" She turned to show me a tiny white kitten, mewing his or her little heart out. I looked back at the drain, expecting to find the rest of the litter, but I saw nothing. The kitten was abandoned.

When I turned back around, Savannah and the kitten were gone. I returned to the store in time to see my dog slash werewolf weaving her way through our guests toward the office. I followed and flipped on the light.

306

My German shepherd had curled up in her bed with the kitten against her chest, covered by her chin. I sat beside them, but Savannah wouldn't let me touch her baby.

Terrific. My dog got a kitten for Halloween, and I knew no more about cats than I did about dogs.

Where's Brittany?

ACKNOWLEDGEMENTS

Many thanks to:

My editor, Amy Mae Baxter, and the entire Avon team for all their hard work making this series a reality.

Julie Golden and Ann Dudzinski for their tireless dedication to helping me not make a fool of myself.

Sadie for just being herself.

She can write the perfect murder mystery... But can she solve one in real life?

Crime writer **Jen** returns to her small hometown with a bestselling book behind her and a bad case of writer's block. Finding sanctuary in the local bookstore, with an endless supply of coffee, Jen waits impatiently for inspiration to strike.

But when the owner of the bookstore dies suddenly in mysterious circumstances, Jen has a real-life murder to solve.

The stakes are suddenly higher when evidence places Jen at the scene of the crime and the reading of the will names her as the new owner of the bookstore ...

Can she crack the case and clear her name, before the killer strikes again?

I wrote murder mysteries. I didn't investigate them. Until now...

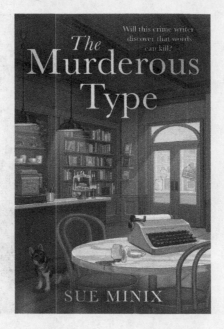

Crime writer turned amateur sleuth, Jen, has taken over the running of the local bookstore in her hometown of Riddleton.

But balancing the books at Ravenous Readers is nothing compared to meeting the deadline for her new novel.

Dodging phone calls from her editor takes a back seat, however, when the local police chief is poisoned. To solve the murder, Jen must dust off her detective hat once more.

With everyone in town seemingly a suspect, and evidence planted to incriminate local police officer and close friend Eric, Jen is working against the clock. Can she find the killer and beat her own writer's block before it's too late?

Don't miss the second instalment in this cosy mystery series – available now!

coffee cups—away from my feet. At least we had one thing in common. Before I totaled it after being pushed off the road, my car always looked like this, too. However, I'd been driving Eric's Jeep ever since, and he'd have a stroke if he found his beloved Wrangler in this condition. I did my best to keep it clean in deference to his health needs.

On the ride out to the resort, Conway and I exchanged information about the case. He knew about as much as I did—with the exception of the paper I'd found in Havermayer's floorboard—leading me to wonder who the source of his info might be. Turned out it was Havermayer herself. He'd gone to visit her right after I left, giving the detainee, who'd had no visitors to that point, two in one day. Add in clean clothing, and it had to feel like her birthday and Christmas combined.

Conway turned into the construction site and parked by the small trailer that functioned as the company office. Directly ahead lay the bones of the two incomplete buildings, adjoined by the occupied one. Three vehicles sat near the completed structure. Not too bad for a resort with no facilities on a Wednesday in late October.

The grassy area between the lobby doors and the parking lot had been decorated with a grave, complete with a fake tombstone and an assortment of witches, zombies, ghosts, and goblins. I doubted the Kirbys had any interest in Riddleton's tiny competition, but at least they'd tried to immerse their few occupants in the Halloween season.

I knocked on the trailer door, standing on the opposite side of the three wooden steps leading to it from Conway. After a muffled "Come in," drifted through the fiberglass, Conway tugged open the door, and I followed him up the rickety steps with no handrail.

Behind the desk facing the door sat a late thirties or early forties woman with platinum blond hair maneuvered into a French twist. Her tastefully applied makeup was topped off with berry-colored lipstick that matched her silk blouse. Someone I'd expect to find in a bank rather than on a construction site. However, since this was the first time I'd ever been in a construction trailer, my assumptions were likely based more on movie and television portrayals than reality.

Standing at a desk to our left were two other women, and Conway included them when he introduced us and told them how sorry we felt for the ordeal they were going through. As he spoke, I watched the blonde behind the desk, Stephanie Robinson, according to her nameplate, scowl, then quickly cover it with a toothy smile that missed her eyes by miles.

The other two women exchanged a glance, then turned back to us, wearing the same fake smile as Stephanie's. Conway had the right idea coming here. It seemed all three had secrets they'd prefer to remain uncovered. Or perhaps they all had the same secret. Regardless of which it might be, nobody seemed happy to see us.

Stephanie introduced herself and offered us seats and coffee. Conway declined both. I followed his lead. She introduced the other two women as Simeon's wife, Virginia Kirby, and Marion Kirby Jenkins, his daughter. Smiles frozen in place, they each nodded, but as I turned away I caught Virginia glaring at Stephanie out of the corner of my eye. Secret number one presenting itself. Now, I only had to figure out the details of why Virginia didn't like her. Given Stephanie's appearance, I suspected I already knew.

Conway rubbed his hands together as he spoke, as if the temperature in the trailer had plummeted since we entered. "Thank you for giving us a few minutes of your time, ladies. I know you're as anxious to learn what happened to Simeon as we are, and I appreciate your willingness to help."

Marion put her shoulders back and her chin forward. "I'm not sure I understand, Mr. Conway. The police have someone in custody. Why do you need to speak with us? We've already answered their questions."

"Yes, ma'am, but there are a few loose ends that need to be tied up."

She crossed her arms over her multicolored diamond-print blouse. "But why did they send *you* for that? Why aren't we speaking with Detective O'Malley? He's in charge of the case, isn't he?"

I was beginning to understand what Eric meant when he said the daughter was difficult to deal with. The steely resolve in her eyes made my skin itch.

Conway glanced at me, then said, "He is, and he's handling other aspects of it at the moment. The department is shorthanded for reasons you seem to be aware of. I'm helping out until the situation is resolved. As an unpaid consultant, so to speak."

"Still, I see no reason—"

Virginia Kirby snapped her head toward her daughter. "Oh, for goodness' sake, Marion, just talk to the man. We have nothing to hide."

Marion pressed her lips into a line, dart-throwing eyes firing first at her mother, then at Conway, who returned fire without blinking.

"What is it you'd like to know, Mr. Conway?" Virginia asked, twisting the sleeve of her white cotton blouse between the fingers of her other hand.

Conway conjured up a fake smile of his own. "We're hoping to get a clearer picture of what happened Friday night. If you could all recount your movements, it would help tremendously."

Stephanie was the first to speak up. "I was home with my husband all night. I believe the police have already verified that."

One spouse giving an alibi for the other. What could go wrong with that?

A nod from Conway in her direction prompted a response from Marion. "I was also home with my husband all night. Also verified by the police."

Two for two.

"I spent the evening with my husband as well," Virginia said. "But we had dinner with friends in Spartanburg."

"And afterward?" I asked.

"Simeon dropped me off at home and came here to meet with Simeon Jr. and Elliott. They'd had a meeting with one of the company's investors, and Simeon wanted to find out how it went."

"Why didn't he just call?" Conway asked.

"He preferred to meet face-to-face."

"Spartanburg is a hundred and fifteen miles from here, Mrs. Kirby. A two-hour drive. That seems a long way to go when a phone call would suffice."

Virginia glanced at Stephanie, then quickly away. "I don't know what to tell you. Obviously, he came here as he said he would." She dabbed a fingertip in the corner of her eye to keep a tear from ruining her mascara.

148